BOOK
SCAVENGER

BOOK SCAVENGER

Jennifer Chambliss Bertman

WITH ILLUSTRATIONS BY Sarah Watts

Christy Ottaviano Books

HENRY HOLT AND COMPANY • NEW YORK

Henry Holt and Company, LLC
Publishers since 1866
175 Fifth Avenue
New York, New York 10010
mackids.com

Henry Holt books may be purchased for business or promotional use.
For information on bulk purchases, please contact the Macmillan
Corporate and Premium Sales Department at (800) 221-7945 x5442
or by e-mail at specialmarkets@macmillan.com.

Library of Congress Cataloging-in-Publication Data
Chambliss Bertman, Jennifer.
Book Scavenger / Jennifer Chambliss Bertman.—First edition.
pages   cm
Summary: Just after twelve-year-old Emily and her family move to
San Francisco, she teams up with new friend James to follow clues in an
odd book they find, hoping to figure out its secrets before the men who
attacked Emily's hero, publisher Garrison Griswold, solve the mystery or
come after the friends.
ISBN 978-1-62779-115-1 (hardback)
[1. Treasure hunt (Game)—Fiction. 2. Books and reading—Fiction.
3. Adventure and adventurers—Fiction. 4. Publishers and
publishing—Fiction. 5. Moving, Household—Fiction. 6. San Francisco
(Calif.)—Fiction. 7. Mystery and detective stories.] I. Title.
PZ.1.C43Boo 2015   [Fic]—dc23   2014045884

First Edition—2015 / Designed by April Ward

Printed in the United States of America by
R. R. Donnelley & Sons Company, Harrisonburg, Virginia

1 3 5 7 9 10 8 6 4 2

To my parents for providing the foundation,
to my brother for being an inspiration,
to my husband for always believing,
to my little champion, for all the reasons

GREETINGS, SCAVENGERS!

Garrison Griswold here to welcome you to the wonderful world of Book Scavenger. We are a community of book lovers, puzzle lovers, and treasure hunters. Are you, too? Then come along and join us!

Here is how you play:

Hide a Book

1. Choose a book to send on an adventure.

2. Pick a public place to hide your book. For example: a local park, a coffee shop, the library, or bus stops.* (*Please be respectful of our environment as well as laws and regulations of the area in which you are hiding a book.) Visit our online store to purchase bookouflage and bookstumes to help conceal your book, or create your own. Or hide your book in its birthday suit—after all, sometimes no disguise is the best disguise of all.

3. Create and upload a clue. Provide other scavengers with a hint for how to find your book. Example: *The lowest branch on the tallest tree.* To increase the difficulty level (and fun!), many users conceal their clue with a cipher or code, or make their clue the solution for a puzzle. Use the

"autogenerate" feature on our website to have a computer encrypt your clue, or get ideas from the Puzzlepedia page and create your own.

4. Register the book you would like to hide. Every registered book is issued a unique tracking code. Apply a tracking badge to the inside front cover of your book. Download your tracking badge from your profile and print it. (You can print onto a label or use paper and tape it to your book.)

5. Hide your book! Track its travels via the "Hidden Books" tab on your profile as other scavengers find, log, and re-hide your book.

Find a Book

1. Select a book. Search for books hidden near you. Select which book to hunt by title, location, or random selection—it's up to you! Alternatively, enter a specific title. If users have hidden that book, you will see a list of the locations.

2. Download the book clue. If you flag the book before you download the clue, you will earn double the points if you reach the book first. This is called declaring a book. See the "Points" section for more information.

3. Solve the clue.

4. Go Book Scavenging!

Points

You earn one point for every book you hide, find, or if someone finds one of your hidden books. As you earn points, you will move up through the ranks of the game. The higher your rank, the more special privileges you earn, like unlocking secret pages and online games and puzzles. You can also cash in your points at the Book Scavenger store for book-hunting supplies—or for more books, of course!

To earn more points and add an element of suspense to your hunt, a seeker can declare a book. To do this, you must select "Declare This Book" before you download its clue. You cannot declare a book you have hidden yourself or one that has been hidden by a Book Scavenger friend. Declaring a book will double the point value. But watch out! Declared books are flagged for all users to see, alerting every book sleuth to the hidden book that is now worth double points. This is where the suspense comes in! Will you capture the book first, or will a poacher? Poachers are book scavengers who target declared books in an attempt to get them before the original seeker.

Ranks

Encyclopedia Brown. (0–25) A bright and brainy young sleuth, Encyclopedia Brown was the go-to detective in his neighborhood who offered his services for the bargain rate of twenty-five cents per day, plus expenses. This is the entry level for all those playing Book Scavenger.

Nancy Drew. (26–50) Your curiosity and keen eye for clues are moving you up in the world! Nancy Drew is a smart and resourceful teenage sleuth who began solving mysteries in the 1930s and continues to solve them to this day.

Sam Spade. (51–100) You are an intrepid book scavenger now. This private detective is the creation of San Francisco's own literary son, Dashiell Hammett, and appeared in his novel *The Maltese Falcon*, as well as three short stories.

Miss Marple. (101–150) Agatha Christie's famous detective is more than meets the eye, and you are now a book scavenger who shouldn't be underestimated.

Monsieur C. Auguste Dupin. (151–200) You're an old pro at this game. Dupin is often considered the original detective. His creator, Edgar Allan Poe, is credited with starting the detective fiction genre in 1841.

Sherlock Holmes. (201+) The highest rank for a book scavenger. You are a master of puzzles, logic, and deduction.

The final, most important, and most *fun* step of all: READ the book! In addition to offering literary treasure hunts, Book Scavenger provides a wonderful online community for book lovers of all ages. Post reviews on your profile, join book conversations in the forums, and bask in the book-loving ambiance.

Those are the rules, fellow scavengers! And don't forget our motto: "Life is a game, and books are the tokens."

Yours in pages and play,

Garrison Griswold
Creator of Book Scavenger
and CEO of Bayside Press

BOOK SCAVENGER

CHAPTER 1

GARRISON GRISWOLD whistled his way down Market Street, silver hair bobbing atop his head like a pigeon wing. He tapped his trademark walking stick, striped in Bayside Press colors, to the beat of his tune. A cabdriver slowed and honked his horn, leaning to his passenger-side window.

"Mr. Griswold! You want a ride? It's on me, my friend."

"Very kind of you, but I'm fine, thank you," Mr. Griswold called back, and raised his cane in a salute. He preferred traveling by streetcar or BART. They were the veins of this city he loved, after all.

A woman clutching a cell phone hurried to Mr. Griswold's side.

"My son is such a fan of Book Scavenger. Can I trouble you for a photograph?"

Mr. Griswold checked his wristwatch. Plenty of

time to spare before he had to be at the main library for his big announcement. He balanced a hand on the woman's shoulder as she held the phone at arm's length to take the picture.

"So is it true?" she asked. "Do you have another game in the works?"

In response, Mr. Griswold pulled an imaginary zipper across his lips and gave her a wink. He continued on his way, through the stream of pedestrians,

whistling and tapping his cane on the brick sidewalk, completely unaware of the two men who'd stepped into his wake.

One was tall and gangly with bushy black eyebrows peeking from the edge of his backward ball cap. His partner was a bulldog of a man who moved as if his chest propelled him down the street instead of his legs. His hands were jammed in his front sweatshirt pocket, and his stare didn't waver from his target.

Mr. Griswold descended into the BART station. When he paused before the fare gate to remove his Fast Pass from his wallet, a voice from behind spoke his name. Mr. Griswold turned and faced the men. His smile faltered. It was early afternoon, off-hours for commuting, and the trickle of people coming in and out of the station was slow. Nonexistent at the moment.

He adjusted his frameless glasses and looked the tall man in the eye. "I'm running late for an appointment, gentlemen." Mr. Griswold wiggled his salt-and-pepper mustache—a nervous habit. The way that short man popped his knuckles and gave him a look that could only be described as *scornful* caused him to put up his guard.

"We have a friend in common," the tall man said.

"Yeah, a friend." The short man laughed hoarsely.

"Ah, I see." Mr. Griswold turned to go through the fare gate, but the tall one stepped in front of him and blocked his way.

"I'm in quite a rush," Mr. Griswold said. "If you wouldn't mind calling my office, I'd be happy to speak with you at a later date."

Mr. Griswold extended his walking stick between the two men, trying to force his way through, but the tall man grasped him firmly by the shoulder.

"We want the book," he said.

Mr. Griswold resisted the urge to hug his leather satchel firmly to his side. Inside was a special edition of *The Gold-Bug* by Edgar Allan Poe that he had crafted himself using the Gutenberg 2004 EX-PRO Printing Press and Binding Machine he kept at his house. He planned to make forty-nine more, but only the one in his bag existed at that moment. He'd brought *The Gold-Bug* as a prop for the unveiling of his new, elaborate game. It would be just enough to give a hint, a small peek, to the public of what would be involved. But these men couldn't be talking about *that* book. Nobody knew about it yet—nobody at Bayside Press, and nobody in his personal life.

Mr. Griswold used the cuff of his suit jacket to dab a bead of sweat from his temple. "I run a publishing company, gentlemen. We deal with hundreds of books. Thousands. You'll have to be more specific than that."

"You know the one we want," the short, stocky man said. He leaned in close, stretching on tiptoe like he was looking up Mr. Griswold's nose. He jerked his neck back to his partner. "He knows which one, right, Barry?"

The tall man stomped his foot. "We said fake names, remember?"

"Whatever," the other responded. "This guy's old. His hearing's probably shot."

Taking advantage of their brief moment of strife, Mr. Griswold swung his walking stick and whacked Barry on the cheek, then pushed past him toward the entrance to the lower level.

"Help!"

His cry echoed in the cavernous station. There was a low crack, like a distant boom of thunder. Mr. Griswold felt something like a punch to his back. He stumbled and fell to the ground, hitting his head on the stone floor. Had he been shot? He struggled to breathe. A numb dampness spread across his lower back, and his head throbbed where it had connected to the ground.

Barry cursed and rushed forward. He stooped beside Mr. Griswold and placed a palm on his forehead, as if he were checking for a fever. "What did you do, Clyde?"

"What happened to 'we gotta use fake names'?" Clyde said.

"I can't believe this!" Barry cried. "You have a gun? You *shot* him? That wasn't part of the plan."

Clyde shrugged. "I improvised."

"What if he doesn't have the book on him?"

"Of course he has it on him." Clyde inspected the hole in his sweatshirt pocket where he'd concealed his gun. "He needs it for that press conference."

An automated announcement drifted up from the level below where the trains and buses arrived. Barry slid his arms underneath Mr. Griswold's and dragged him backward to an empty bench.

With a soft grunt, Mr. Griswold collapsed against the slick granite wall behind him. He crumpled from a seated position to a prone one, his back sliding against the wall, leaving a streak of blood to mark his trail. He tried to land on top of his bag in an effort to keep it from the men, but Clyde tugged it free.

Clyde pulled the book from Mr. Griswold's bag. "*The Gold-Bug* by Edgar Allan Poe." He tossed it to Barry. "That has to be it."

Mr. Griswold's vision blurred the two men together and apart. He wanted to say something, to stop them, but all that came out were moans.

Barry hardly looked at the book before hurling it to the corner, where it rebounded off the wall and slid behind a trash can. "That's a brand-new book!" he shouted.

"It's still a book," Clyde said.

"He's a publisher! He's going to have books on him. We were told to look for an *old* book. A really old book."

A BART train rumbled in one level below. The hum of people leaving the cars carried upstairs.

"We gotta get out of here," Barry said. The two men raced to the exit.

A boisterous group wearing black-and-orange jerseys rode up the escalator. One of them noticed Mr. Griswold slumped on the bench and ran over. A man dialed 9-1-1 on his cell phone. A woman crouched next to him and repeated, "Hang on. Everything will be okay."

As Garrison Griswold hovered on the brink of consciousness, he wasn't worried about when help would arrive. It was the slim edition of *The Gold-Bug* wedged between the trash can and the wall that consumed his thoughts. All that work, all his plans. Everything was in place, but without *The Gold-Bug*, his game wouldn't get launched. His nearly priceless treasure would never be discovered. He hoped desperately that the right person would find his book. Someone who would take the time to understand and appreciate the secrets it held.

CHAPTER

2

THE CLUE was a substitution cipher—Emily was sure. Figuring that out had been the easy part. The hard part was trying to crack it. She rearranged the letters in another attempt to solve it:

Throw ferzu borg the zoey.

That couldn't be right. Who was Ferzu Borg and why would she have to throw him a zoey? And what was a zoey, anyway? This was no way to advance to the Auguste Dupin level of Book Scavenger.

With a huff, Emily ripped the page from her notebook, crumpled it, and dropped it with the other failed attempts littering the cab of the moving van. At the top of a fresh page, she carefully recopied the cipher she'd printed from the Book Scavenger website a few days ago.

"Hey, Sherlylocks," her dad interrupted. "Take a

break and enjoy the scenery. You know who once lived in San Francisco, don't you?"

"Gee, let me guess. . . ." Emily continued writing in her notebook without looking up. Her dad had only mentioned they were moving to the home of his literary idol, oh, sixty million times.

"'There was nowhere to go but everywhere.' Jack Kerouac wrote that in—"

"*On the Road*, Dad. I know."

Emily sighed, frustrated with the cipher and frustrated with her dad for breaking her concentration. She slid her pencil back through her ponytail for safekeeping. They were driving through a valley jampacked with rows of houses wrapped around hillsides like serpentine belts. Emily guessed there were more houses in this one corner of California than in the entire state of New Mexico, where they had most recently moved from.

In the side-view mirror, she could see the family's beat-up minivan trailing behind them. They had nicknamed the minivan Sal, another homage to the great and almighty Jack Kerouac. Their mother gripped Sal's steering wheel and leaned forward the way she always did, like she was so excited to get where they were going, whether it was the grocery store or California. Matthew, Emily's older brother, bobbed his lopsided Mohawk as he listened to music. Most likely Flush, his favorite band. Emily would bet a box of books on it.

9

"Nothing more exciting than a new beginning, don't you think?" Emily's dad asked.

Emily nodded, although she wasn't sure she agreed. Her parents were so proud of this life they'd created, but she didn't get their enthusiasm for new beginnings. It was like starting a bunch of books and never finishing any of them.

California would be the ninth state for Emily in her twelve and three-quarters years, all part of her parents' quest to live once in each of the fifty states. Yes, a quest to live in every state. That always went over well when Emily tried to explain their frequent moving to people.

"Are you in the military?"

"Are you in a witness-protection program?"

"Are you on the run from the feds?"

"You just move around *for fun*?"

Starting before she was born, her parents had bounced from state to state because, in their words, "that's where our paychecks pulled us." When Emily was five, they lived in New York and her dad was laid off from his job at a publishing company. He started to take on freelance copyediting jobs. That same year, her mother was given permission to do her programming job remotely, which meant anywhere she had a computer. Realizing their work wouldn't be tying them to one spot, her parents decided to make their fantasy of living once in every state a reality. They started a blog called *50 Homes in 50 States* and chronicled their moving adventures. The blog had been a hobby to begin with, a way to capture memories from the different places they lived, but it grew into a side business with companies paying to advertise on it, and travel sites and magazines asking them to write articles. The Crane family had been averaging a move almost once a year ever since.

For a while, Emily loved it. It was a big family adventure. Discovering new places, the suspense of where they would go next. And her parents always tried to make it fun. Like their reveal tradition—a surprise dinner they threw for Emily and her older brother, with clues indicating their next destination. Three weeks ago, Emily had walked into their rental after school, brainstorming ideas for a notable New Mexico landmark to feature in her diorama project, and found the kitchen table set with sourdough bread bowls filled with gold-foil-wrapped chocolate coins. Her whole body had tensed up, knowing she'd walked into a reveal dinner, which meant they were moving again. You'd think she would have gotten used to these surprises, but she hadn't.

At first, all she could think about was how she wouldn't get to make her own rock crystal stalactites for her Carlsbad Caverns diorama idea. Then she saw more clues for their next destination: an ALCATRAZ OUTPATIENT MENTAL WARD T-shirt for Matthew; a paperback copy of *The Maltese Falcon* for Emily; the black-and-orange Giants cap her mom wore; her dad dressed like a beatnik in a black turtleneck, beret, and black-framed glasses.

When she deduced San Francisco was their next move, Emily should have flung the gold coins in celebration. The city was not only home to her dad's literary idol, but Emily's, too: Garrison Griswold, CEO of Bayside Press and mastermind of Book Scavenger, the coolest book-hunting game in existence. (Also the only book-hunting game in existence.) Book Scavenger was an online community of people who loved books and puzzles and games as much as Emily did, and it traveled with her no matter where her family lived.

But instead of celebrating, she found herself forcing a smile for her parents. Now that the Cranes had spent years bouncing from state to state, their family adventures were starting to feel . . . Emily wasn't sure what the word was to describe it. All she knew was, a few weeks ago, she'd been sitting with a book and her bagged lunch at her usual spot on the stone planter that surrounded the old oak tree at her Albuquerque middle school. A group of girls she barely knew sprawled near her on the grass. She listened to them complain about how boring their upcoming weekend would be because they were going to the community pool again, and then they started talking about a dance class they took together. Two girls jumped up and tried to remember a routine they'd performed years earlier, doing the moves right there on the grass. Emily, pretending to read her book and not pay them any attention, had felt wistful and a tiny bit jealous. Not because she wanted to take dance classes, or be a part of their group, or go to the community pool so regularly it became boring. What bothered her, she realized as she covertly watched those girls, was that she would never have that circle of friendship. Thanks to her family's traveling lifestyle, she would always be the outsider. She could take dance classes and go to the community pool, sure, but she never stuck around long enough to make real friends, much less relive memories with them years later.

As the moving van exited the freeway and rattled past the baseball stadium, Emily tried to focus on the positive: Book Scavenger! San Francisco!

Sunshine glinted off a silver bridge that arched overhead. Not the Golden Gate Bridge—Emily knew that bridge was red and not silver. Flat water and docks were on one side of their van, and a cluster of skyscrapers on the other. In a way, it reminded her of Lake Michigan when they lived in Chicago, with a city view in one direction and a tranquil spread of water in the other. Although the San Francisco Bay was a swimming pool in comparison to Lake Michigan, with mounds of land on the far side that looked close enough to swim to.

They turned away from the water and headed down a busy street. They were soon engulfed by office buildings so tall Emily couldn't see the tops from where she sat. She double-checked the radio station they were listening to—104.5—making sure it matched the numbers she'd written in her notebook. According to the information she'd read in the Book Scavenger forums, the station would be broadcasting Mr. Griswold's new game announcement any minute now. In addition to running a publishing company, Garrison Griswold organized outlandish events, such as an annual Quidditch tournament in Golden Gate Park and a literary bingo game with so many participants it filled a baseball stadium and earned him a spot in the *Guinness World Records* book. It was why people called him the Willy Wonka of book publishing. People traveled to San Francisco to participate in his games, and now Emily was going to be living there herself. At least for a while, anyway. She would have been there in person to hear the announcement, but by the time she knew they were moving to San Francisco, tickets had all been given away.

"Traffic." Her dad sighed.

They had slowed to a stop and idled in a line of cars. Her mother and brother were one car behind in Sal the minivan. A green trolley rattled down tracks in the middle of the street. They inched forward. The flashing lights of a police car came into view, then a fire truck, then an ambulance. Yellow caution tape was strung in a wide perimeter around stairs descending underground.

An officer directed them around the emergency vehicles. Emily craned her head for a better view.

"Is that a subway station?" she asked.

"They call it BART here," her dad said. "I wonder what's going on."

Emily searched for a clue to what happened, but there was nothing to see besides the flashing lights and emergency vehicles. She bowed her head, ponytail curled around her neck, and resumed her code-breaking work.

CHAPTER 3

THE U-HAUL putted up a hill, leaving downtown San Francisco behind. The sidewalk sprouted trees; the bars on windows were replaced with flower boxes. Her dad turned down a street so steep Emily was amazed everything didn't just lean over and careen downhill through intersection after intersection into a crashing mess at the bottom.

The moving van slowed to a stop in front of a building Emily recognized from the rental website. The new house was taller than it was wide, as if it held its breath to squeeze between the neighboring homes.

"Definitely need the emergency brake for this street," her dad said, shoving the brake pedal down with his foot. "You ready?"

Emily glanced at the clock. One minute to go until

Mr. Griswold's announcement. Her dad tapped his temple, his shorthand for *I can read your mind.*

"I'll leave the radio on. I know you don't want to miss anything," he said.

He swung open his door with a creak and jumped to the pavement, joining the rest of their family on the sidewalk. Emily's mom dug through her purse, the hem of her patchwork sundress chasing itself around her ankles in the breeze. Matthew shuffled in a circle, one hand shielding his eyes from the sun as he took in their new surroundings. His off-center Mohawk could make you do a double take, thinking he was tilting his head when he really wasn't. Her brother couldn't care less that they were moving again. He never cared. Matthew attracted friends like a rainbow attracts leprechauns. And it never bothered him to leave them behind, either. He saw it as building a fan base for his future as World-Famous Rock Star.

The mention of "Griswold" drew Emily's attention back to the radio. The DJ was saying, "We've got a Foghead calling in from the event, and they're saying so far Griswold is a no-show."

"A no-show?" Emily asked the radio.

"You there, caller?" the DJ asked.

A woman's voice said, "Yeah, I'm here at the library, but we haven't seen a glimpse of him. People are getting antsy—this guy near me is ranting about what a waste of time this is. But I don't know. I'm feeling worried myself. Garrison Griswold doesn't seem like a flake, ya know?"

And suddenly Emily knew with certainty why Mr. Griswold hadn't shown up. It was part of the new game! He was faking his disappearance, and the challenge would be to find him, similar to the online murder mystery he'd planned two Halloweens ago. How brilliant!

Her mom rapped on the passenger door.

"Moving boxes are calling your name," her muffled voice came through the glass.

A salty and crisp breeze was blowing when Emily stepped out of the van, carrying with it a faint chorus of brays and barks. She wondered if they might be the Pier 39 sea lions she'd read about. From her vantage point on this steep hill, she could look down across the city and see a slice of the bay beyond the cityscape. Not that she could make out sea lions from this distance—the lone sailboat she could see wasn't any bigger than her fingernail, so a sea lion would be like the size of a freckle.

As she helped her family unload the U-Haul, ideas tumbled around Emily's head of how Mr. Griswold's disappearance could be launched into a game. Maybe there was something to find at the library where he was supposed to make the announcement, or maybe there was a message hidden on the Book Scavenger website.

A third-floor window slid open with a squawk. While their new building looked like a regular, if superskinny, three-story house, Emily knew from the rental website that every floor was a separate apartment. An Asian woman older than her parents leaned out the open window.

"You're blocking the driveway," the woman shouted.

"Hello!" Emily's dad took off his baseball cap to wipe sweat off his brow and waved it. "Ms. Lee, isn't it? We're the Cranes—your new tenants? Just unloading our things, then we'll return the U-Haul and it'll be out of the way."

"Move that truck or I'll call the police," their landlady said, and slammed the window shut.

"Mental note: Do not mess with her driveway," Matthew said. He straddled the ground with one foot against the garage door and the other nearly in the gutter. "Can't really call this a *drive*way, though, can you?"

"Not even a parkway," Emily said.

Matthew sat cross-legged on the ground. "Sitway might work."

Emily smiled. Sometimes she forgot how funny her brother could be, when she wasn't the butt of his jokes.

The house had three front doors opening onto the porch, one for each apartment. While her mom worked the key in theirs, Emily noticed the door to the right was wide open. A private staircase stretched up and out of view to Ms. Lee's floor. Partway up the staircase sat a boy, about Emily's age, who she assumed must be Ms. Lee's grandson. He carefully wrote in a *Puzzle Power* magazine.

Emily's mom pushed their front door open, revealing their own staircase. While the rest of her family went inside, Emily hung back. The boy had shiny black hair that poked up at the back of his head as if he'd slept on it funny. He looked at Emily.

"Moving in?" he asked.

Emily startled a little and blushed. Had she been staring at him long?

She raised the plastic bin filled with clothes. "I'm delivering a pizza."

The boy blinked at her twice. She'd been going for funny, but maybe that just sounded snotty. She turned to her own doorway, but not before seeing the corner of the boy's mouth curl up in a smile.

Upstairs, Emily's dad dropped his moving box in the front room. He spread his arms wide and rotated in a circle. "Does this feel like Home Sweet Home or what?"

"It feels like a sparsely furnished apartment," Emily said, dumping her bin next to his.

"Dibs on this room," Matthew called from down the hallway.

"Hey, no fair!" Emily ran past Matthew's claimed room to see the leftover bedroom. It was narrow, like their building. A closet door cut off one corner, and Emily was surprised to see the inside was a triangle instead of the expected square. She'd never had a triangular closet before. There was also a window that stared at the building next door. Emily slid the window up and reached an arm out. Her fingertips almost brushed the neighboring house.

The window directly above hers slid open. Emily snapped back inside, fearing Ms. Lee would pop out and yell at her about touching the neighbor's building. Instead, she heard a repetitive squeaking.

She'd been so focused on the next-door house that Emily hadn't noticed the rope strung alongside her window. The rope wound around a pulley attached to the outside of the building and ran up to another pulley fixed beside the window directly above hers. A rusted tin sand pail was being lowered, and once it reached her, the window upstairs shut.

Bewildered, Emily tilted the bucket to see what was inside. She removed a scrap of paper that had a three-by-three grid drawn on it with the message *Fly into flamingo theater, enter empty nest.*

Emily reread the message. It made no sense. She leaned out the window and peered up, but there was no one to see.

The boy on the stairs must have sent this. But what in the world was a flamingo theater, and how was she expected to fly there? And what about this grid? Tic-tac-toe had nine squares, but then why not mark an *X* to start the game?

Emily pulled the pencil from her ponytail and sat on the floor to study the paper further. The sentence didn't strike her as being a cipher since it was made up of actual words, not a garbled mix of letters. Emily played around with rearranging the letters, thinking maybe it was an anagram.

Her mom leaned in her doorway. "You'll have plenty of time for sleuthing later, Em."

"This isn't for Book Scavenger," Emily muttered. But sometimes taking a break helped her see a puzzle in a new way, so she tucked her pencil back into her hair and went downstairs.

The boy sat in the same place as before, absorbed in *Puzzle Power*. He gave no indication that he'd just delivered a puzzle via sand pail, but now he wore a bulky purple scarf. Odd, since it was warm enough for Emily to wear a tank top.

At the moving van, Emily dawdled, debating if she should ask the boy about the bucket and the note. But what would she say? *Did you send this to me?* Duh. Who else would it be from? Ms. Lee? *What am I supposed to do with it?* If she said that, then she might as well just say *I give up*, and Emily wasn't one to give up.

"What are you doing?" Matthew said from behind her.

Emily blushed, realizing she'd been making gestures while she imagined her conversation. She grabbed the closest thing to her in the truck bed—her suitcase filled with books.

"Looking for this," she said, and lugged it to the ground.

"Oh-kaaay."

The suitcase was so packed with books Emily had to drag it up to the front porch one step at a time.

"Can you go any slower?" Matthew asked.

"This is heavy." Emily grunted. She looked inside their doorway at the endlessly long flight of stairs. "If you're in such a rush, go around me," she said.

Matthew sidestepped her and clomped by with his skateboard and backpack. Emily sat on the edge of her suitcase to catch her breath. She peeked in Ms. Lee's door. The boy now wore swim goggles along with his scarf. Emily snorted in surprise and then clamped a hand over her mouth. He continued to make marks in his magazine and acted oblivious to her being there.

It seemed like an hour passed dragging her suitcase up the stairs, during which all three of her family members passed her going up or down and none offered any help. Unless you counted her mother saying, "I told you not to pack all your books in one bag, Em."

She debated the puzzle as she climbed, sorting through her mental file cabinet of puzzles solved for Book Scavenger. The grid had to be the key. Why include it? Logic puzzles used grids, but she didn't see how that scrap of paper added up to being a logic puzzle.

Emily rolled the suitcase into a corner of her room and pulled out the paper and her pencil once again. When she tried reading it backward, it was gibberish. What if she took the first letter of each word . . .

"'Fifteen,'" she read aloud.

The first letter of each word spelled out *fifteen*. That couldn't be a coincidence. But fifteen what? Was that the solution, and if so, what did that mean? And that still didn't explain the grid.

"A magic square!" Emily threw her pencil triumphantly in the air.

In a magic square, a grid was filled with a consecutive set of numbers so every row, column, and diagonal added up to the same number. With a three-by-three grid and the numbers one to nine, the solution was always fifteen. She had learned about magic squares when she hunted *Shakespeare's Secret* in Colorado. The clue was a partially finished magic square. The numbers used to solve the square ended up being the combination for a lock on a hidden box that contained *Shakespeare's Secret*.

When Emily finished solving the boy's magic square it looked like this:

8	1	6
3	5	7
4	9	2

She dropped the note back in the bucket and pulled the rope to raise it up to the boy's room. Then she ran downstairs and jumped on the landing. This time the boy had added reindeer antlers to his ensemble. Emily giggled.

"Halloween already?" her dad murmured as he passed by on his way inside.

Ms. Lee's voice rang down the stairs. "James!" she said. "Come help me, please." Without so much as a glance Emily's way, James jumped to his feet and ran upstairs, the bells on his reindeer antlers jingling with every step.

"Check your bucket," Emily called after him, hoping he'd heard.

CHAPTER 4

LATER THAT AFTERNOON, Emily went to the U-Haul to grab her Book Scavenger notebook, but the empty cab reminded her that she'd already taken in her stack of books and papers. She checked her new room, but the notebook was nowhere to be found. She went through the apartment, panic simmering when the notebook remained lost.

This was not just any notebook. It was Volume 9 of her Book Scavenger notebooks. It was where she wrote the rough drafts for the book reviews she posted on Book Scavenger. It was where she wrote journal entries about memorable book hunts. It was where all her ideas for puzzles and ciphers and hiding books exploded on the page, and where she tried to work out the clues for the books she was hunting. Combined with her online profile, it basically documented her entire life.

She ran outside and threw open the U-Haul door one more time. She dug out a granola bar wrapper and a pen from underneath the seat, but no notebook. The panic was now in a full-frenzied boil when someone said, "You set a new record."

Emily spun around. That boy—James—stood on the porch. The scarf and goggles from before were gone, but he still wore the reindeer antlers.

"Otis never would have solved that one as fast as you did. But then again, Otis always said he was allergic to numbers."

"Are you speaking reindeer?" Emily asked. This kid made no sense, and she was impatient to get back to her notebook hunt.

"Otis. He lived in your apartment before you. He was more of a word puzzle guy than a math puzzle guy. He moved to the East Coast to be near his grandchildren. Otis was great—don't get me wrong—but I'm glad to have someone my age moving in. At least you look my age—are you in seventh grade, too? I'm James, by the way."

James shifted his weight, and Emily noticed an important detail she'd overlooked before: her notebook in his hands.

"Where did you find that?" She charged up the concrete steps, pulled the notebook from him, and hugged it to her chest.

The antler bells tinkled lightly as James stepped back. With a touch of defensiveness, he said, "It was on the ground outside your door. I knocked earlier but nobody answered. I was going to send it down in the bucket, but then I looked out the window and you looked like you'd lost something and . . ."

Emily didn't know what to make of this guy. He wore reindeer antlers and delivered puzzle challenges via a rusty, old sand pail. He seemed genuinely offended that she might have thought he'd stolen her notebook, but he still seemed friendly. Even the cowlick on the back of his head stuck up like a wing waving hello.

"Are you hypnotized by my hair?" James asked.

Emily felt her face heat up, but James waved her off.

"It's cool. He likes the attention."

"He?"

"His name is Steve."

"Your cowlick is named Steve?"

"I was going to name him Geronimo, but that seemed ridiculous," James said.

Emily laughed, her skepticism chipped away.

"Nobody would take you seriously with a cowlick named Geronimo."

"Exactly," James said. Then he added, "That puzzle you were working on was interesting. Did you like the one I sent in the bucket?"

"The magic square? You had me stumped with the flamingo theater. I was like, what in the world is a—" Emily's brain caught up with her rambling mouth. "Wait. How did you know I was working on a puzzle?"

The spiral spine of her notebook dug into her fingers. She flipped the notebook open, irritation rising with every whipped-over page. Beneath the Ferzu Borg cipher was unfamiliar block-letter handwriting: **THIRD BENCH DOWN THE PIER.**

Emily gasped. "You solved it?"

"You almost had it. You just missed a letter."

She didn't *miss* a letter. Emily inspected the original cipher and her work. She sucked in sharply when she saw, almost immediately, that James was right.

She'd missed a letter.

The cipher text had two *N*s and she'd assigned a different letter to each one. An amateur mistake.

In a reassuring voice, James said, "It's easy to miss stuff like that. That's why two eyes are better than one. No offense to the Cyclops."

Emily's cheeks flashed with the heat of embarrassment. "My eyes are fine. I've been in a car for two days—that's all."

She looked at the slashing lines of James's handwriting practically taunting, **THIRD BENCH DOWN THE PIER**! That was pretty nervy of him. Solving a puzzle that clearly wasn't his to solve. If she'd wanted help with it, she would've sent it up in that dinky little bucket. What a show-off! She knew his friendliness was too good to be true.

"So what are you, anyway?" Emily demanded. "A poacher? I suppose you'll want to go capture the book for me now, too?"

James's smiling eyes turned crestfallen. "What are you talking about? A poacher? And what do you mean, 'capture a book'?" He continued apologetically, "The puzzle was staring up at me, chanting *solve me.* . . ."

His antlers seemed to droop. Even Steve seemed to droop.

"*Poaching* and *capturing a book* are Book Scavenger terms. Doesn't everyone in San Francisco play?"

James shook his head. "I've heard of it, but I don't play."

Emily gaped at James. Living in San Francisco and not playing Book Scavenger was like living in a chocolate factory but not eating any sweets.

"You obviously like puzzles." Emily eyed James suspiciously. "Don't you like to read?"

"Sure," James said.

"Then you have to try it. Book Scavenger is all about people who love books and puzzles and games. Plus having adventures and exploring new places."

"What do you do?"

"People hide their used books somewhere public, like a park, and then post a puzzle or clue on the website to lead others to it. You earn one point for each book you hide or find, or if someone finds one of your hidden books."

"What are the points for?"

"The points move you up through the levels. Everyone starts at Encyclopedia Brown, then there's

Nancy Drew, Sam Spade, Miss Marple, Auguste Dupin, and Sherlock Holmes. The higher you go, the more you unlock on the website, like bonus material for different books, secret puzzles, and games. You can also trade in points to buy stuff from the Bayside Press store."

"So 'third bench down the pier' leads to a book? How do you find it from that?"

"Books are listed on the website by location. This one is hidden at the Ferry Building. There must be a pier there with benches and—" For a split second Emily paused, took in James's tilted head and concentrating eyes, and even Steve leaning forward like he wanted to hear more. Impulsively, Emily said, "Maybe I could show you. Want to go scavenging this weekend?"

The words were out there now, hanging in between them. Emily held her breath waiting for James's response.

He smiled. "Sure!"

Emily felt like she'd drunk a soda really fast— sugar-buzzed but a little sick at the same time. So much for her practiced avoidance of making friends she'd only have to leave. But James was good with puzzles—he'd proven that. And he was funny. Maybe it wouldn't be such a bad thing to have a book-hunting partner, even if only for a while.

"Did you hear about Garrison Griswold?" James asked.

"How is it possible that you don't play Book Scavenger but you know who Garrison Griswold is?" Emily asked.

"Everyone knows Garrison Griswold. I even met him at his book carnival last spring."

"You *met* him?" Emily asked. "What's he like? What's the carnival like?"

She had been dying to go to Griswold's famous San Francisco book carnival since she first heard about it five years ago. Hopefully her family would still be living in San Francisco next spring.

"He walked around in this burgundy-and-blue-striped suit and top hat with a matching cane. He gave me tickets for the games. And every kid who goes to the carnival gets a free grab bag full of books."

"He really is the Willy Wonka of book publishing," Emily said with awe.

"It's awful what happened to him, isn't it?" James said.

Emily waved a hand dismissively. "Him not showing up today? I'm not worried. I think his disappearance is part of his next big game."

James tilted his head, antlers jangling. "You haven't heard? They just announced it. Garrison Griswold didn't disappear. He's in the hospital."

CHAPTER 5

Y OU SAID you needed a messenger," Barry hissed into his cell phone, wincing when it brushed the gauze taped over his split cheek. "That's all I agreed to."

It was maybe an hour after they'd left Griswold in the BART station. Barry and Clyde had jumped on a streetcar and hightailed it to Pier 39, where they could get lost in the crowds. They were on the wooden walkway behind the stores and restaurants. Through a breezeway came the buzz of tourists, the carousel cranking out its song. At the end of the pier, a cluster of people looked down at the sea lions sunning themselves on floating platforms in the harbor, braying like a bunch of rowdy men arguing at the horse races. And there was Clyde, sitting a few feet away from Barry, just out of earshot, cool as a cucumber and shoveling doughnut holes into his mouth.

"Who is this guy you partnered me with, anyway?"

A voice barked through the phone. Barry ducked his head like a scolded dog. "It's all over the news, man!" Barry said. "I'm kind of freakin' out over here. Even bums on the street know Garrison Gri—you know who."

Barry pressed the knuckles on his free hand against an eyeball and listened. "Yeah, we got rid of it. Clyde said he wiped it clean and threw it in the bay."

Crazy Clyde stared down a seagull perched on the railing in front of him. He pelted a doughnut hole at the bird. The seagull flapped up and then down to retrieve its prize.

"Look," Barry said into his phone. "Can I just get my money? You can find someone else. Or let Clyde take over from here."

He listened for a moment and then slapped his thigh. "But that's not my fault! He didn't have it on him. I might have been able to talk to the guy about it if the Sundance Kid hadn't shot him."

"We did look everywhere," Barry argued. "There was only one book in his bag, but it was brand-new."

"But you said it would be super old. You made that very clear."

"I don't know. It was by Poe. *Gold*-something-or-oth—"

"Well, I didn't know! You said an *old* book. If you'd said 'take any book'—"

"No, it's not with Griswold. I threw it in the trash."

"I'm sorry, okay? We'll go back and look. Then you give me my money and I'm out. Right?"

"Fine. But we can't go now. That place'll be swarming with cops. We'll go this weekend. Tomorrow. That's the best I can do—take it or leave it."

CHAPTER 6

ON SATURDAY MORNING, Emily checked the Book Scavenger forums for updates on Mr. Griswold, but the news was still the same: in critical condition at St. Mary's Hospital after being mugged in a BART station. Any plans for a new game were postponed indefinitely. The words *critical condition* had worried Emily.

"It means he's seriously injured, but beyond that it's hard to say without more information," her mom had said. "People recover from being in critical condition all the time."

In addition to worrying about Mr. Griswold, Emily couldn't help feeling disappointed about his game. The timing had been so perfect with their moving to San Francisco. She was glad she'd made plans to go book scavenging with James that afternoon. It would be a good way to distract herself from constantly refreshing the Book Scavenger forums for game rumors or updates on how Mr. Griswold was doing.

But before she could actually go to the Ferry Building, she had to ask her parents for permission. They were hanging the family motto her dad had years ago stenciled onto scrap wood: LIVE, TRAVEL, ADVENTURE, BLESS, AND DON'T BE SORRY. By Jack Kerouac, of course.

"Please?" Emily pleaded again.

"Not today, Em," her mom said around the nail gripped between her lips while she hammered another one into the wall.

"We need to get the lay of the land before we let you go off by yourself," her dad said. Knowing the objection Emily would raise, he rushed on to add, "Even if James goes to the Ferry Building on his own all the time. Your mom and I have a full day of unpacking and settling in. Of course, there is another alternative." Her dad tipped his head toward Matthew's door.

Emily sighed. She was hoping to avoid that alternative. Funny, if she traveled back in time a few years, it would have been Matthew dragging her along for an adventure. That was back when they were inseparable, when they were both into geocaching, a treasure-hunting game that uses a GPS to find hidden stashes of goodies, and the early days of Book Scavenger. Then Matthew went into the sixth grade and his classmate wanted to start a band, so her brother took up the guitar. Once he discovered Flush, he was all music, all the time. Treasure hunts were beneath him. Good-bye, best friend and partner in crime; hello, pain-in-the-butt brother.

Emily took a deep breath and knocked on her brother's door. She could feel the bass of a Flush song through the soles of her feet. Matthew's guitar screeched wrong chord after wrong chord as he practiced along with the music. She knocked again. The song abruptly stopped and then restarted from the beginning.

She pushed his door open and shouted his name but, if he'd heard, he didn't turn around. Emily tapped him on the shoulder, and Matthew spun, surprisingly plucking the right chord for once. He wore his favorite Flush T-shirt, the one with the band's name printed above a toilet.

"What?" he shouted over the music.

"Want to go to the Ferry Building?" Emily shouted back.

"Nope." He turned back around and raised the neck of his guitar.

"Matthew!" His stereo sat near her on the floor, and she kicked her toe at the power button, turning it off.

"What?" he said. "You asked if I wanted to go and I don't. Maybe if you asked if I wanted to make five bucks . . ."

"Look, I can't go without you. James says we can take cable cars to get there. I know you've never been

on one before—don't you want to explore San
Francisco a little?"

Matthew repetitively plucked a guitar string,
thinking.

"Fine," he said.

They joined James on the porch, and the three
walked up the hill. Matthew held out his smartphone,
taking a video as they walked. He panned a faded
striped sofa on the sidewalk with a FREE sign, a Giants
pennant fluttering on a rooftop deck. About a block
away from the peak of the hill, a hum like a massive
swarm of bees rose above the distant sounds of traffic.

"What is that?" Emily asked.

Before James could answer, they reached the top
and Emily could see for herself. Tracks ran down the
intersecting street, vibrating with cables even though
no trolley was in sight.

"This is where we'll board," James said. "There
should be a cable car any minute now."

The street they'd walked up dipped downhill after
the cable car tracks. A cluster of tourists on motorized,
standing scooters approached. Matthew recorded the
Segway riders rounding past them in a single-file line.

"They're doing a tour of Lombard Street," James
explained. "A famous curvy street that's up that way."

"'Frisco is sweet," Matthew said.

"Don't call it 'Frisco," James said with a shake of
his head. "Locals hate that."

"Noted." Matthew zoomed in on an old-fashioned light-up sign jutting out from an ice cream shop across the street.

"I can use some of this footage for my Flush videos."

"Flush?" James raised his eyebrows.

Emily rolled her eyes. "He means *fan* videos. My brother thinks the members of Flush actually know him and pay attention to what he does."

"Oh, they do. They know me as FiveSpade." Matthew tapped his screen, and his recording stopped with a ding. "Trevor—that's the drummer," he explained for James's benefit, "once commented on a video I posted on the Swirlies site. And then he shared it on his own blog. It was stop-motion animation with LEGOs—pretty sweet, if I do say so myself."

"But none of that means Trevor or any of Flush actually know *you*. You talk about them like they're your best friends."

James, who was standing between Emily and Matthew, had been swinging his head back and forth between brother and sister as their debate went on. Before Matthew could retort, James blurted, "Steve likes your hair."

Matthew tucked his chin down, considering James. "Oh yeah?" He smoothed his lopsided Mohawk with one hand. That morning he'd added three shaved lines over his left ear. "Who's Steve?"

James pointed to the tuft of hair standing up on the back of his head.

Matthew studied the cowlick, then nodded.

"Steve's got good taste," he said.

A bell clanged, and a red-and-tan trolley crested the hill, stopping at the intersection with another clang of the bell. Emily was unsure where to board or who to pay, but James led the way, stepping up at the front and showing a pass to the conductor. They sat on the wooden benches that ran along the outside of the cable car, facing the sidewalk. Matthew wanted a good video of the ride, so he stood next to them rather than sat, with one arm hugging a pole.

When the cable car jerked into motion, Emily curled her fingers around the edge of the bench. There was no seat belt or anything. Once they'd rolled down a couple of blocks, she relaxed and realized she wasn't going to fall off.

Everything James pointed out had a story attached to it. A dry cleaner's run by his uncle who pretended to sneeze quarters. A gigantic cathedral with a labyrinth but not the cool kind made out of hedges. A market where his grandmother buys oysters for Chinese New Year.

"How long have you lived here?" Emily asked James.

"My whole life."

"You've never lived anywhere else?"

"Not even a different home. My family has lived in our building forever. I think my grandfather bought it in the sixties. My bedroom was my mom's when she was a kid. Even before that building, my family has been here since my great-grandparents came from China."

Emily tried to imagine that—year after year in one house, one neighborhood, one school, with memories that went back for generations. She couldn't wrap her head around that. All she came up with was a crazy patchwork mishmash of all the different places she'd lived: their sunny tiled kitchen in New Mexico, their fireplace in Colorado that you could flip on with a switch, the slanted hallways in their Connecticut house, the carpeted staircase in their South Dakota house that she and Matthew bumped down on their rear ends.

"The longest I've lived in one place was almost three years," Emily said. "And I don't even remember that. It was right after I was born."

"Seriously?" There wasn't a jeering tone to James's question, but Emily bristled anyway. Sometimes she forgot how weird her family seemed to other people. Matthew had been listening, his arm looped casually around the post as if he were waiting for a bus instead of hurtling down a steep hill. Well, the cable car didn't exactly hurtle; it was more like clattering down a hill.

Her brother jumped in, eager to give the rundown of their moving history. He loved doing this—he almost sounded braggish about their family's oddballness.

"I was born in Arizona, Phlegmily was born in Washington. Then it was Massachusetts, and about the time we lived in New York, our parents realized— thanks to a few states they lived in before the Phlegm and I existed—they'd already lived in a fifth of the US. So they thought, *Why not live once in every state?* After New York, we did South Dakota, Illinois, Connecticut, Colorado, New Mexico, and now we're, like, totally vibin' Cali, brah." Matthew shook a fist

44

with his thumb and pinkie raised. "Shaka-brah, brah."

"That's Hawaii, doofus," Emily muttered.

"Our parents both do freelance work, so they can work from anywhere," Matthew said. "They're total dorks about this moving stuff."

Emily waited for James to double over in laughter or compare her family to a traveling circus, but all he did was shrug and say, "That sounds cool. My dad travels a lot, too."

"You don't think it's weird?" Emily couldn't help asking.

"Not any weirder than having your dad live out of hotels on business trips while you're at home with a mom and grandma who are obsessed with their catering company. Our couch is usually covered in sheets of soup dumplings."

"How often do you see your dad?" Emily asked.

"A couple of times a month, maybe. It varies." James looked away, up the hill they'd traveled down.

Emily couldn't imagine her parents traveling without her and Matthew, let alone by themselves. They liked to say they were the Swiss Family Robinson minus the shipwreck, or the Partridge Family minus the music.

They got off the cable car, and James led Emily and Matthew through a nearly deserted outdoor mall, then a palm-tree-lined plaza. The Ferry Building sat across a busy street, perched on the edge of the bay. It was a simple but stately building. Long, two stories

45

high, and crowned with a giant clock tower at its center. White tented booths for a farmers' market lined the sidewalk in front and wrapped around the corner.

They had made it halfway across the plaza when Matthew stopped in front of a man setting up a half circle of buckets, some overturned with a pot on top, some buckets right-side up with an upside-down, empty water jug tucked inside. The man pulled drumsticks from his vest pocket and gave a practice *rat-a-tat* run before readjusting some buckets.

"Matthew, come on," Emily said. "We're almost to the Ferry Building."

Matthew refused to leave, so Emily and James agreed to meet him by the bucket man after they found their book. They crossed the busy street and followed the white tents around the side of the building to the pier, where a maze of additional tents stretched ahead of them.

They wove through the crowds, and Emily felt a trill of anticipation. This was her favorite part of book hunting. The puzzles and riddles were fun, and she devoured the books, but the actual seeking was what brought her back to this game again and again. She could check out books from the library or she could buy puzzle books from the grocery store if that was all she was interested in. But combining those things with a hunt was like living a real-life board game, with a book as the prize.

"What do we do now?" James asked once they

stood in front of the third bench down the pier. Gray-green water lapped softly on the other side of the railing.

"We look for the book. It should be hidden somewhere around here. We're looking for *Tom Sawyer*."

Emily crouched next to the bench on her hands and knees, her ponytail dipping to the ground. There was a small piece of paper taped to the underside of the bench.

"No!" She slapped the ground in frustration.

"What's wrong?" James asked.

Emily pulled the calling card loose and stood up. It had the Book Scavenger logo on the front, and the back said:

> TOO SLOW!
> THIS BOOK HAS BEEN FOUND BY:
> # BABBAGE

"This Babbage guy poached our book, that rat," Emily said. "He knew I was hunting it, and so he got to it first." And her double points, too, while he was at it, she thought glumly.

"Who's Babbage?"

"I don't actually know him. It's a username for another Book Scavenger player. He could be anyone. Babbage could even be a she."

Emily dug a card from her small backpack pocket. "See? This is my card. You leave them when you hide or find a book, so people know you were there."

Her card was nearly identical to the one they'd found, but instead of *Babbage* it said *Surly Wombat*.

"'Surly Wombat'? How'd you come up with that?"

"It's an old joke with my brother. When we were living in Connecticut, we were hunting *The Golly-whopper Games* and the clue told us to go down this path through a bunch of trees. I don't know why, but the path creeped me out, and I didn't want to go. Matthew said, 'Don't be a surly wombat,' and went tromping down the path. It was such a random name to call me that it cracked me up. I mean, they're these cute, pudgy animals, and picturing one with an attitude, all surly . . ." Emily smiled at the memory. "So that got me over my nerves, and I followed him down the path to find the book. Later that day, I logged onto Book Scavenger but had to leave the computer for some reason, and Matthew changed my username to Surly Wombat. My first username was something generic, like booknut123. I never changed it back."

"Surly Wombat. I like it." James compared her Surly Wombat card and the Babbage card for a second more before handing them back to her. "How did this Babbage person know you were hunting *Tom Sawyer*?"

"I declared it before I downloaded the clue. Doing it that way, you get double points if you find the book.

But declaring a book means it's flagged on the website, so every other Book Scavenger user knows it's worth twice the points if they find it first. But it's only been a couple of days since I declared it, and there are a bunch of flagged books, so I thought there was no way someone else would solve the cipher and get to it first. I guess I thought wrong."

They made their way back to Matthew, stopping a couple of times for James to pick up some produce and other items from the farmers' market for his mom and grandmother. They had to pry Matthew from the crowd watching the bucket man *rat-a-tat* around his makeshift drum set, and then they headed back to the cable car stop by a different route than the way they'd come. They walked in between the same gray corridor of office buildings Emily's family had driven through the day before. It was a ghost town on the weekend, with only a few cars and the occasional passersby. A colorful bouquet of flowers abandoned on the sidewalk stopped Emily in her tracks. There was another one just ahead, and then another. A staggered trail of bouquets, like Hansel and Gretel's bread crumbs, led to an iron railing surrounding an underground staircase.

"What's with the flowers?" Matthew asked.

A torn yellow streamer tied to one of the iron bars wafted up in the breeze, waving the word *caution*. Emily gasped, realizing the yellow tape was a remnant from the perimeter that had barricaded the underground stairway the day before.

"This is the BART station," she said in a hushed voice, as if they were standing outside a cemetery and not a public transit stop. "We drove by this yesterday. All the emergency vehicles were here." This was where Garrison Griswold had been mugged. Even though the sun beat down on them, Emily felt a chill.

CHAPTER 7

I F IT WEREN'T for the pile of mementos honoring
Mr. Griswold, a person might pass this corner and
never guess something horrible had happened there. A
poster board leaned against the railing. It read: GET
WELL SOON, MR. GRISWOLD! YOUR CITY NEEDS YOU!
Flowers, candles, stuffed animals, and cards were in
the pile, but more than any other item, there were
books. Lots of books as if all the people in the city had
brought their favorites just for Mr. Griswold.

"I feel like we should leave something," Emily said.

James looked in the nylon bag that held his grandmother's vegetables. He pulled out a bundle of leafy
greens.

"Bok choy?"

Emily dropped to one knee and opened her backpack. She tore a piece of paper from her notebook and
folded it into a makeshift card. She and James crouched

on the sidewalk to write a note and sign it. James also
signed *Steve* with three little lines coming up from
the second *e* like a cowlick. Emily held the card up to
Matthew.

"What?"

"You should sign it, too."

"I don't even know the guy."

"Sign it, Matthew."

With a grumble, Matthew held out his hand for a marker. When Emily took the card back, she read what Matthew wrote: *My sister is bummed about what happened to you, so she's making me sign this. Get well soon, Mr. Candyman!*

"Matthew! You can't write that. And I've told you before—the Willy Wonka nickname has nothing to do with candy. He makes books."

"Fine, I'll fix it." He took the card back, crossed out *Mr. Candyman*, and wrote in *Old Book Dude*.

"That's even worse!" Emily snatched the paper from Matthew and crumpled it in her hands.

"So where did it happen, anyway?" Matthew asked. "Do you think he was standing right here?"

Emily shivered. "Creepy! I don't want to think about that."

"I think it was down in the station," James said.

"I'm going to check it out." Matthew was halfway down the stairs before Emily or James could say another word.

"Matthew, get back here!" Emily yelled after him.

"It's not closed or anything," Matthew shouted from below. "This would be a sweet spot for a music video."

Emily and James clambered down the stairs after him. The air grew warmer and more stale with every step until they were underground, standing next to

Matthew, who panned the area with the video on his smartphone. The station was an expansive, slick-walled cave with flickering overhead lighting. Slow, faraway notes from a clarinet player Emily couldn't see made her think the station must stretch pretty far back from where they stood. Bright advertisement posters for Beach Blanket Babylon, Teatro ZinZanni, and other San Francisco businesses were framed and hanging along the walls and on columns. Fingerprint-smudged glass walls and electronic gates separated them from the escalators and stairs that went down to the level where the trains came and went.

A woman walked down the stairs behind them and straight through the fare gate, like she did this all the time. Up ahead, a group entered from a farther entrance and turned to walk away from them to the opposite end of the station. Did these people even realize where they were or know what violent thing had happened here just one day before? Thanks to her brother's earlier question, Emily couldn't stop wondering where Mr. Griswold had been when he was mugged. Was he arriving on a train or downstairs waiting for one? She didn't want to be thinking like that, which of course made it all the more difficult to stop.

"Let's get out of here," Emily said. As she turned to leave, she lobbed the crumpled ball of her ruined card at a trash can, but it came up a few feet short. When she bent down to pick up her litter, she spotted the maroon edge of a book jammed between the can and the wall.

"No way!" she said. She pried the book loose from its spot and held it up. "A hidden book!"

"Is that for Book Scavenger?" James asked.

"*The Gold-Bug*," Emily read the title. It would totally make up for Babbage poaching her book if this was, in fact, for Book Scavenger. She flipped the cover open. "There's no tracking label on the inside. You're assigned a unique tracking number when you register a book with Book Scavenger," she explained to James. "You print the number on a label and put it inside the book. But sometimes people forget, or they don't care about tracking the book so they don't print the label and put it inside. But this must have been hidden, right? Why would someone throw this away? It looks brand new."

She considered the book again. The gold beetle embossed on the front glittered at her.

"I'll leave my card, just in case."

She crouched by the trash can, but before she could place her card, James nudged her.

"Um, your brother . . ."

Emily looked up to see Matthew applying a bumper sticker for Flush to the face of the ticket machine.

"Matthew! What are you doing? You actually carry those around in your pocket?"

"A devoted Swirly carries Flush paraphernalia at all times. That's rule number one. Rule number two is Flush adornment makes the world a better place. Besides, sticker slapping never hurt anyone."

"Do you not see the sign?"

Directly above him was a sign that read: NO VAN-DALISM. VIOLATORS WILL BE PROSECUTED.

Matthew waved a hand dismissively. "That's like a 'Beware of Dog' sign for Chihuahua owners. Nobody's even here—this place is practically empty."

"Practically is not the same as totally," James said, shifting from foot to foot as he eyed two men who had come into view on the far side of the station.

"Cut it out, seriously," Emily said. She hastily slid her calling card behind the trash can, adjusting it so it could be seen by someone looking for it but not spotted as trash. She stood and nodded toward the approaching men. "Those guys are watching us."

One was short and squat, the other tall and thin as a lamppost. The men were uncomfortably focused on them. If there was any doubt about that, it was squashed when the short man punched his friend on the arm and stabbed a finger in their direction.

The tall one cupped a hand around his mouth and shouted: "Hey, you kids! Stop!"

"Matthew, you idiot!" Emily said.

"Undercover security! Run!" Matthew shouted.

They flew to the staircase, Emily still clutching her new book. James pushed past Matthew when they hit the sidewalk.

"Follow Steve!" James shouted. His spiky tuft bobbed wildly as they ran.

James headed back in the direction of the Ferry Building. They hurdled flowers and stuffed animals, pounding down the brick-laid sidewalk until they reached a wall of people lining up to board a bus.

"Excuse us!" James shouted as they dove through the line. James turned a corner by the bucket man, who was still beating his makeshift drums in a frenzy. They ran toward the empty outdoor mall, the splattering of an immense concrete fountain urging them on. Emily looked over her shoulder. The men were still behind them, rounding past the bucket man.

"Keep running!" she shouted to James and Matthew.

James turned past a bakery and entered the mall. Glass-fronted stores passed by in a blur, then James turned sharply and hustled upstairs. There was nothing but the sound of their feet pounding until, finally, they slowed to a stop outside the public restrooms.

"I think we lost them," Matthew said between gasps.

"Quiet!" James held a finger to his lips.

Emily, James, and Matthew hugged the wall next to the restrooms to stay out of view of anyone on the lower level until footsteps thundered beneath them and then faded. A man swore, which echoed in the empty shopping center. Another voice said, "I told you they circled back to the park. Come on!"

Emily counted to one hundred in her head and

then, when she was certain the men were gone, turned to her brother, her face hot from running and growing hotter with anger.

"Matthew!" She thwacked him with the maroon book still gripped in her hand. "I can't believe you!"

"Jeez, chill out." Matthew wiped sweat from his forehead with a corner of his T-shirt. "Who would have thought security guards would get so worked up over a stupid bumper sticker?"

CHAPTER 8

E MILY WANTED to look up *The Gold-Bug* on the Book Scavenger website, and because there was almost always someone on the Cranes' computer and James had his own, they left Matthew at the front porch and went up to James's apartment. With every step up James's staircase, the smells of spices and roasting meat grew stronger. It had been a long time since Emily had been in a friend's house. She thought of James's grandmother and her scolding tone, and she started to feel anxious that she would do or say the wrong thing. She followed James's lead when they reached his entry landing, sliding off her shoes like him and adding them to the row that lined the wall.

Voices speaking Chinese came from the front room, and when Emily peered in, she saw they were from a flat-screen TV perched on a cabinet. An elderly Chinese woman, dwarfed by the floral armchair she sat in, was fixated on the screen. Every so often she'd flap her hands and say something too quiet for Emily to hear over the TV noise, like she was carrying on a one-sided conversation.

"Hi, Tai Po." James crossed the room and gave the woman a sideways hug. "My great-grandmother," he explained to Emily. "She lives over on Pacific with my auntie, but Saturdays she usually comes here because my cousins have weekend tournaments and stuff. You know how that is."

James tossed those sentences out so casually, totally unaware of how such simple statements could make Emily's head spin. First of all, what tournaments? She assumed he meant some kind of sport or maybe chess, but no, she didn't know how those could be. Moving so often, organized sports and school clubs weren't really something she did. Her free-time activities were sightseeing with her parents, reading, puzzles, and Book Scavenger.

And then there were all the people James mentioned in one sentence—a great-grandmother, auntie, cousins—all right here, nearby? Like he saw them all the time? Emily saw her grandmother who lived in Vermont maybe once a year, and the rest of her grandparents had passed away. She had an uncle who was in Europe, at least she thought that was where he was. He and her dad weren't super close. And her mom had a sister she talked often with on the phone, but it had been years since they saw her.

There was a clatter from the kitchen at the other end of the apartment. Emily turned to look down the hall and saw another woman pop her head out of the doorway. "You're back!" she said.

"Hey, Mom." James walked down the hallway to hand over the two bags he'd brought back from the farmers' market.

"Did you guys eat? The kitchen's a disaster zone, so don't come too close, but I can get you something. We're in the middle of prep work for that anniversary dinner we're catering tonight." James's mom had long, glossy black hair and wore hoop earrings that rocked like swings when she talked.

"We're good," James said, looking to Emily for affirmation. "Emily's going to show me the Book Scavenger website."

"Oh, Emily! I haven't even introduced myself. I'm so sorry. I'm James's mom. I'd shake a hand but . . ." She waved her flour-coated hands. "How are you liking San Francisco?"

"It's nice." She had to raise her voice to be heard over the roar of a stove fan that had been switched on in the kitchen. Something sputtered as it dropped in hot oil. From inside the kitchen they heard James's grandmother shout something over the oil and fan.

James's mom held her palms up and shrugged, like she was saying, "What can you do?" and ducked back into the kitchen.

It was a little overwhelming how different James's

apartment felt from Emily's, which was nearly identical in layout but nothing else. The Cranes' rentals were always furnished with the basics, and that was it. Stark and bland. James's apartment was layered with objects and smells and noises. There were rugs and couches and decorative pillows. Tables with fabric draped over them, and then frames and trinkets on top of the fabric. Real plants that you had to take care of. The walls were painted colors, not rental white, and covered with art, photographs, and a collection of paper fans. Some things looked brand-new, like the flat-screen TV, and some things looked like they belonged in a museum. James had said his family had been living in this building for generations, and you could feel it.

James's room was no different from the rest of the house. Filled to the brim. Blue walls covered with superhero and comic book posters, a solar system slowly revolved from the ceiling, a stuffed boa constrictor stretched across the foot of his bed. Multiple bookshelves with not just books but collections. Neat and orderly LEGO models, toy monsters, a tower of board games, sand dollars. Emily and Matthew were limited to one suitcase of "nonessentials" and one suitcase of books. Emily couldn't even calculate how many suitcases it would take for all of James's things.

James pushed back a curtain concealing a closet filled with a desk and computers.

"You've got to be kidding me," Emily said.

"I never kid about computers." James patted each one on top like obedient puppies. "One computer for schoolwork and regular stuff, one for video games, and the third—I built this one."

"You *built* a computer?"

"It's not really a big deal," James said with a shrug. "So how do we see if that *Gold-Bug* book is part of the Book Scavenger game?"

They went to the Book Scavenger website, and Emily clicked on "Embarcadero BART station." There were no books listed under Hidden. She did a search for *The Gold-Bug*, but nothing turned up in the results.

"Maybe somebody really did throw it away and missed the trash can," James said.

"Who would throw this away?" Emily asked. The book was entirely too special-looking: a hardback bound in linen cloth the color of a pomegranate, a gold beetle embossed on the front with flecks that sparkled when you tilted the book. It opened stiffly, as if she was the first to do so. Nobody would dump a book like this.

Emily flipped to the copyright page. The only thing on it was a small drawing of a black bird in front of a bridge and ocean waves, and a short string of numbers. The drawing gave her an itchy-brain feeling, like she'd dreamed about finding this book or had seen that symbol before.

Maybe someone hid it so recently he or she hadn't had time to register it online, or maybe he or she even forgot. She clicked on the forum and posted a message.

She typed: "I found a copy of THE GOLD-BUG by Edgar Allan Poe in a San Francisco BART station. Did anyone hide it and forget to register it? Please, pretty please, say yes because I need the points." She didn't really *need* the points, but she was only fifteen points away from advancing from Miss Marple level to Auguste Dupin, and she'd been counting on getting those two points by finding the *Tom Sawyer* book today.

After posting her message to the forum, Emily gave James a tour of the Book Scavenger site, updating her profile information so it listed San Francisco as her city and Booker Middle School for "school/work."

"What about that card you found?" James said. "At the Ferry Building? What did you call that guy? A . . . poacher? Can we find out anything about him?"

Emily pulled the card from her backpack and typed "Babbage" into the user search. She clicked on the profile and was surprised to see that Babbage ranked Sherlock Holmes level, the highest possible level.

"That rat! He didn't even *need* those points. Selfish poacher," Emily muttered.

"Points don't matter when you're at the top level?" James asked.

"Well, you can still use them at the Book Scavenger

and Bayside Press stores. And some people are just competitive and want to see how high they can get their point total."

It would take her a long while to get to Sherlock Holmes level, but once Emily did, she'd probably be one of those competitive people.

"Has Babbage declared any books?" James asked. "Maybe we could beat him to one of the books he's hunting."

Emily clicked on Babbage's profile to look at his hidden books but was stopped by another discovery.

"Booker Middle School!" James read. "He goes to our school?"

"Or she," Emily said. Knowing Babbage was a middle schooler just like them made her all the more irritated that he or she had poached *Tom Sawyer*.

"Can't we see their picture?"

"There isn't one uploaded." Babbage used a generic avatar, just like Emily.

She scanned Babbage's book listings. The user hadn't declared any titles, but he or she had hidden several recently. When you hid a book and uploaded the clue, you selected a detective category to give other users an idea of how tricky it might be to find your hidden book. Babbage had rated all of his or her clues at Sherlock level, so they were almost definitely beyond Emily's cipher-cracking capabilities.

The computer dinged, and an instant-message box popped up.

RAVEN: Can I be of service?

"Who asks if they can be of service?" James said. "Is Raven a butler or something?"

Emily shrugged. "Beats me."

SURLY WOMBAT: Service with what?

RAVEN: You inquired about THE GOLD-BUG.

"Oh!" Emily straightened. "That was fast. Raven knows about the book! See? I knew it was a Book Scavenger book."

SURLY WOMBAT: Did you hide it in the BART station?

RAVEN: I cannot reveal the locations.

"The location's been revealed, you weirdo," Emily said. "How else would I know about it?"

SURLY WOMBAT: I already know the location. I found THE GOLD-BUG in the BART station. I'm trying to get credit for it.

RAVEN: THE GOLD-BUG is a short story by Edgar Allan Poe, originally published in 1843. Poe won a short story contest and the prize was publication in a local paper. It was a popular story in its day and brought attention to cryptograms and secret writing.

"What's with the history lesson?" James asked.

Emily sighed. "I don't think Raven actually hid this book. She's probably one of those know-it-alls who likes to flaunt every fact in her head. Yippee for you, you know a lot about Edgar Allan Poe." Emily closed the instant-message box with a sharp click of the mouse.

"Let's see if there's anything new about Mr. Griswold in the hospital," Emily said.

In the forums, there weren't any news updates, but Emily did see a thread under the "Garrison Griswold" category titled "What if..." A user from South Carolina had posted: *Don't want to be a downer, but I just had a sad thought. What happens to Book Scavenger if Mr. G doesn't make it?*

Emily breathed in sharply. She had been worried about Mr. Griswold and what it meant that he was in critical care, but it never crossed her mind that something happening to him could mean something happening to Book Scavenger, too. She skimmed the posted reactions, finding an assortment of replies. Most people were positive about the future of both Mr. Griswold and Book Scavenger. But one user's reply might as well have been boldfaced the way it jumped out: *A friend of a friend works at Bayside Press, and* *let's just say it's been love, not $, keeping Book Scavenger up and running. And that was before all this went down with Big G. I want to be bright and cheery about what the future holds, but I'm thinking we should get our book-hunting kicks in now while we still can. Hope I'm wrong.*

A world without Book Scavenger? Six years ago she didn't know any different, but now it was such a huge part of her life. Without Book Scavenger, Emily wouldn't be able to follow a book's journey, see who found it and where it traveled to next, read the adventure logs that other sleuths posted, trade reviews after they read the book.

Reading would be lonely without Book Scavenger. Moving again would be unbearable without Book Scavenger.

"Well, it looks like nothing's changed with Mr. Griswold," James said, breaking up her thoughts. "We talked about making up a secret language. Want to do that now?"

Emily blinked at James a few times, like she couldn't quite get her eyes to focus. "Right," she finally said. "Looks like nothing's changed." Emily glanced at the forum message once more before closing the browser window.

CHAPTER 9

THAT NIGHT IN BED, Emily distracted herself from worrying about Mr. Griswold and Book Scavenger by reading the new book she'd found. Thanks to the odd exchange with Raven earlier that day, she knew *The Gold-Bug* was an old story of Edgar Allan Poe's. She thought that was weird at first, an old story in a clearly brand-new book, but her dad reminded her that classics get republished all the time, often with a new cover to "make them more accessible to modern readers," as he put it.

Emily dipped her nose in *The Gold-Bug* and breathed deeply. It had a new-book smell with the faintest hint of lemons. The pages turned crisply as she went back to the beginning of the story to start over. The language was old-fashioned, and Emily noticed a spelling mistake right off the bat and then another a few sentences later, so she was having trouble getting into the story.

She'd flipped ahead and read enough snippets to know it was about a secret message and a treasure hunt. That sounded good, so she stuck with it, but the mistakes bothered her. Using one of her dad's purple editing pencils, she corrected the misspellings like he did, marking through the incorrect letter and writing the correct one above. Some people thought it was strange or even destructive to write in books, but it was a habit Emily had picked up when she was seven and used to play "editor" while her dad worked. Back then she mostly wrote nonsense or drew pictures of cats, but now her notes made up a reading diary of sorts.

Emily sighed with frustration as she came across what was probably the twentieth typo.

From the ceiling she heard a thud, then three fast thuds, followed by another thud. That was the signal she and James had agreed on when they made up their secret language earlier that day. It meant a bucket message was coming. Emily crossed her room and slid open her window.

For their secret language, they had decided on a substitution cipher. James knew from keyboarding class that the sentence "The quick brown fox jumps over the lazy dog" used every letter in the alphabet, so they made that their cipher key. To end up with twenty-six letters to match the alphabet, they skipped any

that were repeated. Their secret code looked like this:

Regular Alphabet:
ABCDEFGHIJKLMNOPQRSTUVWXYZ

Cipher Key:
THEQUICKBROWNFXJMPSVLAZYDG

S was still *S*, but they decided that was okay. If they could memorize their new alphabet, they'd be able to read each other's messages without using an answer key for reference.

The bucket lowered beside Emily, and she removed James's note. It said, ZKTV TPU DXL QXBFC? Gibberish to anyone else, but Emily knew what to do. She tugged her pencil free, and soon she'd translated his message: *What are you doing?*

Emily wrote her reply:

PUTQBFC CH. IXLFQ 20 VDJXS. DXL?
(Reading GB. Found 20 typos. You?)

She used the handle of the broom she'd found in the kitchen to repeat the knock on the ceiling before sending the note up. James's reply came a few minutes later:

KXNUZXPO. ETF B SUU CH?
(Homework. Can I see GB?)

72

Emily placed the book in the bucket. While she waited for James to send it back, she thought about how weird it was for a book to look so perfect on the outside, but have so many mistakes on the inside. Whoever made it must not have hired someone like her dad to fix the errors. James knocked, and the bucket lowered back to her window.

DXL ZPBVU BF HXXOꞨ? PUHUW!
WXXO ZKTV B IXLFQ—KTKT.
(You write in books? Rebel!
Look what I found—haha.)

Emily opened the book and saw that James had circled consecutive letter corrections in order to spell out the words *fort*, *wild*, and *home*. Leave it to James to turn a bunch of boring typos into a crazy word search game. She sent him a note back:

DXL TFQ DXLP JLGGWUS. ☺
(You and your puzzles. ☺)

Sunday morning, Emily woke to the sound of someone bowling outside her room. She groggily shifted under her covers. Wait—did she just hear someone *bowling*? She threw off her sheet and cracked her door just in time to see Matthew careening toward her on his skateboard.

"Breakfast!" he hollered as he coasted by, beaning her on the forehead with a plastic-wrapped muffin. He skidded to a stop in front of his own room. Emily picked up the blueberry muffin from the floor.

"You're such an idiot," she snapped.

"Tough break for you, then," Matthew said with a shrug. "Same gene pool."

Emily shuffled to the kitchen. It was a narrow room with a small table squeezed in at one end.

"Where's Mom?" she asked her dad, who sat at the table surrounded by sections of newspapers.

"Out taking pictures for the blog."

"Already?" They'd been in San Francisco less than two days.

"The blog won't create content for itself, I suppose," her dad murmured.

Emily searched for a juice glass among the various moving boxes and bags that still cluttered the counter and floor, lost in thought about *The Gold-Bug*. She'd made her way through the whole story last night. With every typo she found, she crossed out the incorrect letter and wrote the correct one above. On the last page her handwritten corrections spelled out the word *belief*. Even though she had teased James about his knack for spotting a puzzle anywhere, it kind of spooked her, as if the book itself were trying to talk to her. But that would be crazy.

"Hey, Dad? When you're copyediting, have you

ever noticed the typos spelling out a word?" She found a juice glass and joined him at the table.

"Hmm?" Her dad unfolded the section he was reading and then refolded it in quarters so he could read a different part of the page.

Emily poured herself some juice. "You know how you cross out the incorrect letter and write the correct one above it? Have those corrected letters ever spelled out words?"

Not looking up he said, "They're already part of a word."

"No. What if the typos themselves were part of a second word, too—made up of only the corrected letters that you wrote. That's never happened?"

"You mean the corrections spell out a word by chance?" Her dad looked at her, baffled. Then he gave a soft grunt, like he was amused by this idea. "That would be quite a feat. Unless you're talking about two-letter words like *be*, or maybe *the*, I don't think it could happen." He gave it some more thought then shook his head firmly. "No, it would be impossible to do accidentally."

Emily was about to tell him it wasn't impossible and in fact had happened many times over in the book she was reading when her dad said, "Thought you'd be interested in this." He riffled through the stacks of paper and pulled out a folded-up section. "A profile on Garrison Griswold today, and a little about Book Scavenger."

"Oh! Let me see!" Emily opened and closed her hand like a little kid wanting a toy.

Her dad stood from the table and handed the paper to Emily with a smile. "I love that you're so passionate about books and publishing. Speaking of, it's back to work for me."

"It's Sunday," Emily said.

"I need to make up for the time I took driving us out here so I can meet my deadline. No rest for the weary. But don't worry, we'll have a family adventure this afternoon."

"You do know *adventure* means something unusual and exciting, right?" Emily asked her dad. He crinkled his nose and tilted his head in response, looking bemused. "If sightseeing and exploring new places is our family norm, then maybe *adventure* isn't the right word choice."

Her dad chuckled. "Interesting theory," he said and left the kitchen.

Emily unfolded the newspaper. A photo of Garrison Griswold accompanied the article. He stood in front of the Bayside Press building in the same burgundy-and-silver-blue outfit James had described him wearing at the book carnival: top hat, suit, and walking stick all in Bayside Press colors. He was a very tall man—from the photo it looked like he'd have to duck to go through the front entrance if he had on his hat. He wore frameless glasses, had floppy silver hair, and a salt-and-pepper mustache that was like a miniature duster broom balanced under his nose.

Emily skimmed the article:

Griswold moved to the San Francisco Bay Area in 1952 at age twelve. At the age of eighteen, propelled by his admiration for the Beat Generation of writers, he moved out of his parents' house and into the city itself. Inspired by Lawrence Ferlinghetti's endeavors with the City Lights Booksellers and Publishers, Griswold began publishing an alternative weekly paper called the *Bayside Weekly*, which eventually developed into one of the most prominent publishing companies in San Francisco.

Also known for his spirit of fun, Griswold has been affectionately nicknamed the Willy Wonka of book publishing. In 2004 he launched a book trading game called Book Scavenger that has grown in popularity, amassing over 500,000 users in sixteen participating countries, with an average of 100,000 books to be found on any given day. In addition to Book Scavenger, he's hosted several smaller-scale games around the city and occasionally in farther-off locations.

Mr. Griswold had also moved to the Bay Area when he was twelve? Emily hadn't known that. She wanted to cut out Griswold's profile and photo, but she couldn't find any scissors. After rummaging through bags and boxes, and yanking open kitchen cabinets and drawers, she sighed to the ceiling separating her apartment from James's. She bet the Lees had a specific location for scissors. All normal kids who didn't live like gypsies probably did. She bent the paper over the corner of their laminate countertop to rip it, but accidentally tore off the corner of Griswold's photo.

She was about to flick the small piece into the trash bag hooked over a cabinet door but stopped when she saw the Bayside Press logo on the building. She'd ripped right through it—the circular crest with a seagull soaring over water in front of a bridge. The logo wasn't new to her, but now it was like seeing it for the first time.

Emily raced down the hallway to find her dad settling in front of the family computer.

"Dad," she said, her voice breathless as if her run had been a mile long. "About my typo question—could someone do it intentionally? Publish a book with the typos in it on purpose?"

Her dad readjusted his glasses as he considered her question.

"They could," he said slowly, "although I don't know why they would. Publishers pay me to keep typos out of books. Why would they want to leave them in?"

Why *would* someone want to leave them in? Emily

left her dad perplexed by her sudden interest in the editorial process and raced back to her room. She picked up *The Gold-Bug* from the top of her stack of books, the word *belief* echoing in her head as she flipped to the copyright page.

The emblem on the copyright page was nearly identical to the Bayside Press logo, but instead of a seagull there was a black bird.

"No way," Emily whispered. This was Mr. Griswold's book. It had to be. He must have hidden it in the BART station before he was mugged. And there was only one reason Emily could think of that Mr. Griswold would purposely hide a book and not enter it on Book Scavenger.

To start a game.

CHAPTER 10

EMILY HAD TO TALK to James. She looked to the window where the sand pail dangled, but this was too urgent for that. She bundled *The Gold-Bug* with her notebook and the news clipping.

"I'll be right back!" she called to her dad as she thundered down the stairs.

She thrust the article at James when he opened his front door. The damp chill of morning fog had Emily hopping from one bare foot to another, and she realized in her haste she hadn't changed out of her pajamas, but she didn't care.

"You'll never believe this! You know the words you circled in *The Gold-Bug*?" Her words tumbled out in an excited rush. "I found another one last night. And then, when I was talking with my dad this morning, I saw this."

James looked confused and possibly like he'd just

woken up, although Steve's presence plus pajamas could have that effect. He leaned over to study the torn news clipping. "Mr. Griswold?"

"We found his next game!" Emily blurted out.

James's expression reminded Emily of the main character in *The Gold-Bug*, who thought his friend had gone insane.

"I guess you should come in," James said, opening the door wider.

In James's room, Emily said, "Look at the logo on the wall behind Mr. Griswold and compare it to this." She flipped *The Gold-Bug* to the copyright page.

James looked back and forth between the two emblems. "They're almost identical."

"Exactly alike, except for the bird. This book is Mr. Griswold's new game—I'm sure of it."

James inspected the emblems even closer, mulling the idea over. "And the hidden words are part of a clue," he said.

Emily nodded, her ponytail bobbing encouragingly. She flipped open her notebook and showed James the hidden words she'd found: *fort, wild, home, rat, open,* and *belief.*

"Do you think it's a puzzle?" James asked. "A word scramble, maybe? *Open wild rat home . . . Rat fort belief . . .*"

They bowed their heads over the list in concentration. James combed his fingers through Steve, deep in thought.

"I wonder why Poe?" James asked. "Why pick this story to start his game?"

"Maybe Poe is his favorite author?"

James nodded to the newspaper clipping still in Emily's hand. "What about that profile? Does it say anything about his favorite authors?"

Emily shook her head. "We could look online. Search both their names and see what comes up."

They moved to James's computer, and he typed in "Griswold and Poe."

Emily was surprised to see more than fifty thousand hits. "Well, I guess there's a connection." The top one was titled "The Rivalry of Poe and Griswold."

"They knew each other?" James asked. "I thought Poe was . . . dead. Like, a long time ago."

"I did, too." Emily clicked the link, and the two leaned toward the screen and began reading. "Oh, it's about a *Rufus* Griswold. Different first name." According to the article, Rufus Griswold and Edgar Allan Poe were both East Coast writers in the mid-1800s who were familiar with each other but didn't get along. After Edgar Allan Poe died, Rufus Griswold published a mean-spirited obituary about Poe. It began, *Edgar Allan Poe is dead. He died in Baltimore the day before yesterday. This announcement will startle many, but few will be grieved by it.* And then, to the surprise of a lot of people, he became Poe's literary executor, which meant he had access to all of Poe's papers. He later published a biography about Poe that was full of lies and attacked his character.

"He must be related to Garrison Griswold, right?" James asked. "I mean, what are the chances their last name is just a coincidence?"

"They must be," Emily said. "I don't understand what that means, though. Why hide a Poe book for his game when his ancestor hated the guy?"

"Maybe Mr. Griswold feels badly about it," James suggested. "Maybe choosing Poe is his way of making amends."

"That's possible." Emily scrolled down the web page. "Or maybe he simply likes Poe and doesn't care what this Rufus guy felt about him. But I'm not sure how knowing any of this tells us how to play Mr. Griswold's game." Emily studied the book on her lap, as if the beetle on the cover might start talking and give them the answer.

"Well . . ." James twisted his computer chair back and forth as he thought. "Maybe the question to ask is, Why *The Gold-Bug*? We read 'The Tell-Tale Heart' last year at Halloween. I've never heard of *The Gold-Bug* before yesterday. So why not use the more popular story? Or any other story of his? There's got to be a reason why he chose this particular one."

Emily flipped through *The Gold-Bug* again, sorting through what she knew about Mr. Griswold and his games, and the little she knew about Poe.

"This story is about a treasure hunt. A man finds a

gold-bug and a piece of parchment, and then he discovers that when he heats the parchment a cipher appears. He cracks the cipher and it leads him and two friends to buried treasure. So . . . maybe Mr. Griswold is planning something like that."

James's eyes widened. "And the hidden words are part of a message that leads to buried treasure. Do you think that's it?"

Emily's mouth crooked up in a half smile. "After he organized the life-sized Mastermind tournament at Crissy Field last winter, people kept asking Mr. Griswold what game he had planned next. He said he had something in the works, something major. A secret message that leads to buried treasure sounds pretty major to me."

Emily returned to her apartment later that morning, still trying to wrap her head around her big discovery. She couldn't believe she'd found Mr. Griswold's next game. Ever since she joined Book Scavenger years ago and read all the stories shared on the forums about his San Francisco games, she'd hoped that somehow she'd get to participate in one in person. And now she had not only stumbled across his game, but it was also entirely possible she and James were the *only* people who knew about it so far.

As excited as she was that she'd found Mr. Griswold's game, and her hunch that it would be a treasure hunt like in *The Gold-Bug* story, she still didn't know what to do with the hidden words. Puzzling over everything she'd just learned, Emily walked into their kitchen to find her mom knee-deep in shopping bags and cardboard boxes.

"Do you know where I put that magic unpacking wand?" her mom asked. "I'd like to zap this stuff and have it put itself away. If the dishes could also sing and dance while they're at it, that'd be great."

Emily knew from experience that her parents would be dutiful about unpacking for approximately one or two more days and then something would come up to distract them—work deadlines, a local festival they didn't want to miss out on since they probably wouldn't be there the following year, or the urgent need to research an unusual bird they saw. Their possessions would gradually find their way out of their moving containers and be put away—clothes would move to closets after they were worn and washed, that sort of thing. Emily sometimes suspected her parents had an unspoken competition about who could ignore the moving boxes the longest. When they were in Colorado, there was an entire box that never got opened. Her parents donated it without even looking inside when they moved to New Mexico. They figured it must not be important if they hadn't been compelled to open the box for a whole year, and since they were on a perpetual quest to live with as few belongings as necessary, off went the box. At the time, their decision had seemed logical enough to Emily. But now she wondered what had been in that box. She thought of James's apartment and all the photos and trinkets. What if the box had been full of old family photos or heirlooms—something special that you wouldn't technically need for a year, but was still important all the same?

"Finished!" Emily's dad announced from the front room. His footsteps echoed down the hallway. He rapped loudly on Matthew's door before entering the kitchen. "I propose a treat!" he said.

"A treat?" Emily's mom asked. "Does it involve leaving the house? Because I would be so sad if I had to stop unpacking right now." She dropped the spatula she'd been holding and stepped away from the bags and boxes to grab her purse off the kitchen table.

Flush music amplified as Matthew came out of his room and joined them.

"Let's venture down to North Beach," Emily's dad said. "I've been dying to see City Lights."

Emily perked up. "The bookstore?" She remembered reading the name in Mr. Griswold's profile.

"The one and only," her dad replied. "Or I should say, the one and only City Lights. I imagine there are many bookstores in San Francisco. But City Lights is at the top of my list for Jack Kerouac and Beats-related spots."

"I'm in!" Emily said.

"Me too!" her mom said.

"Can we get lunch?" Matthew asked.

The family took a bus down their hill to a neighborhood called North Beach. Emily wasn't sure why it was called North Beach, because there wasn't a speck of sand in sight. They got off the bus near Washington Square, a flat stretch of grass that sat in front of an old church. That day there was an Italian heritage parade, so the square and streets were filled with people. A marching band, followed closely by floats of Christopher Columbus's ships, circled the square. Elsewhere in the city was a Fleet Week celebration, and every so often the Blue Angels flew overhead as part of the air show.

Heading to the City Lights bookstore, the Cranes walked a weaving path around café tables that packed the sidewalk. The sky erupted with another thunderous roar as a pyramid of six jets flew high above the twin white spires of the Saints Peter and Paul Church. Emily and her parents clutched their ears, but Matthew didn't seem as fazed. Maybe the music that constantly pulsed through his earbuds dulled the sound a bit.

Her dad, leading the way, turned to them and walked backward. "Only in San Francisco!" he shouted. Her parents said that so often with every place they lived, it had become an inside joke. When their parents made a remark about a sunny day or a sale on tomatoes, Emily or Matthew would say, "Only in . . . (fill in the blank of wherever they were living)." It usually flustered their mom like she'd been scolded and she'd snap, "Well, not everything can be an enriching experience."

They walked under sculptures of open books dangling from wires like birds in flight and soon found themselves in front of City Lights. Emily's dad wanted a picture taken of him standing under the CITY LIGHTS BOOKSTORE painted on the front window; then one with him, Matthew, and Emily; then he asked a stranger to take one of the whole family. He was so excited you'd think he was visiting Disneyland.

They filed through the entrance into a small room shaped like a pizza slice.

"Amazing to think this room made up the whole bookstore in the beginning, isn't it?" And it *was* kind of amazing, since the original pizza-slice-sized store would have fit maybe ten people tops, and that would have been shoulder-to-shoulder. The bookstore was now a hodgepodge of rooms that spanned nearly a whole block. "As other businesses left this building," her dad explained, "City Lights gradually took over the whole space."

They stepped up into a larger room washed in sunshine from tall windows. Matthew nearly collided with a college-aged guy, who did a double take of Matthew's shirt—the one with five diamond playing cards on it. "Flush!" the guy said, and Matthew said, "Yeah, man."

"You hear about the underground concert? At the Fillmore?"

"Seriously?" Matthew pulled at his Mohawk,

trying to play it cool, but Emily could tell by her brother's bouncing knee that this was new and exciting news. "I knew they were doing an underground tour, but I didn't know they'd be here."

"Yeah, man," the guy said. "You have to buy tickets for Shoot the Moon, but Flush will be playing, too."

Matthew waited until the guy walked out of the store before hurrying to their dad.

"Dad, did you hear that?" Their dad studied notes written on Post-its tacked to a bulletin board that asked, WHAT'S THE ONE BOOK YOU ALWAYS RECOMMEND?

"Flush at the Fillmore, Dad. That's, like, *my* Jack Kerouac and *my* City Lights. I have to go to that concert. I'll never have this chance again!"

It sounded melodramatic, but her brother was probably right. By the time his favorite band came back to that venue, the Cranes would probably be long gone, living in Ohio or Mississippi or wherever their parents' whims took them next.

"We can talk about it."

"But it's Flush!"

"You're causing a traffic jam, Matthew," their mom said. "Your dad didn't say no. We just need more information. Now's not the time."

Matthew plugged his earbuds back in and stepped through an arched doorway leading to another room of books. The rest of the Cranes split into different directions to explore the bookstore on their own.

Emily walked from small room to small room, up and down the three levels that made up City Lights. She noted the mismatched flooring; the hand-lettered signs with sayings like A KIND OF LIBRARY WHERE BOOKS ARE SOLD; an oval mirror with a lion's head on top; framed art, photos, and memorabilia from the Beat poets. Emily trailed her fingers along the varied book spines and thought about young Garrison Griswold, freshly moved to San Francisco, and how this bookstore and its owner had been an inspiration to him.

She'd hoped coming here might help her understand the hidden words she and James had found in Mr. Griswold's book. *Fort, wild, home, rat, open, belief,* she chanted to herself as she wandered among the bookshelves. No bolt of inspiration struck, and the bookstore didn't magically offer up a solution as she'd hoped it would, but she was quite content to roam. She passed Matthew sitting on a footstool flipping through a book with black-and-white photographs of musicians. Her mom smiled at a book of poetry. Her dad studied a group photo of his beloved Beats for so long Emily wondered what he must be thinking about.

If Mr. Griswold hadn't been attacked, this would have been a perfect first weekend in a new place. Book hunting on a pier with a new friend, discovering Mr. Griswold's game, and spending an afternoon browsing in an iconic bookstore. She only wished there wasn't a giant, invisible timer lording over her family, ticking down to when they would inevitably move again.

CHAPTER 11

*T*HUD. *Thud-thud-thud. Thud.*

It was Monday morning, Emily's third day in San Francisco. It was also the Columbus Day holiday, which meant no school. Her first day at another new school would wait one more day.

Emily slid open her window and listened to the pulley squeak as the bucket was lowered. Even though James had his window open upstairs, too, they seemed to have made an unspoken agreement that there would be no verbal conversations when the message bucket was in use. Encrypted conversations only.

She unfolded the paper and read:

ZTFV VX KBGU T HXXO? B OFXZ
T CXXQ KBQBFC SJXV.

She translated the message in no time at all: *Want to hide a book? I know a good hiding spot.*

Emily had lucked out moving into James's building.

Twenty minutes later they walked up their hill and down the other side, ending up in the middle of a stretch of shops and restaurants. Emily had brought her backpack with her to hold her Book Scavenger notebook and the book they planned to hide (Emily's second paperback copy of *Inkheart*, the one she'd found at the Albuquerque Zoo), and at the last minute Emily threw in *The Gold-Bug*. You never knew when you might have time to sit down and study a book for more typos.

"If we were walking to school, we'd turn that way," James said, pointing down the sloping street. Far down the road, apartment buildings framed a view of the bay with Alcatraz island smack dab in the middle.

Emily stood still. "It's like out of a movie," she said.

"What is?" James looked at the parking meters, the liquor store across the street, the bus stop in front of them.

"The view." Emily pointed.

"Oh." James absentmindedly threaded his fingers through Steve as he looked again toward the water. "Yeah, I guess so. You should see it on a sunnier day, though."

James turned away from the water to walk up the street. "Hollister's bookstore is up this way."

James's idea had been to hide the book in a bookstore. "Like hiding a leaf in a tree," he said. There was one bookstore in particular that he had in mind, a place he stopped in regularly on his way home from school. "Ever since Hollister learned I like puzzle magazines, he's kept a good stock of them."

As they approached, the door to the bookstore swung open with a jingle and out stepped a black man with gray-frosted dreadlocks tied loosely at the nape of his neck. The man studied the store window as if he were assessing a painting, and then went back inside. His upper body rocked like a metronome when he walked, swinging his ponytail of ropes side to side across his back.

"That was Hollister. He owns the store," James said. Soon they reached it and could see for themselves the display Hollister had been studying. The entire expanse of window was filled with books arranged by color and stacked atop one another like LEGOs to create the Bayside Press symbol.

James whistled long and low.

"How did he do this?" Emily asked.

"This must have taken him forever," James said.

They pushed open the door. "Hollister, your window looks amazing!" James said.

The bookstore owner slapped his thigh and said, "Well, hey there, James! You finish the latest *Puzzle Power*? I hope not, because the next issue isn't due for another month." Hollister nodded in Emily's direction. "Who's this young lady?"

Up close she could see one eye drooped and didn't

look in quite the same direction as the other. She wondered if that lazy eye made it difficult for Hollister to read, and if so, how torturous that would be, surrounded by books all the time.

"This is Emily. She just moved here."

"Hello, Emily-Who-Just-Moved-Here."

"Your window is really cool," Emily said. "I never would have thought of using the colors of book spines and covers to make a picture, like art."

"Ah, well." Hollister rubbed his neck. "Small token of respect for a good man. It's the least I can do for an old friend."

"Old friend?" Emily repeated. She looked to James questioningly.

He shrugged. "You're friends with Mr. Griswold?"

"I said *old* friend. It's been at least thirty years since we've had a sensible conversation. Although I do have a regular customer who works for him. A rare-book collector who manages his library. So I sort of feel like I keep in touch with him that way. Or in touch with his reading interests at least, but that's what matters most, am I right?" Hollister chuckled. For a minute he looked like he might say more, but then he dropped to one knee and sorted through the pile of books he'd gathered. A morose cloud had settled around the man's shoulders, and Emily didn't know him well enough to understand if that was normal or due to his dwelling on Mr. Griswold. "This window display is the least I can do right now, that's all."

It occurred to her that if Hollister once knew Mr. Griswold, he might be able to help them figure out the secret message they'd discovered. But the way he acted, talking about Mr. Griswold, made her worry that maybe it was a touchy subject. And if she was honest, part of her felt protective. Right now *The Gold-Bug* and the words she and James found belonged to them. Sharing that might ruin the fun somehow. They should stick with their original reason for coming to Hollister's store. She cleared her throat.

"Could we hide a book in your store?" Emily said. "For Book Scavenger? It's got a badge inside, so no one will mistake it for one of yours."

Hollister nodded. "Sure, sure. Have at it."

The bookshop was narrow with tall bookcases creating tunnels that twisted and turned. A ladder leaned against one bookcase to reach the topmost titles. Every nook was occupied by a chair, a teetering pile of books, or both. In the back half of the store there was a loft and a spiral staircase that led up to it. Emily and James wandered through the store, scouting for the best hiding spot.

"It can't be too difficult," Emily said. "I do want someone to actually find it, since I'll get a point when they do, and it's no fun tracking a book that never moves."

"How about this?" James pointed to a bookcase raised on knobby feet that made up the arts and crafts section. James took *Inkheart* from Emily and slid it

underneath the bookcase so the pages were visible instead of the spine. "Can I see your notebook and a pen?" he asked.

Emily pulled her pencil from her ponytail and her notebook from her backpack and handed both to James, curious to see what he'd come up with.

"The clue can be . . ."

crafts
_____

wrong side out

"I get it." Emily grinned. *"Wrong side out under crafts.* That's perfect. We can take a photo of this puzzle and upload it for our clue when we get back to our building."

Emily returned her notebook to her backpack and saw *The Gold-Bug.* She looked to the front where Hollister was. Maybe they wouldn't tell him about the game or ask about Griswold specifically, but he still might be able to point them in the direction of some helpful information.

"Let's ask Hollister if he has any books by or about Edgar Allan Poe," Emily whispered to James.

Hollister led them to a round table decorated for Halloween with a giant paper spider, a witch's cauldron, and cotton-strewn webs.

"Most of my Poe is out here now. He's popular this time of year," Hollister said.

Emily chewed on this as she looked over the book display. Maybe that was all Mr. Griswold's Poe choice came down to: a popular author for Halloween season. Maybe her treasure hunt suspicion was way off—but then why not pick one of Poe's spookier stories if Halloween was the point?

There were various collections of Poe's work on the table, along with other mysteries and scary stories. A stack of books in a familiar maroon color stood out to Emily. Hastily, she pulled *The Gold-Bug* from her backpack and stepped closer to the pile. They weren't the same. She exhaled a breath she didn't realize she'd been holding. The cover color was almost an exact match, but hers had the sparkly gold-bug, whereas the one Hollister was selling had an oval portrait of Poe himself. She opened Hollister's and flipped through it. Her book had only one story and the one on the table had close to ten.

"That one of your schoolbooks, Emily-Who-Just-Moved-Here? Looks fancy." Hollister's voice made her jump. She'd gotten lost in thought comparing the two books. Instinctively, she wanted to stuff *The Gold-Bug* into her backpack to hide it, but Hollister had already seen it.

"There's no way our schoolbooks would look half that nice," James replied to Hollister. If it made him nervous to think Hollister might catch on to Mr. Griswold's game, James wasn't showing it. "Our schoolbooks are so old, my science textbook says there are still nine planets. They're so old, I found my mother's name written in one from when she was a kid."

"Mm-hmm." Hollister nodded. "So old they're written on stone tablets? In hieroglyphics?"

"This is just a story by Edgar Allan Poe about a gold-bug," Emily said in her best casual, it's-no-big-deal voice. "I'm reading it for fun. I thought it might be the same copy you have here, but it's not."

Hollister whistled. "Fun indeed. Now, Poe had a twisted sense of fun, didn't he—people being buried alive, going crazy. You say it's just that one story?

Haven't come across one like that before. Mind if I take a look?"

"Sure," Emily said, her voice squeaking ever so slightly.

"This is very nice." Hollister turned the first few pages like they might tear if he flipped them too fast. Emily held her breath as he opened to the copyright page where the raven version of the Bayside Press symbol was. Seeing as he'd been in the middle of constructing a gigantic tribute to the original, she thought for sure he'd spot the similarity and make the Griswold connection, but Hollister didn't linger at all and kept turning pages. "You reading this? You like it?"

"I finished it last night," Emily said, relaxing a little. "It's not the easiest story to read, the way it's written and all. Like that first line: 'I contracted an intimacy with a Mr. William Legrand.' Why not say 'I met'?"

"Seems highfalutin nowadays, doesn't it." Hollister closed the book and handed it back. "It was written in a different time, that's for sure."

"Don't you contract diseases, not people?" James asked.

Emily giggled. "Maybe *Mr. William Legrand* is code for 'chicken pox.'"

"In that case, I met Mr. William Legrand when I was four."

"I had a shot so I'll never have to meet him," Emily said.

Hollister tsked. "Poor Mr. Legrand. People going

out of their way to avoid his acquaintance." Hollister offered Emily the collection of Poe stories from the Halloween table. "On the house. A 'welcome to San Francisco' gift for a budding Poe enthusiast."

"Oh . . . I couldn't," Emily said, even though it killed her to turn down a book.

Hollister pressed the book on top of *The Gold-Bug*. "I insist. The more Poe you read, the more familiar his language will be."

"Well, thank you." Emily flipped through the book. The collection included "The Gold-Bug" as well as several other short stories, like "The Tell-Tale Heart" and another one called "The Black Cat." There were poems in the collection, too, including one called "The Raven." This poem was accompanied by an illustration of a black bird almost exactly like the one used in place of the seagull in the Bayside Press symbol. She hadn't stopped to consider why Mr. Griswold had chosen a black bird to replace the seagull, but now she realized it must be a nod to this poem.

"Raven." Emily didn't intend to say that out loud, but she did.

"One of his most famous works," Hollister said, before shuffling back to his window display.

"Raven?" James lowered his voice to Emily. "Like the Book Scavenger user who messaged us with all the gold-bug info?"

"That can't be a coincidence," Emily whispered back.

James raised his eyebrows. "Someone else knows about the game."

"Not just knows about it," Emily said. She was remembering the odd way Raven had greeted them—asking if they needed anything in that really formal way that made James joke about her being a butler. And then the comment about not being able to reveal where the book was hidden, even though they'd already found it. "Raven was trying to help us."

Emily and James left Hollister's store with hasty good-byes and hurried back to James's computer (as quickly as you can hurry when a hill with an incline as steep as a roller coaster separates where you are and where you have to go). The sky was overcast, but Emily was pink-faced and wiping sweat off her temples by the time they reached their building.

As they settled in front of James's computer, Emily fanned herself with her notebook. She logged into her Book Scavenger account and did a user search for Raven.

"Yes! She's online," Emily said.

SURLY WOMBAT: Can I ask you about THE GOLD-BUG?

It didn't take long before Raven's reply popped onto the screen.

RAVEN: THE GOLD-BUG is a short story by Edgar Allan Poe, originally published in 1843. Poe won a short story contest and the prize was publication in a local paper. It was a popular story in its day and brought attention to cryptograms and secret writing.

Emily groaned. "Hello? We know. You told us that last time." To James she asked, "Do you think I should just be straight with her? Maybe then she won't be so weird."

James shrugged. "It's worth a try."

SURLY WOMBAT: I know about the game.

RAVEN: I can't help you with that.

SURLY WOMBAT: What do you mean?

RAVEN: I do not have the information you seek.

Emily slapped a hand on James's desktop. "I don't understand this! She was so eager to help the other day."

SURLY WOMBAT: I thought you wanted to help us with THE GOLD-BUG?

RAVEN: THE GOLD-BUG is a short story by Edgar Allan Poe, originally published in 1843. Poe won a short story contest and the prize was publication in a local paper. It was a popular story in its day and brought attention to cryptograms and secret writing.

Emily groaned, but James straightened in his seat.
"She's playing a game with us," he said.
"No kidding."
"No, seriously. There's a pattern to how she replies. See how every time you mention *The Gold-Bug*, she gives that exact same answer? Here, let me test this out." James took over the keyboard.

SURLY WOMBAT: Do you like soda?

RAVEN: I do not have the information you seek.

SURLY WOMBAT: Plaid pants look nice on you.

RAVEN: I can't help you with that.

SURLY WOMBAT: Who hid THE GOLD-BUG?

RAVEN: THE GOLD-BUG is a short story by Edgar Allan Poe, originally published in 1843. Poe won a short story contest and the prize was publication in a local paper. It was a popular story in its day and brought attention to cryptograms and secret writing.

Emily gasped. "You're right!"
James scrolled back through the conversation. "Look, when we ask a question she replies, 'I don't have the information you seek,' like maybe if she *did* she would answer the question. But if we say

something that's not a question, then she'll say, 'I can't help you with that.' And asking a question with *The Gold-Bug* in it always gets the same reply."

"Here, let me try something."

Emily took over the keyboard and typed, *Do you know what* fort, wild, home, rat, open, *and* belief *mean?*

RAVEN: Your query is incomplete.

And before Emily and James could think of another question to ask, the chat feed updated again.

RAVEN: That is all the assistance I can offer today.

"That's it?" James and Emily cried in unison.

"I guess there's a limit to how many questions she'll answer," James said.

"Well, she did tell us something at least. She didn't say our query was wrong, just incomplete."

"So maybe the words need to be in a different order?" James suggested.

"Or," Emily said, "maybe there are more words left to find."

CHAPTER

12

I T HAD BEEN two days since they'd seen those kids take the book, and Barry and Clyde were still hanging around the plaza across from the Ferry Building. They'd been stalking the area since Saturday, hoping the kids would come back, but no luck. Barry sat on the steps next to what had to be the ugliest fountain in all of San Francisco. It looked like a gigantic knocked-over game of Jenga sitting in a pool of water.

"They're not coming back," Clyde said. Over and over he flipped the card he'd found by the trash in the BART station, every so often palming it as if he were practicing a magic trick.

"Well, we don't have any other leads." Barry stabbed a stick into a crack in the concrete step.

"This card is our lead," Clyde said.

Barry snorted. As much as he couldn't wait to be done with this whack, he couldn't walk away. He needed the extra work—it's not like they handed out jobs on street corners—and his bookie scared him more than Clyde did.

"Fat lot of good that card does us. It's got nothing on it—no address, no name, no number. Just that picture of Earth and *Too Slow! This book has been found by: Surly Wombat.* What does that even mean?"

"I told you, I saw the girl put it there. After she took our book," Clyde said.

"It's not *our* book," Barry muttered.

"Whatever. That's just cement tactics."

"What?" Barry wanted to jab Clyde with his stick, but he wouldn't dare. The guy was just . . . Three days after shooting Garrison Griswold and he still hadn't shown any emotion. Didn't talk about it, didn't seem worried about it. Almost like he didn't even remember. The way you might be if you swatted a fly, and then a couple of days later someone asked about the fly and your brain had to run a few circles to even remember that insignificant bug.

"I said: That's. Just. Ce. Ment. Tac. Tics." Clyde drew out each syllable like molasses dripping off a spoon.

"Cement tactics? That fugly fountain is cement tactics. Bad cement tactics. What the heck is cement tactics?"

"What are you talking about?" Clyde looked at Barry like he was the one who'd lost his mind.

"What are *you* talking about? You lost me with cement tactics," Barry said.

"*It's our book, it's their book.* It's just words, you know?"

"Oh," Barry said. "You mean semantics, numbnut. Try reading more books instead of stealing them."

Clyde shrugged. "I prefer cement tactics. It's poetic."

Barry sighed and held out his palm. "Let me see the card."

Clyde handed it over, and Barry studied it for the gazillionth time.

"I'm telling you," Clyde butted into his thoughts, "let's look it up online."

"Look up what? There's nothing useful here. You want to look up *Surly Wombat*? Or this picture?" The picture was a drawing of Earth and a treasure map blended together.

Clyde shrugged. "Maybe."

"Fine, better than the nothing we've been doing. You got a phone with Internet?"

"You got a Benz?"

"Yeah, it's in the shop, wiseguy." Barry pushed himself up from the steps. "Follow me. I know someone."

Barry had a friend who worked as a bellhop at a hotel in the financial district. Luck was on their side, because that friend was working his shift and he let Barry and Clyde into the guests-only computer room.

"Good, it's empty," Clyde said as they woke up the computer.

Barry looked over his shoulder, grateful for the giant glass window that made the room visible to the lobby. He may tower over Clyde, but he still didn't want to be alone in a dark alley—or a computer room—with the guy.

They typed in *Surly Wombat* but only found a bunch of stuff about the animal.

Barry flicked the logo. "That must be for a business or something. But how do you tell what business if the picture doesn't say?"

The more Barry stared at it, the more the dotted lines on the treasure map/Earth blurred together. And then, quick as a lightbulb flicking on, Barry could see a letter hidden in the drawing. "These dotted lines outline letters! See?" He traced a finger showing a *B* on one side and an *S* on the other. It was like a hide-and-seek game with letters. He was proud of himself for spotting them. "It's still not much, but maybe if we enter *BS* and then all the words we can think of that have to do with this card . . ."

Barry typed in *BS*, *logo*, and *book*.

Clyde tapped the screen. "Make that *hidden book*."

"We didn't hide it. That was just luck it missed the trash." Good or bad luck, Barry still couldn't tell.

"But when that girl pulled the book out, she yelled to her friends, 'a hidden book.' I heard her. She thought it was hidden there on purpose. That's why she left that card. It was, like, a message for whoever she thought hid it in the first place."

Barry frowned at Clyde. "Why didn't you say any of this before now?"

Clyde shrugged. "Didn't seem important."

Barry changed *book* to *hidden book*, and also added the word *game* to his search list. He punched Enter and up popped a long list of hits. There was one about the game Liar's Dice, another about a game called Cheat, another about a video game, and the rest of the page of hits were about something called Book Scavenger. Barry clicked one and the Book Scavenger home page opened up. There, front and center of the screen, was the logo from the card.

CHAPTER 13

TUESDAY MORNING marked Emily's second first day of school this year. In Albuquerque, she'd started school on the official first day of school in August, and now she was starting school again in San Francisco, almost two months later than the rest of the kids.

At some point, Emily hoped she'd stop getting jitters, but today seemed worse than ever. She didn't want to disappoint James or do something that made him realize he didn't want to hang out with her anymore. She couldn't remember the last time she'd started school with a friendship already made. It was hard breaking into a new school. The other kids had history—they'd been in the same class the year before, or soccer league, or Sunday school, or Girl Scouts, or had grown up on the same street. Even if two kids didn't get along, they usually opted for each other over the strange new girl. Knowing they'd be moving again soon enough helped Emily not care what people thought of her, but she still couldn't help the first-day jitters.

When she opened her front door, James was waiting to walk with her. She'd wondered if his cowlick would be slicked down with gel for school, but Steve poked up in all his glory.

"Kids wear Converse here, right?" She didn't know why she'd blurted this question. She wasn't even the type to care about what she wore. And it wasn't like she had a variety of wardrobe options anyway if for some reason her jeans and hoodie were socially unacceptable.

James pressed an index finger to his lips as he looked her up and down. "Hold on," he said, and ran back upstairs.

If Emily felt jittery before, she was full-fledged Mountain Dew soda plus five packs of Skittles jittery now. A San Francisco middle school must have a very rigid idea of acceptable clothes if James had taken her question so seriously.

Emily heard a tinkling noise she couldn't put her finger on until James jumped back onto the porch and held out his reindeer antlers.

"I'm not wearing those!" Animal headgear couldn't be a school trend . . . could it? There was that group of girls in Colorado who wore knit hats with cat ears.

James shook the antlers with a shushing chime,

looking amused at her alarm, and Emily laughed, finally realizing he was teasing her.

"Take them," he insisted. "Keep them in your backpack in case you need a smile. Or something to barter with."

Emily's front door reopened and her mom waved the camera.

"Oh good! I caught you two before you left."

Emily stifled a groan. Her mom had already insisted on pictures with Matthew before their dad drove him to the high school. Not to mention the first-day-of-school pictures they'd taken in New Mexico. How many first-day-of-seventh-grade pictures did a person need?

"Mom—"

James grabbed the antlers back, plunked them on his head, and swung an arm around her shoulders. "Cheese!" he said. "Or what do reindeer say? Moo!"

"What?" Emily laughed. "I think it's something like this."

She grabbed the antlers and put them on her head and made a noise like a horse neighing. They leaned their heads together and tried to make themselves a two-headed reindeer with the headband straddling them both. Her mom captured all of this, laughing along with them, and with every click of the camera, Emily's nerves eased.

Booker Middle School was a monstrous brick

building that took up an entire block. It reminded her of the Newbury Public Library in Connecticut, one of her favorite libraries of all the places they'd lived. Both buildings were enormous and historic-looking and made of brick, but the Newbury library was surrounded by a hillside of dense trees on one side and a strip mall on the other, while Booker Middle School was surrounded by the high-strung wires of the city's electric buses and squatty apartment buildings.

The hallways were decorated for Halloween with orange-and-black crepe paper strung in sagging zig-zags across the ceiling. Students' spiderweb art clung to a concrete brick wall. As Emily moved through the crowded hallways during passing period, she felt largely unnoticed, except for when she accidentally bumped into someone. A perk of going to such a big school was that you didn't stand out as the new girl.

One of her tactics for distracting herself from new-school nerves was to try to spot other Book Scavenger users. This was particularly tricky at Booker because the hallways were so crowded and loud—slamming lockers, high-pitched laughter, voices shouting in different languages. Her attention bounced all over the place. Not that pinpointing another Book Scavenger user was an easy thing to deduce, even in the smallest and quietest of schools. You might occasionally see someone in a T-shirt or hat with the logo on it. More common was the Book Scavenger pin, which Emily herself wore on her hoodie. But it was easy to miss a detail that small. The few times she'd actually spotted other users, she didn't have the nerve to approach them and say anything. Instead, she would rearrange her hoodie so her pin was visible and then position herself somewhere that she might be noticed, thereby leaving it up to the other person to do the approaching. So far that tactic hadn't worked.

Here at Booker, she knew there was at least one other Book Scavenger player: Babbage was prowling around somewhere. Maybe that poacher had even already been in one of her classes. Poaching was perfectly legal in the Book Scavenger world, and some users claimed the competitiveness made it more fun, but Emily didn't like to do it. She thought it was more mean-spirited than competitive. If you knew somebody had their hopes up to find a certain book, why would you want to beat them to it and squash their hopes, just because you could?

Emily slid her books into her locker, lingering longer than she needed to while slams and stomps and shouts filled the hallway. *Fort, wild, rat, home.* Having a puzzle to work through always helped distract her from all the new swirling around. She closed her locker door and found James standing right behind it. Emily yelped.

"Geez, you surprised me!" But she smiled as she said it.

"They don't call them sneakers for nothing." James kicked up the toe of his shoe. "Ready for social studies?" It was the one class they had together all day. The bell rang, and the two fell in step.

"Any breakthroughs yet?" James asked.

They had talked about Mr. Griswold's game the entire walk to school, and during lunch they'd sat on the blacktop with their backs against the school building and *The Gold-Bug* open between them, poring over the pages to find more typos. The twins James normally sat with, Kevin and Devin, were there, too, but they were too distracted by their argument over the best way to defeat the bosses in a video game called *Rocket Cats* to pay them any attention.

Emily shook her head in response to James's question.

"Me neither," he said.

They turned the corner and stopped in front of Room 40, their social studies class, to wait with the other students until the teacher arrived.

"Can I see *The Gold-Bug* again?" James asked.

Emily handed it over and looked up to see a girl in the crowd scowling at her. The girl was tall enough to pass for a high schooler. Her short-cropped hair puffed away from her head like a mushroom cap. James studied the pages of *The Gold-Bug* for the millionth time, oblivious to the mushroom-cap girl and everything else. Emily tried to study the pages with him but couldn't shake that feeling of being watched. Sure enough, when she looked up again, the mushroom-cap girl's glare was so intense Emily actually looked behind herself, assuming there must be someone else, but there were only lockers.

Emily studied the floor, the ceiling, anything but the mushroom-cap girl. *Fort, wild, rat, home.* Her eyes landed on Vivian, a girl with stick-straight black hair so long it reached the tops of her khakis' pockets. She'd met Vivian in an earlier class, and Emily relaxed at seeing a familiar face besides James's. After their shared second period, Vivian had strode up to Emily, held out her hand, and said, "I'm Vivian Chu, seventh-grade class president. I make a point of knowing everyone in our class. Welcome to Booker Middle School. Please let me know if there is anything I can do for you as your class president."

Emily had shaken Vivian's rigid hand and said nothing else. Now, in front of Room 40, she flexed her fingers in a small wave hello, to which Vivian gave a tight-lipped smile in return. It struck Emily how different it was, attending a new school with James already her friend. On her previous first days, she had always kept her head in a book, and here she was waving to almost-strangers.

Now the mushroom-cap girl gnawed on her thumbnail and glared at the linoleum. Maybe she hadn't been intensely focused on Emily after all. Maybe that was just her normal expression.

A man strode toward the cluster of students, keys jangling in his hand. The crowd parted as he boomed, "Let's go, people. We've got dead men to discuss."

Their teacher, Mr. Quisling, planted himself at the front of the room, legs apart, arms crossed. Muscles bulged from beneath the short sleeves of his red T-shirt. His silvery-gray hair was cropped close to his skull, and icy-blue eyes watched each student enter and take a seat. He held up a hand like a traffic cop, stopping Emily.

"New face," he barked.

Emily didn't know what to say to that, so she just stood there.

"Emily Crane?"

"Yes," she mumbled.

"Grab a textbook from the bookshelf. I hope you've been learning about the Roman Empire; otherwise you will have a lot of catching up to do."

Emily pulled a textbook from the shelf Mr. Quisling had indicated and slid into the seat James had saved for her.

"So, Emily Crane," Mr. Quisling said. "Where are you from?"

A simple question, but it always threw her. She wasn't *from* anywhere. She never knew if she should say where she was born or the last place she lived. If she said something vague like "all over," a teacher like Mr. Quisling might interpret that as attitude. The rest of her teachers had just welcomed her to the school and left it at that.

"Um . . ."

There were snickers behind her. Emily looked

back to see the mushroom-cap girl with her mouth covered and taunting in her eyes. So much for thinking she'd imagined her negative attention earlier.

"I'm not grading you on your response, Ms. Crane," Mr. Quisling said.

"I moved here from New Mexico," Emily finally replied as the tardy bell rang.

Mr. Quisling clapped his hands twice to get everyone's attention.

"Excellent. A-plus for that. Just kidding, no grade." Mr. Quisling rubbed his hands together. "Let's get to work. Open your books to chapter eight."

Emily's pen was poised over her open binder, ready to take notes. She copied the words Mr. Quisling wrote on the whiteboard, but her mind wandered back to Mr. Griswold's game. *Fort wild home rat . . .*

"Psst."

The Gold-Bug perched on the edge of James's desk with an origami frog peeking from the pages. Making sure Mr. Quisling still faced the board, James held the book out to Emily.

She grabbed it and slid out the frog-shaped note. Placing the note in her lap, she unfolded each section as Mr. Quisling spoke so he wouldn't hear the rustling. The note was a garbled mixture of letters, but Emily recognized it immediately as their secret code.

When Mr. Quisling looked down to read aloud from his textbook, Emily eased the note from under the desk. At the same moment, something hit the ground with a loud *boom*.

Mr. Quisling's head snapped up. Emily tucked the note inside *The Gold-Bug*.

"Is there a problem?" Mr. Quisling said sharply. "Maddie?" Maddie, it turned out, was the name of the mushroom-cap girl.

"I'm sorry, Mr. Quisling," Maddie said. "I accidentally knocked my book off my desk."

Emily did her best to discreetly slide *The Gold-Bug* inside her binder as Mr. Quisling walked down her aisle. He picked up Maddie's textbook and handed it back. Emily's heart thundered so loud she was sure he'd hear it.

Instead of returning to the front of the room, Mr. Quisling hovered over Emily's desk. With his index finger he flipped open her binder and revealed *The Gold-Bug*.

"I don't recognize this," Mr. Quisling said. "You're not doing homework for another class on my time, are you, Ms. Crane?"

Emily jerked her head back and forth so emphatically her pencil flew out of her ponytail and clattered to the floor. Mr. Quisling picked up *The Gold-Bug*, flipped through it, and pulled out the unfolded note. She couldn't bring herself to peek at James. Mr. Quisling studied the paper a bit before saying, "Interesting form of note-taking you have. Is this how they did it in your previous school?"

He returned *The Gold-Bug* to her desktop with no additional attention. Emily would have felt relief about that except that he carried James's note with him as he strode back to the front of the class.

"So you're an Edgar Allan Poe fan and you take encrypted notes."

Someone returned her pencil to her desktop, but Emily was too mortified to move or say thanks. Mr. Quisling gestured to his lecture outline about the Roman Empire and said, "Then surely you know what Edgar Allan Poe and Julius Caesar have in common?"

She had no idea other than they were both dead and had been for a long time.

"Anyone?" Mr. Quisling asked the class.

A chair squeaked and someone coughed, but other than that the classroom was silent.

"Who knows what a cipher is?" Mr. Quisling asked. He sounded genuinely interested, not like he was merely torturing a student. He turned to the whiteboard and wrote *cipher*.

"A cipher," he underlined the word, "is when you substitute individual letters with other letters, numbers, or symbols."

"Like a code," someone said.

"A code is similar: It's a way to conceal a message. But a code can be more expansive, with word or phrase substitutions rather than individual letters."

Some of the students looked uncomfortable, like

they might be embarrassed for Emily; others were writing in their notebooks, possibly copying Mr. Quisling's board work.

"Will we be tested on this?" asked a boy slumped in his desk in the far row next to the wall.

Mr. Quisling blinked with lizard-like slowness. "You can consider anything we discuss in this class possible fodder for an exam, José."

And then, to Emily's great horror, Mr. Quisling began copying James's note onto the whiteboard.

CHAPTER 14

THIS IS WHAT Edgar Allan Poe and Julius Caesar had in common. They were both fans of the monoalphabetic substitution cipher."

Emily desperately hoped the bell would ring or someone would pull the fire alarm as she watched Mr. Quisling transcribe the note. She couldn't even bring herself to look at James.

"Julius Caesar developed one of the earliest substitution ciphers," Mr. Quisling said. "Today we call it the Caesar Shift. Edgar Allan Poe was not only a famous writer but also a cipher enthusiast. So enthusiastic, in fact, he organized a cipher challenge when he was the editor of a literary magazine. He claimed he could solve any cipher submitted."

Despite herself, Emily found this interesting. It made sense, really, since his story "The Gold-Bug" included ciphers. She resumed cringing in horror once Mr. Quisling finished copying James's note:

NTDHU VKU OUD BS IXPV.
B ETF VKBFO XI VKPUU.

Mr. Quisling tapped the whiteboard. "What we have here is called a ciphertext. When decoding a secret message like this, letter frequency analysis is a good place to start."

Starting on the far left of the whiteboard, Mr. Quisling wrote out the standard alphabet. He was almost jogging as he scribbled his stubby capital letters. He's enjoying this, Emily thought. He is, he's enjoying humiliating her! James intently studied the pencil he rolled back and forth under his fingertips.

"Ciphers play an interesting role in the history of our world. Battles have been won and lost because of them. Assassinations have been diverted because coded plots were intercepted and deciphered, or conversely, assassinations have been successful. The twists and turns history has taken have often relied on secret messages and whether those messages were able to remain secrets."

José raised his hand. "Are you sure we should be doing this? Breaking this code?"

Emily gave José a small smile of gratitude, but his interjection didn't deter Mr. Quisling.

"Your syllabus plainly states that passing notes or doing any work other than class work is done at your own risk." Mr. Quisling waved to the board behind him. "This is what you risk."

"If Ms. Crane were plotting an assassination, let's see how we'd fare in diverting the course of history."

Using the alphabet he'd written on the board, Mr. Quisling drew a hash mark under a letter for each time it appeared in James's message.

"The three most common letters in the English language are *e*, *t*, and *a*. By looking at our frequency chart we see that *u* is used five times in this message, *v* four times, and *k* and *b* three times. It's highly likely at least one of these letters represents *e*, *t*, or *a*. But which is which?"

This was the same tactic the character had used to solve the secret message in Poe's story.

"Let's look at our three-letter words: *vku*, *oud*, and *etf*." Mr. Quisling stood back and rubbed his chin. He circled the *vk* in *vku*.

"The *th* combination found in *the* is commonly found at the beginning of other words. In this message, you see *vk* is also used in *vkbfo* and *vkpuu*. This might suggest that *v* equals *t* and *k* equals *h*, making *vku* equal *the*. Let's go with that and see what happens."

Mr. Quisling filled in letters of the message like a game of Hangman. Students began calling out guesses for the words. Before Emily knew it, Mr.

Quisling and her social studies class had cracked James's message:

MAYBE THE KEY IS FORT.
I CAN THINK OF THREE.

"Assassination diverted!" Mr. Quisling cried.

Emily's face burned so furiously she thought her eyes might act like magnifying glasses in the sun and set her binder paper on fire. At least James hadn't mentioned Mr. Griswold or his game in his note.

A student called out, "It doesn't make sense!"

Another said, "Maybe it's supposed to read *fart*," and laughter filled the room. Mr. Quisling clapped his hands and shouted "Enough!" The laughter sputtered until a boy stage-whispered, "The three farts of Christmas past, present, and future."

James joined in the renewed titters, but the tips of his ears looked suddenly sunburned.

Mr. Quisling paced the aisles for so long the laughter faded into suppressed giggles, then uneasy silence and shifting in seats. Emily ran her finger around the diamond carved onto her desktop, avoiding eye contact and hoping no more humiliation was in store.

Mr. Quisling smacked the desk of a girl, who yelped in surprise.

"I propose a challenge!" Mr. Quisling proclaimed. "A cipher challenge, in the spirit of Edgar Allan Poe.

Here's how it will work: You may submit substitution ciphers to the class. One cipher per student per week. You can turn in your first ones tomorrow, which is Wednesday, if you wish. After this week, Monday will be the day to submit ciphers. The class will have the week to attempt to break the submitted ciphers. Any ciphers left standing by the end of the week will earn you a free homework pass to use on any assignment this semester. You may earn a maximum of three homework passes."

Chatter and excitement permeated the classroom.

"Don't lose your heads, people," Mr. Quisling bellowed over the din. "Be prepared to explain your cipher for the class if it goes unbroken, in order to prove it's validly constructed."

The bell rang, and above the scraping chairs and zipping backpacks, Mr. Quisling shouted, "Bring enough copies for the whole class."

As people filed out of the room, Mr. Quisling tapped papers into an even pile on his desk. Without looking up, he said, "Starting off on a bad foot, Emily Crane. Do better tomorrow."

Emily nodded obediently, even though Mr. Quisling wasn't looking at her.

"You aren't mad at me, are you?" she asked James in the hallway.

"Mad at *you*?" James said. "You should be mad at me. It was stupid to pass the note in the first place. At least this cipher challenge sounds cool."

"Don't get too excited." Maddie stepped away from the lockers like she'd been waiting for them. "Your cute little code was broken like that." She snapped her fingers. "I doubt you'll win any homework passes."

"And you will?" James asked.

Maddie smirked. "How about a side bet? Whoever earns the most homework passes or gets to three first wins."

James rolled his eyes. "It's always about winning with you, isn't it? It's only worth doing if there's a ribbon in it."

For the briefest moment Maddie winced, but with a shake of her motionless hair, she said, "Sounds like someone who's afraid of losing."

"*I'm* not afraid of losing. Are *you* afraid of losing, Steve?" James tilted his head to the side as if he were listening to his cowlick's reply.

"What's in it for the winner?" Emily interjected.

Maddie's calculating smile took on a slightly evil cast. "Maybe it's not about what we win, but what the other has to lose."

"What does *that* mean?" Emily asked.

Maddie moved two fingers like alligator jaws across James's hair. "If you lose, you have to shave off that stupid tuft of hair you treat like an imaginary friend. And just that—I want a bald spot in its place."

Emily sucked in a breath. *Not Steve!* she thought. She'd grown attached to the spiky guy. But James didn't look worried.

"And if you lose?" he asked. "Will you shave your head?"

It was clear from Maddie's expression she hadn't considered the flip side of this wager.

"You can dye it," Emily blurted out. "Red, with white polka dots. Like a toadstool."

James bit his lip to keep from laughing.

"Like I'm doing that," Maddie said.

"It's better than having to shave part of your head," James said.

"Way better," Emily added. "You can wash the color out the same day. James will have to wait weeks for his to grow back."

James held up his hands. "Hey, I understand if you're worried you can't beat me."

"Fine." Maddie held out her hand to shake. "Start planning a farewell party for Stan."

"It's Steve," James called to Maddie's retreating back. "And the only thing he'll say farewell to is your brown hair when you have to dye it red!"

On their way back to their building after school, Emily and James walked through the stretch of shops and restaurants that surrounded Hollister's bookstore. A coffee shop, a fancy restaurant, an old movie theater converted into a fitness center, a dry cleaners, another coffee shop, a clothing boutique, a sushi restaurant, and so on. All these businesses were on the ground level of buildings with floors of apartments above. There was more activity squished into those few blocks than the entire New Mexico town Emily had left behind.

"What's Maddie's problem, anyway?" Emily asked. She and James broke apart for three women with yoga mats slung on their shoulders and then came back together.

James shrugged. "She thinks she's better than everybody. Good old Mop-Top Maddie Fernandez. Not that I'm one to talk about distinctive hairstyles, of course."

"I thought her hair looked more like a mushroom cap than a mop," Emily said.

James snorted. "A mushroom! Is that why you came up with the toadstool look if she loses? Why didn't I see that before?" He looked at Emily slyly. "She's an evil mushroom queen."

"Her Royal Fungus?" Emily suggested, and they cracked up. Three adults waiting at a bus stop eyed them suspiciously. James clamped a hand over his mouth, and Emily straightened her posture, but their attempts to look serious just made them break down in laughter even more.

On Wednesday, almost the entire social studies class submitted ciphers for Mr. Quisling's challenge. On Thursday, every last cipher had been cracked, including James's, Maddie's, and Emily's.

"What did I get myself into?" James moaned as they walked after school Thursday afternoon. "I can't believe *all* the ciphers were broken. This is going to be way harder than I thought. I don't want to shave off Steve."

"Don't worry! Her Royal Fungus is struggling with the challenge, too. You're not losing to her yet."

"Emphasis on *yet*," James said.

Emily bumped her backpack against his. "You're a puzzle master! You've got this. And I'll help you. Not that I'll be much help, seeing as I've made zero progress with Mr. Griswold's secret message."

"Have you tried talking to Raven again?"

"Yeah. She wouldn't reply until yesterday, and then all I got was 'I don't have the information you seek.' I wish I could stop by Bayside Press and snoop for information about the game."

James stopped walking. He stared absentmindedly at a window washer on a platform dangling outside an apartment building. "Well. Why can't we?"

Emily looked from the window washer to James, confused.

"Visit Bayside Press," James said. "It can't hurt to try, right?"

CHAPTER 15

AFTER DROPPING their school stuff off at their apartments, grabbing snacks, and getting permission to go downtown, Emily and James found themselves riding the bus to the financial district. They walked from the bus stop to the Bayside Press building. The rattle of streetcars, honking horns, and the bustle of people made this part of San Francisco much noisier than where Emily and James lived. When they turned into the narrow courtyard outside the main entrance of Bayside Press, all the city noise seemed to hush. Emily held up a hand to stop James from walking farther.

"This is, like, sacred Book Scavenger territory," Emily said. "Let me absorb this for a minute." She took in the gleaming tower of an office building, the blue sky reflected off its sides. The surrounding buildings were dull and serious in comparison. "Okay, I'm good," she said, and they pulled open the glass doors to enter Bayside Press.

The ground-level lobby was an open space with gray walls, stone floors, and a uniformed security guard standing behind a desk.

"Hi," Emily said when they approached the security guard. "We'd like to speak with someone at Bayside Press."

"All right," the man said. "Who are you here to see?"

"Um . . ." Emily and James looked at each other.

"We're here to see Joe?" James said hopefully.

The man looked over his glasses at them. "Joe," he said.

James nodded confidently. Emily wasn't sure about "Joe," but she marveled at how quickly James committed to his story.

The man flipped open a binder and scanned a list of names. "Joe Beatson, Joe Field, Joe Fu, Joe Kothari, Joe Mason, Joe Shah, Joe Vigil, Joe Vince, Joe Young . . . Any of those your Joe?"

James swallowed. "The last one? Joe Young?"

The man closed his binder. "I made him up. As I suspect you made up your *Joe*. Sorry, kids, but this is a business. We can't let just anyone go gallivanting through our hallways."

Emily gripped her backpack straps. They'd come all this way and were so close to seeing the inside of

Bayside Press, she didn't want to turn around and leave. Even if they didn't find an answer to Mr. Griswold's *Gold-Bug* puzzle, now that she was here, she craved just a peek behind the scenes where Book Scavenger was created.

She slid her backpack off her shoulders, unzipped it, and pulled out *The Gold-Bug*. "What if I told you we've found Mr. Griswold's next game? Could we talk to someone then?"

James stared at her, eyes wide. They hadn't talked about sharing their discovery of the book with anyone. It might have been her imagination, but Steve seemed a little extra splayed himself.

The security guard barely looked at the book. "I don't doubt you found the next game," he said in a voice that suggested he actually *did* doubt it, quite a bit in fact. "But I still can't let you upstairs without an appointment."

"Excuse me," someone said from behind Emily and James. They turned to see a man about Emily's parents' age wearing a burgundy-and-blue-argyle sweater-vest. "I couldn't help overhearing."

"Hey, Jack," the security guard greeted him. "I told them they need an appointment. They say they've found Griswold's next game, but you know. We've heard that one before."

They'd heard that before? It hadn't occurred to Emily that there might be other *Gold-Bugs* out there waiting to be found.

"I've got this," Jack said to the guard. To Emily and James he said, "So, I take it you're fans of Mr. Griswold?"

"And Book Scavenger," Emily said.

"She's really good at it," James chimed in. "She's almost reached Auguste Dupin level."

Jack whistled low and nodded. "Dedicated," he said.

Emily looked down but smiled. She was still fourteen points away from Auguste Dupin, so she wouldn't say she'd *almost* reached it. Still, the compliment and praise were flattering.

"And what's this?" Jack pointed to the *Gold-Bug* book in Emily's hand.

Even though he was a grown-up, Jack had a round, boyish face that made him look kind and trustworthy. But she didn't know who he was, other than someone who worked at Bayside Press. What if the book was some sort of valuable Bayside Press item and he took it away? Maybe it hadn't been such a good idea to pull *The Gold-Bug* out of her bag.

"It's . . . it's a book we found while playing Book Scavenger."

"And you thought it might have something to do with Griswold's next game?" Jack didn't say this in a mocking or condescending tone. Just more like that was a logical thing for them to assume. "Let me show you guys something. Come on."

He led them to the elevator. As they stepped inside, he said, "I didn't actually introduce myself, did I? I'm Jack. I'm Mr. Griswold's assistant."

"For real? You actually work with Mr. Griswold?" James asked.

"Like, every day?" Emily added. "How's he doing?"

"Ah." Jack looked down for a minute. "Not very well, I'm afraid." He looked up again, his eyes bright. "But all the well wishes and positive thoughts you can muster for him will help."

Not very well, I'm afraid rang in Emily's ears. She thought of the forum messages she'd read last weekend, when Mr. Griswold was first mugged, and that Book Scavenger user who had said they should enjoy Book Scavenger while they could. She hugged *The Gold-Bug* to her chest.

An instrumental version of "Monster Mash" filled the elevator for an awkward moment until they reached the seventh floor. The doors opened to reveal a lobby drenched in Bayside Press colors.

"Whoa," Emily breathed out. "This is cooler than I'd imagined it would be."

She turned slowly, taking in the silver-blue carpet butted up against burgundy-and-silver-blue-striped walls. A gigantic metal Bayside Press emblem hung behind the stark wall of a receptionist's desk.

Jack raised a hand to the receptionist and waved Emily and James through a doorway and down a hall.

"I'm afraid this tour may not be as exciting as you might hope, if you're fans of Mr. Griswold," Jack said as they walked. They passed doorway after doorway revealing grown-ups hunched in front of computers or talking on the phone, messy stacks of paper piled around them. "With his Willy Wonka reputation, a lot of people might imagine our offices to be like an amusement park. But no chocolate river or Oompa Loompas here. There are signs of his whimsy, of course."

Jack gestured to the hallway lined with painted portraits of famous San Francisco writers wearing somber expressions and silly costumes. Daniel Handler in a bunny costume, Amy Tan as a farmer, and Allen Ginsberg as a clown.

Jack stopped in front of a glass-walled conference room with a table piled high with a collection of stuffed animals, flowers, balloons, and books—not unlike what Emily, James, and her brother had come across outside the BART station last Saturday.

"What's all that?" Emily asked.

"Well, in the giant pile are the things people left outside our building for Mr. Griswold. We'll be donating them to the children's floor of the hospital where he's located. But that second pile is what I wanted to show you."

They stepped into the room and walked up to a smaller pile. Mostly it looked like a collection of notes or letters, some folded like the one she and James got caught passing in Mr. Quisling's class. Some of the pages were typed, some torn out of a notebook. There were also odds and ends of books, and then unusual things, like tangrams glued onto poster board and a laminated map of San Francisco that had sticky notes attached to it with letters and numbers scrawled on them.

"These are all the 'games' other people have found and sent to us. We've been inundated with them, as you can see."

"Are these"—James held up a bag with eight bouncy balls inside, each with a letter written on it—"really Mr. Griswold's games?" James manipulated the balls in the bag so they spelled out the word *anteater.*

"I doubt it," Jack said. "I can't say definitively, of course. Only Mr. Griswold could and he's—well, he can't do that right now. But I do know a couple of absolutes about Mr. Griswold. One: His games are rarely simple. That World's Largest Bingo Game he staged at the Giants' stadium? A logistical nightmare to pull off. Night. Mare." Jack tugged at the wavy hair that flopped on his forehead, like even the memory was stressful. "And two: he is *highly* secretive about his games. He'll keep his plans to himself until he can't go any further on his own. And even then, he often enlists help without people realizing what they're helping with. As for this rumored latest game, nobody knew what he was planning. I work with him closer than anyone, and I don't have the slightest clue."

They studied all the papers and odds and ends. James picked up a worn paperback that had been frontside down.

"'*The Maltese Falcon* by Dashiell Hammett,'" he read aloud.

"Oh, my parents gave me that!" Emily said.

Jack nodded. "One of San Francisco's most notable writers."

"Why are people sending these things?" Emily asked.

Jack took a moment before he replied. "Books and games are how people feel close to Mr. Griswold. That's what connects them to him. They want his game to exist, and so they find it in the unlikeliest of places. All of these"—Jack waved a hand over the odds and ends—"are examples of what Mr. Griswold has instilled in people: the ability to see something in nothing, to find a puzzle in what someone else would call trash." He held up a matchbook.

"Of course, some of these are from people who maybe have an unhealthy fascination with Mr. Griswold, or who are trying to trick us into awarding them a prize. But others are from people who genuinely believe they've found something. Like that *Maltese Falcon.*" Jack pointed to the book James had placed back on the table. "The person who sent us that didn't want anything in return. They found it hidden through Book Scavenger and were convinced it was part of Griswold's new game. They just thought we should know about it. They couldn't bear the thought of an unfulfilled promise, a game that never gets launched."

Still holding *The Gold-Bug*, Emily studied the pile and considered which category of fan she fell into until she realized she was different. She really *had* found Mr. Griswold's game. She wasn't just hoping it to be true. And similar to that person Jack had described, she also couldn't imagine ignoring *The Gold-Bug* puzzle now that she'd found it. It had to be solved.

"So you don't believe the person who turned in *The Maltese Falcon*? You don't think it's part of the game?" Emily asked.

Jack smiled sadly. "No. But it doesn't matter even if I did. Whatever Mr. Griswold was planning just isn't a priority for us at this point, I'm sad to say. Things were hectic before everything happened, and now . . ."

These game submissions piled on the table were a physical representation to Emily of how many people would wish to be in her shoes. She was glad Jack didn't believe her about *The Gold-Bug*.

"You know, it's been a nice break talking with you two." Jack looked through the glass walls of the conference room. "I'm glad I happened through the lobby when I did. You two are the epitome of the types of readers Mr. Griswold was most hopeful about reaching—young, enthusiastic, dedicated. In fact . . .

"Oh, what the hey," he said as if he'd settled an internal debate. "I've got something else to show you. If Mr. Griswold were here, he'd show you this himself."

CHAPTER 16

EMILY AND JAMES scurried out of the conference room after Jack. The hallway opened to a large space filled with cubicles, the hum of computers, the rustle of papers, and a few low voices. A woman sat at a long table with two stacks of paper in front of her. Emily recognized what she was doing from watching her dad work. She was proofreading a book. One stack of papers was a copyedited manuscript—basically a printout from a computer file that had been marked up in colored pencil with a bunch of edit marks. Long, rectangular sheets made up the other stack. Her dad called them *proofs*. They showed the book as it would look when it was published, with the pages printed side by side on each rectangular sheet. The proof-reader ran her finger from edit mark to edit mark across the manuscript pages and then checked the other stack to make sure all the edits had been made in the almost-a-book version. Emily had seen her dad do this sort of work dozens of times, but now, as she was surrounded by everything Griswold, it sparked an idea. The collection of Poe stories Hollister had given her included "The Gold-Bug." So why not compare that "Gold-Bug" against Griswold's? Maybe if she checked word by word she would uncover more typos, or something else that would help her solve the puzzle once and for all.

The idea put a little hop-skip in her step, and James looked over, a questioning smile on his face. "Do you know what he's going to show us?" he whispered.

"No. I'm just glad we came here, that's all."

After leading them through a maze of cubicles, Jack slowed in front of one and said, "That's my space." There were dog photos tacked behind his computer, and some of the same editing books Emily recognized from her dad's shelves sat next to a bobblehead collection. But it was his name on the placard that really caught Emily's attention.

"You're Jack *Kerouac*? You're my dad's favorite author! We named our minivan Sal after one of your characters."

She wouldn't have guessed Jack Kerouac would be this young, and from her dad's descriptions she hadn't pictured him as someone who wore argyle.

Jack blushed. "Ah, well . . ."

She needed to have Jack sign something. "Do you have a pen?" In her excitement, she'd forgotten she was wearing her backpack. She unzipped it and dropped *The Gold-Bug* inside so her hand was free to dig for a pen.

"I'm not *the* Jack Kerouac," Jack explained. "Not the one who wrote *On the Road*. He passed away decades ago. My mom was a fan of the Beat poets, and she made my name legally Jack Kerouac in homage to my father, who was involved in the movement himself. Not that he knew I existed—my father, I mean. Although the original Jack Kerouac wouldn't have known I existed, either, of course."

Jack fiddled with his collar.

"Your mom gave you your own first *and* last name?" James asked. "You can do that?"

"It was the sixties," Jack said, as if that explained it. "It's served me well, though. Mr. Griswold got a kick out of it. I think part of the reason he hired me was so he could tell people Jack Kerouac worked for him. Come on, what I want to show you is right behind us."

They turned to a closed set of double doors. Jack jiggled a key in a lock, then opened them to reveal an enormous room decorated in burgundy and silver-blue, just like the lobby. Mr. Griswold's office. Emily knew it at first glance. Windows spanned the far side of the room, showing a view that encompassed the Ferry Building and the bay beyond. Bookcases lined the walls and were filled with books, of course, but also a variety of games and puzzles and toys: a miniature

Ferris wheel, a chessboard with the pieces placed mid-game, a large wooden elephant assembled with carved wooden pieces. Something whirred and ticktocked at an uneven pace, and Emily finally zeroed in on a glass case with a structure inside designed to keep marbles perpetually moving up in buckets, down slides, and around sprockets. Emily could envision Mr. Griswold roaming this room, flipping through his books and playing with his toys.

Something moved in her peripheral view, and Emily turned to see an actual man standing there, scanning the titles on the bookcase alongside the entrance. For a fleeting, hopeful second—before she got a good look at him—Emily thought it was Mr. Griswold himself. But then Jack said sharply, "What are you doing in here?"

The man held his battered briefcase in front of himself, almost protectively. His sweaty dome was crisscrossed with long strands of ginger hair, and his suit was rumpled. The man practically leaped forward and extended a hand.

"Leon Remora. So sorry if I startled you. I work with Mr. Griswold—at his home, not here at Bayside Press. But I have his keys, you see?"

Mr. Remora held up a ring of keys and jangled them. "I'm a rare-book collector. I work for Mr. Griswold—I said that already, didn't I? Well, I'm trying to locate one of his missing books, and when he and I last spoke before his, ah"—Mr. Remora twirled his fingers in the air, searching for words—"his *you know*. Before what happened happened . . ." The man pulled a handkerchief from his pocket and mopped his face with it. "Mr. Griswold told me he'd left it in his office. This book I'm looking for. And since I have access to his keys—with his permission, of course—I came here to retrieve it."

Jack's arms were crossed now, and he studied Mr. Remora the way you might an abstract painting. "And you locked the door behind you because . . . ?"

"Did I do that? I don't recall doing that. Are you sure they don't automatically lock?"

"No, they don't."

"Well, I must have locked it out of habit. Absentminded and all that, you know?" Mr. Remora tapped his skull with his index finger.

"Did you find the book you were looking for?" Jack asked.

"No, but if I could just look a bit longer—"

"I'm sorry, but no," Jack said. "We aren't allowing anyone in here."

Mr. Remora's puppy-dog pleading eyes darkened. "Aren't children *anyone*?" he said.

"That's enough, Mr. Remora," Jack clapped his hands. "You've had your chance to look over these books. If you need more time, you'll need to make an appointment, and perhaps someone can assist you."

"But I'm his book collector! I should have full access to the books in his office!"

"Mr. Remora, you might manage his personal collection, but you have no business here. Now, please, don't make me call security."

Jack stepped back, prompting Emily and James to move with him. Mr. Remora strode past, dabbing his handkerchief around his neck and not making any eye contact whatsoever.

Once Jack had watched the man walk out of view, he turned back to Emily and James.

"Sorry about that, guys. He put a damper on my fun surprise now, didn't he?" Jack flourished his arm and said, "I give you Mr. Griswold's sanctuary."

A sculpture of a man's head sat in front of the expansive windows, and thanks to the small illustration on the cover of the short story collection Hollister had given Emily, she recognized it immediately.

"Is that Edgar Allan Poe?" she asked.

"Impressive!" Jack said. "It is indeed. Mr. Griswold has a special affinity for his work."

"You could say that again," James said.

Jack looked quizzically at James, but Emily spoke up. "He's a fan of his, then?"

"Big-time," Jack said.

Well, that solved one mystery, at least, Emily thought. Emily and

James had puzzled over why Griswold chose Poe for his game.

"Why is Poe wearing a necklace?" James asked. The statue wore a golden pendant in the shape of a rabbit. The rabbit had elaborate scrollwork making up its middle, and bells hung off its feet.

"One of Mr. Griswold's most prized possessions," Jack said. "You've heard of the hunt for the golden hare?"

Emily and James gave him blank looks.

"Of course you haven't. That was a silly question. Your parents were probably as young as you then."

"What was it?" James asked. "Were people searching for a wig spun out of gold?"

Jack laughed. "Not *hair*." He threaded his fingers through his bangs and tugged. He pointed to the necklace. "A hare, a rabbit. This was in the seventies. An eccentric artist and a publisher worked together to create a book called *Masquerade*. It was a picture book with clues, hidden in the illustrations. If you solved the clues, they led you to a buried treasure—the necklace that you're looking at, to be precise. Mr. Griswold wasn't the one to find it originally. He bought it at auction several years ago."

Clues hidden in a book that led to buried treasure? That was similar to "The Gold-Bug" story and what they had guessed the game would be. This had to be what Mr. Griswold had planned. Emily gently stroked the golden hare necklace, trying to mask her excitement as best as she could, but inside she was jumping up and down.

"The treasure hunt became something of a phenomenon," Jack continued, "but it bombed when the clues proved to be too difficult. It took three years, and in the end the person who found the treasure cheated. But it spawned a whole genre called armchair treasure hunts.

"Mr. Griswold loved this bit of publishing lore. To him that rabbit represents how one idea—whether it's a book or a game or something else—can capture the fascination of so many people at once, to the point where a community is built up around it where nothing existed before."

"Like Book Scavenger," Emily said.

Jack paused, head cocked to the side, and thoughtfully nodded as he considered this. "Yes. Exactly. Mr. Griswold would have been thrilled to hear you say that."

Emily smiled shyly at the golden hare. It thrilled her to know that.

CHAPTER 17

EMILY AND JAMES spent their Friday lunchtime in the school library. James wanted to research ciphers for Mr. Quisling's challenge in order to come up with something super hard for others to break. The rest of their sixth-period social studies class must have had the same idea, because nearly every table of the library was full. After learning about the challenge, the school librarian assembled a cart of books related to ciphers and codes and made a temporary "no check-out" rule for them, to ensure they stayed available for everyone's use.

Emily had said she'd help James research ciphers, but first she wanted to finish comparing the two editions of *The Gold-Bug*. She'd started last night after they got back from Bayside Press, and now it was almost the end of lunch period and she still wasn't done. Comparing texts word by word turned out to be quite the consuming task.

"I can't believe you keep finding them," James said, looking up from *Mysterious Messages*.

"That makes seven total during this lunch period alone," Emily said.

On her right was Garrison Griswold's *Gold-Bug*, and on her left was the same story printed in the Poe collection from Hollister. Emily tapped her pencil back and forth from a word in one *Gold-Bug* to the same word in the other. She found another typo in Griswold's: *exsessively*—a misspelling she had missed all the previous times she'd pored over this story. She crossed out the first *s* and wrote *c* above the word.

"I'm almost at the end of the story, so I better have them all. This is tedious." She compared the last few paragraphs and didn't find any additional typos. "Now what?" Emily muttered, more to herself than anything else.

"Have you tried writing all the letters on a separate page, in the order they show up in the book?" James asked. "It might be easier to make out the words if we're looking at just the found letters together on one page."

That was a good idea. Emily started copying the letters onto her notebook. James stopped her after the fifth letter to say, "Look, we found *fort* before, but an *h* comes next. Maybe the word isn't *fort* but *forth*? As in 'go forth, my son, and find my hidden message'?"

When Emily finished, the string of letters read:

forthemostwildyetmosthomelynarrativewhichI-
amabouttopenIneitherexpectnorsolicitbelief

James took a stab at reading it aloud, "'Forth em'—no . . . *'For* the most wildy—wild yet home . . . homely narrative which I am about to open in either expect nor solicit belief . . .'"

"That doesn't make sense," he said.

"You doubled an *o*," Emily said. "See? It's not *to open*; it's *topen. To pen.*"

They tried the sentence again, reading together out loud: "'For the most wild yet most homely narrative which I am about to pen, I neither expect nor solicit belief.'"

"That's the craziest thing I've ever seen," James said, flipping through the pages of *The Gold-Bug*. "Or I should say, 'the most wild and homely' thing I've ever seen!"

"It sounds like there should be more, doesn't it?" Emily asked. "It's like he's saying, 'Wait until you hear this wild and crazy story . . .' but then there's nothing else."

"And the wording is funny," James said. "Old-fashioned. I mean, who says they're going 'to pen' something?"

"Maybe that's the way Mr. Griswold talks?" She threw it out as an idea, but she'd watched videos of him online before and she didn't remember him sounding like this.

James shook his head. "No. He gave a welcome speech at that book carnival. He talks like a regular grown-up. Maybe a little happier and more dramatic, but he didn't sound like he time-traveled from a hundred years ago or anything."

"How is a hidden sentence a game?" Emily muttered out loud.

"It's too bad there isn't anyone we could ask for help," James said.

"That's it!" Emily pointed to James.

He looked around himself to see what she was pointing at. "Me?" his voice squeaked.

"Help," Emily said. "Someone who's willing to help—*Raven*."

"You're right!"

They ran to the computer bank at the back of the library. James dropped into a chair and shook the mouse to wake up the computer. They pulled up the Book Scavenger site, Emily logged in, and fortunately for them, Raven was online.

"Here." She slid her notebook next to the keyboard. "Type the sentence and see what Raven says."

Emily read the sentence aloud as James typed.

RAVEN: I can't help you with that.

"Nuts," James muttered. "I forgot it has to be a question."

SURLY WOMBAT: Is "For the most wild yet most homely narrative which I am about to pen, I neither expect nor solicit belief" a clue for Mr. Griswold's game?

RAVEN: Congratulations! You have found the first clue in Garrison Griswold's literary scavenger hunt launched on November 10. If you made it this far, you have found one of the fifty copies of THE GOLD-BUG hidden across the city. You have also located my game assistant, Raven. Raven is willing to offer you a small measure of help on your journey, provided you ask the right questions.

Emily blinked at the screen. She had fantasized about this—moving to San Francisco and participating in one of Mr. Griswold's games. She'd done it. She'd found his next game. She reread the message again.

"There are supposed to be fifty hidden copies of *The Gold-Bug*," James said. "How many do you think he hid before this one?"

"It's only the middle of October. He wasn't planning on the game officially starting for another three weeks. Maybe there aren't others out there yet." At least Emily hoped that was the case. She liked thinking of *The Gold-Bug* as her own personal connection to Garrison Griswold.

"We only have five minutes left until the bell rings, and we still don't know what to do with the hidden sentence. Quick"—Emily nudged James—"ask Raven about that."

SURLY WOMBAT: What do we do with the first clue?

RAVEN: One good story deserves another.

"'One good story deserves another'—what does that even mean?" James asked.

Before Emily could answer, a message from a guest user popped on her screen.

GUEST: I think you found my book.

Emily scrunched her nose. "Uh, hello? Who *are* you?"

"Why would you hide a book for Book Scavenger if you're not a registered player?" James added.

SURLY WOMBAT: What book?

GUEST: You said you found a Poe book in the BART station. That's my book. I need it back.

Emily and James looked at each other. The Poe

book belonged to somebody? That couldn't be. It had the Bayside Press symbol with the raven, and they'd just uncovered the secret message. Raven had even confirmed it was part of the game. Emily was a hundred percent sure the book was Mr. Griswold's. Which meant that either this mysterious person was Mr. Griswold, somehow managing to log in from the hospital even though yesterday Jack had said he was in very poor condition, or this guest user was mistaken. Or—a possibility that made her anxious to even consider—someone knew about the game and was trying to get the book for that reason.

SURLY WOMBAT: I find a lot of books. Tell me about yours.

GUEST: It's by Poe.

SURLY WOMBAT: Title?

The cursor flashed over and over until finally another message popped up.

GUEST: THE GOLD-BUG.

Emily's stomach tightened.

James nudged her. "Hollister said it was unusual to see a book with only one of Poe's stories. Maybe there's another collection by that name. Maybe this is a coincidence," he said.

SURLY WOMBAT: How many stories?

The cursor blinked endlessly. Emily held her breath.

GUEST: Three.

Emily exhaled.

SURLY WOMBAT: Sorry. I don't think I have your book.

CHAPTER 18

BARRY SLAMMED a fist onto the computer station, making the librarian at the information desk look over.

"Sorry," Barry muttered, and ducked his head.

"You shouldn't have guessed three," Clyde said. He sat back in the chair next to him, swiveling the seat from side to side.

"You *told* me three," Barry said through gritted teeth.

Clyde shrugged. "What do I know?"

After they'd found the Book Scavenger website on Monday, they'd switched gears from staking out the area around the BART station to spending the rest of the week staking out this website. Or at least staking it out as much as they could manage, seeing that Barry didn't have a computer at home and worked at a liquor store in the evenings, and Clyde . . . Barry had no idea what Clyde did when they weren't around each other.

In any case, it had taken them five whole days of checking in on a computer either at the hotel where his friend worked or here at the main city library when his friend wasn't working.

The green light next to Surly Wombat's name switched to gray and read "unavailable" instead of "online."

"Of course," Barry said. "We scared her off."

Barry dropped his head into his hands. Man, was he screwed. It was bad enough he'd thrown that book away in the first place. But Barry had neglected to tell his boss about the kids. He'd led him to believe they had a better handle on the book situation than they actually did. Although their boss had already threatened to take matters into his own hands if they didn't hurry up, so maybe Barry hadn't done such a good job of convincing him he had a handle on things.

Barry clicked on the name "Surly Wombat," and the page jumped to the girl's profile. At least he assumed this was that girl—she was the one Clyde had seen leaving the card in the first place. This profile gave very little personal information and no photo. Barry forced his eyes to scan the whole page this time instead of glazing over a couple of lines in. At the bottom of the page there was one important detail Barry had missed before.

He leaned close to the screen and blinked his eyes to make sure he was seeing straight.

"There we go." He stabbed the words. "'School: Booker Middle.' We can go there."

"Field trip," Clyde said.

CHAPTER 19

EVEN THOUGH the guest user hadn't known the right details about her book, Emily still felt uneasy.

"You okay?" James asked.

"Yeah, just . . ." The person had specifically said they were looking for a book with three stories, and Mr. Griswold's had only one. Still, it rattled her to have someone else insist *The Gold-Bug* was his or hers.

"That was just weird," she said.

James nodded his agreement. "But we *did* find out the first clue."

"We did!" Emily said brightly. "'One good story deserves another,'" she repeated. "What could that mean?"

The bell rang. James walked his cipher book back to the library cart, reading it until the very last second. Emily had left her binder, *The Gold-Bug*, and the Poe short story collection on the table when they went to chat with Raven, so now she closed those. She stacked them with the Poe collection of stories on top.

Story. One good story—*The Gold-Bug*—deserves another . . . *story*?

Emily reopened the collection of stories and flipped through it.

"Ready?" James asked, hoisting his backpack onto his shoulders.

Emily continued to flip pages, stopping every third page or so. About halfway through the book Emily turned to a short story called "The Black Cat."

"James!" she said and pressed the book to the tabletop. James leaned forward and read out loud: "'For the most wild yet most homely narrative—'" He looked at Emily, his mouth hanging open.

"'One good story deserves another,'" Emily said with an incredulous laugh. "The clue is the first line of another Poe story."

Emily walked on air throughout the weekend. Even though she didn't yet know what to do with the next clue, the fact that she'd come this far was satisfying enough. For now.

James was in high spirits after school on Monday as well. The first week of Mr. Quisling's challenge was a wash, since everyone's submitted ciphers had been broken. Already about half the class seemed to have lost enthusiasm for the challenge once they realized how tricky it would be to come up with something unbreakable. Emily didn't even submit one herself. She had been too wrapped up in homework, reading "The Black Cat" in hopes of figuring out what she was supposed to do next in Mr. Griswold's game, and her family's adventures. But James and Maddie were both as committed to their bet as they had been the week before. They each submitted ciphers, and James felt great about his chances this week.

"Her Royal Fungus is going down!" James crowed as they trudged up the sidewalk after school. He held Maddie's cipher sheet in front of him as they walked:

"I'll be able to crack this in no time," James said.

A canopy of trees provided momentary relief from the October sun blasting on high. The fog had burned off from the morning, and Emily's sweatshirt looped uselessly around her waist. If she were back in Albuquerque or Denver, there would be a crisp bite of fall accompanying the warm sunshine.

"Did you know," James said as they stepped around

162

a woman exiting an apartment building with a stroller, "that a long time ago, if a ruler had a secret message he wanted to send, he shaved the head of his servant, wrote the message on the servant's scalp, waited for the servant's hair to grow back, and then the servant traveled to the message recipient and had his head shaved again so the guy could read it?"

"If you have to shave off Steve, you could try that out," Emily said.

James threw his hands up to either side of his cowlick as if he were covering Steve's ears.

"As if I'll lose! Have some confidence."

Emily patted Steve on his pointy tips. "My deepest apologies, Steve! Of course you won't lose."

"Those guys might have spent their whole life going back and forth with messages on their heads, like a living piece of notebook paper," James said.

They approached Hollister's bookstore. His window display homage to Bayside Press was still in place. Emily stopped and peered inside through a gap between two books.

"Hollister's in there, talking to someone. Do you think he might help us with the Black Cat clue?"

"It can't hurt to ask. He knew a lot about Poe last week."

They pushed open the door just in time to hear the customer say, "You said the Welty would be in! I came all the way across the city."

Sparse strands of ginger hair gripped the irate

customer's balding head like a claw. James stopped short, Emily right behind. This was the same man who had been in Mr. Griswold's office last week.

"What is he doing here?" James whispered to Emily.

"No, no, now," Hollister was saying. "I said I'd *found* the Welty we discussed. I wish you had called first, Leon. I don't know what else to tell you." Hollister looked over and saw Emily and James standing just inside the front door. His shoulders dropped from his ears, and a smile split his face. "Ah, James and Emily-Who-Just-Moved-Here. Just finishing up with my friend, Mr. Remora. In fact, he's the one I mentioned to you earlier. The rare-book specialist who works with Mr. Griswold." To Mr. Remora Hollister said, "These two are fans of Gary and Book Scavenger."

Gary? It sounded funny to hear Mr. Griswold referred to as a Gary.

Mr. Remora barely glanced in their direction. If he recognized Emily and James, he didn't show it. "This is unacceptable!" He hammered his index finger into the counter, like he was pounding a miniature gavel. "I told my client I'd deliver the book to her this week."

"Well, I'll check on the status as soon as possible. And I tell you what, Leon. I will personally hand deliver it to you so you don't have to trek back to my shop."

One strand dipped in front of Mr. Remora's eyes, and he blew at it repeatedly, only to have it flop back down. Finally, he pushed the strand of hair back on his head. "Fine."

Emily and James leaned against the counter, waiting for their turn to talk to Hollister. A tray filled with magnetic poetry sat beside a rack of bookmarks. Emily and James pushed around words while they waited. *Ferocious. Fish. Eyeball.* It reminded Emily of first discovering Mr. Griswold's hidden words in *The Gold-Bug*.

Hollister pulled a pen from the mug by his register. "Now what's your address?"

"1717 Fillmore Street—"

"Ah, you live by the Fillmore?" Hollister said, jotting it down.

"Yes. Lucky me. Traffic and noise, hoo-rah."

Hollister clamped his mouth shut and focused on writing the address, drawing a long inhale of breath through his nose. When he finished, he tucked the notepad with the address onto a shelf under the counter and turned to Emily and James. "So what brings you kids in today? More book scavenging?"

"Oh, um." Emily glanced at Mr. Remora. He was sorting through a pile of books on Hollister's counter.

"We wanted to ask you about 'The Black Cat.'"

"The Black Cat!" Hollister hooted. "Haven't thought about that place in years. That's where I met Ferlinghetti."

"No," James interjected. "It's not a place. We're talking about . . ."

165

His voice trailed off as he and Emily looked at each other. There was a *place* called the Black Cat? Maybe that was what the clue was telling them to do. Go to the Black Cat.

Mr. Remora slapped his hand on the counter three times. "Hollister. We're not done here. I'd like these rung up." He waved to the small stack of books he'd sorted from the original pile. "And what about that Carver you had last month? Is that still here?"

"I believe so. Let me go check the stacks." Hollister gave the kids an apologetic smile. "I can answer your questions in two shakes of a lamb's tail."

Emily nudged James. "We can look it up online," she said.

James called after Hollister's retreating figure. "Don't worry, Hollister! We'll google it!"

CHAPTER 20

EMILY AND JAMES sat side by side in the accordion section of an extra-long city bus on their way to the Black Cat restaurant. On one side of the bendy part was a woman with a crate on wheels packed tightly with plastic grocery bags, and on the other was a man painted head-to-toe in silver, reading a newspaper. Whenever he turned a page, robotic sounds mysteriously accompanied his movement. Emily tried not to stare, but she swore his mouth wasn't moving to make the noise.

James didn't give the silver man or plastic-bag lady a second glance. Emily wasn't sure how much of that was due to him having lived in San Francisco his whole life and being immune to these kinds of sightings, and how much was due to his absorption in cracking Maddie's cipher. How he could be focused on anything other than Griswold's game right now was a mystery to her. Emily practically bounced in her seat, she was so excited, straining to read every street sign the bus approached in hopes that they would reach their stop already.

Finally, they approached the intersection for the Black Cat restaurant, and James stood up to pull the bell wire. They exited through the back door and jumped to the sidewalk, and the bus whirred away.

"It should be up here at the next corner," James said.

They crossed the intersection of a busy, four-lane street and soon found themselves standing under a neon sign that jutted over the sidewalk.

Jazz music tumbled out when they pushed the front door open. Emily's eyes adjusted to the dim interior. The hostess stand was unmanned, so Emily peered into the bar area where a heavyset man with a bald, shining head wiped down a table.

"We don't seat until five o'clock," the man said in a deep baritone voice without looking up.

"We're not here to eat," Emily said. She sounded like a mouse compared with him.

"Then what exactly are you here for, babies?" he said, not unkindly, his rag hovering over the tabletop.

"We left something," James said.

"Last night," Emily added. "We need to get it back."

"You two were here last night?" the man said.

"With our families," James jumped in. "It was a large group."

"Well, not that large," Emily added. What if there hadn't been any large groups last night? "But large."

"A large but not large group, huh?" The man considered this with a skeptical pout. "All right, I'll bite. What did you leave?"

"A, um, book," Emily said.

James poked her in the back. Okay, so maybe a book wasn't the best imaginary thing to leave at a restaurant. But she didn't know how Mr. Griswold's scavenger hunt was supposed to work—did this man know about it and he had a clue waiting for them? Or did they have to find it hidden somewhere? Maybe if she mentioned a book, he'd ask which one, then she'd say *The Gold-Bug*, and he'd offer her the next clue.

But the restaurant manager didn't ask any questions, and if he thought it was ridiculous to have left a book in a restaurant, he didn't show it. He crossed to the hostess podium and picked through items that lay behind it.

"I've got a cell phone, sunglasses, and an umbrella. No book."

"Could we look around for it? We won't take long," James said.

"We won't mess anything up," Emily added.

"Fine, fine." The man waved them into the back dining room.

"So what are we looking for exactly?" James

whispered. Emily lifted a tablecloth and peered under a table.

"I have no idea," she said. "I'm hoping we'll know it when we see it. Keep an eye out for anything that looks out of place. A note taped under a table or something like that."

They worked their way through the dining area, lifting tablecloths and peering under chairs, scrutinizing wall hangings and the small clusters of carnations on every table.

When they met in the middle, James asked, "Have you read 'The Black Cat' yet? Maybe there's something in the story that's a hint for what we should be looking for."

"Well, it's about a guy who drinks too much, kills his cat in a drunken rage, and then thinks the cat comes back from the dead. Then the guy goes even crazier and kills his wife and buries her in their basement, but he accidentally buries the zombie cat with her and gets himself caught. So I hope the story has nothing to do with what we should be looking for because I'd rather not dig up dead bodies or zombie cats."

"Geez. Hollister wasn't kidding. Poe really did have a twisted imagination, didn't he?"

Emily placed her hands on her hips and surveyed the restaurant. They had looked over every inch with no luck. "Maybe we should say something to the manager about the game? Maybe he's supposed to give us our next clue."

It was the best idea they had to work with, so they went back to the bar where the manager shuffled papers behind the counter.

"You find your book?" he asked without looking up.

"Um, no," Emily said. She wasn't sure what to say next, but she didn't have to worry, because James took the lead.

"Did you know there's a story called 'The Black Cat'?" James asked, climbing onto a bar stool. Emily hesitantly climbed onto the one next to him. "Is that what this place is named after?"

The man set down the stack of papers and lowered his gaze to James. "Nope," he said.

"Nope, you didn't know there's a story with that name, or nope, that's not what this place is named after?"

The manager didn't respond.

"Well, have you read it?" James asked. "It's by Edgar Allan Poe, and it's about this guy who—"

"So you didn't find your book?" the man asked again.

"It's actually an Edgar Allan Poe book we're looking for. Have you heard of"—James leaned forward eagerly—"*The Gold-Bug*?"

The manager walked around the bar, gripped

their backpacks, and pulled James and Emily down from the bar stools.

"You kids didn't leave a book here, did you?" He steered them toward the door. "So what have you been doing? You get into the liquor? You leave a stink bomb somewhere?"

"No, no, no," James said hurriedly.

"We found a secret message in a book," Emily blurted out. "Do you have our next clue?"

The manager dropped his handle on their backpacks.

"What?" he said with a shake of his head. "No, I don't have a clue for you kids. Go play your game somewhere else, okay? I've got work to do."

Emily and James sat in disappointed silence as they rode the bus back to their building. She'd been so certain that was where they needed to go.

Finally, Emily said, "Well, at least we can cross the Black Cat restaurant off our list."

The movement of the bus rocked them side to side. James had his binder open again to Maddie's cipher. Emily looked out the window and watched the city pass by. Gray buildings, liquor stores. They approached a corner park that was raised and built over a parking garage. Its sign read PORTSMOUTH SQUARE. Bright red pagoda-style awnings covered picnic tables. Lantern lampposts turned on for the evening as dusk settled in. A man climbed the stairs from the sidewalk up to the park. He moved in a sideways sway, long dreadlocks swinging across his back, and he carried a duffel bag.

"Hey, James." Emily elbowed him. "Isn't that Hollister?"

James looked up. "It is. I wonder what he's doing all the way over here."

They passed the park and continued to stare out the window. James absentmindedly plucked at Steve. "Hey, Emily," he said. "What if Mr. Griswold never finished his game? What if getting to 'The Black Cat' story is all there is right now? Raven said the game wasn't supposed to start for a few weeks."

"No way." Emily shook her head firmly. "He finished the game." She couldn't prove this, of course, but she just knew it was true. It had to be.

"Well, maybe we should focus on Mr. Quisling's cipher challenge for a little bit instead. Admit it—wouldn't it make your day to see Her Royal Fungus with an official mushroom-top hairdo? Besides . . ." James punched a fist in the air and shouted, "We must defend Steve's honor!"

There were only two other people on the bus, but they both turned to look at them. James gave an apologetic wave. "Sorry!"

"Steve has nothing to worry about," Emily reassured him. "We'll make sure of that."

James gave a tight-lipped smile and returned to scribbling notes about Maddie's cipher.

CHAPTER 21

IN MR. QUISLING'S class the next day, Emily eyed James slumped in his desk next to her. He was irritated because he hadn't cracked Maddie's code yet.

"It's only Tuesday," Emily reassured him. "We have all week."

But James slumped even lower when his was one of the two ciphers broken. After class, Maddie stood behind James and drew an imaginary circle around Steve.

"Once you shave that off, you could draw an eight in its place and your head would look like a Magic 8 Ball," she said.

James smacked Maddie's finger away from his head.

"What, no plucky retort?" Maddie asked.

James yanked his backpack zipper closed with a ferocious tug.

"Don't let her get to you," Emily said as they left a

smirking Maddie behind. "There's plenty of time to solve hers."

"Easy for you to say," James said. "It's not your hair on the line."

By Thursday, James had made a breakthrough with Maddie's cipher and was back in high spirits.

"She didn't make it up herself," James said at lunch. They sat at what had become their regular spot in the library. "It's an alphabet from the Dark Ages called Ogham. I found it when I was researching ciphers online. Look, I printed out a copy." James slid over a sheet of paper filled with various hash marks.

⊤	⊤⊤	⊤⊤⊤	⊤⊤⊤⊤	⊤⊤⊤⊤⊤	⊥	⊥⊥	⊥⊥⊥	⊥⊥⊥⊥	⊥⊥⊥⊥⊥
B	L	F	S	N	H	D	T	C	Q

╱	╱╱	╱╱╱	╱╱╱╱	╱╱╱╱╱	┼	┼┼	┼┼┼	┼┼┼┼	┼┼┼┼┼
M	G	NG	Z	R	A	O	U	E	I

✕	◇	⊏	⋈	▦	=	＞	—	＜
ea	oi	ui	ia	ae	P	start of text	space	end of text

"She copied it straight out. If you know Ogham, you'd understand her message. But who knows Ogham, right?"

Emily looked over the Ogham alphabet sheet. It wasn't all that different from hers and James's secret code, but somehow using symbols instead of letters made it seem more foreign and intimidating.

James continued. "The only clever thing Maddie did was use a sentence that wouldn't work well with frequency analysis: *Zelda Zombie eats zinnias*. Using that many *z*'s makes letter-frequency analysis difficult because you assume the symbols that appear the most often will be an *e*, *t*, *a*, or another frequently used letter, not *z*."

That afternoon in Mr. Quisling's class, James gave a satisfied smile when Maddie's name was crossed off the board.

"The score's still zero-zero, Fernandez," he said to her after class.

Maddie gave a mock-scared face and waggled her fingers before walking away.

"Ms. Crane," Mr. Quisling called over. "I need to speak with you before you leave."

Speak with her? Emily's lips felt dry all of a sudden. She wasn't behind on homework. She hadn't done anything to get on Mr. Quisling's bad side since she was caught passing the note last week. At least she didn't think she had. James gave her a questioning look. She shrugged and gave a small wave as he left for his next class. Kids filtered in for Mr. Quisling's seventh period as she approached his desk.

"Emily," Mr. Quisling said. "Are you a Book Scavenger user?"

"I . . . uh." That wasn't what she had expected him to ask. She didn't know what she *did* expect him to ask, but it definitely wouldn't have been about Book Scavenger.

"In our faculty meeting the other day, Principal Montoya mentioned that a man had contacted our school believing a valuable book of his was mistakenly found by a Book Scavenger player who listed Booker as his or her school in their profile. He said this player posted on the Book Scavenger forums about finding a book called *The Gold-Bug* by Edgar Allan Poe. I recall you had an unusual-looking Poe book on your desk last week."

Mr. Quisling leaned an elbow on the arm of his chair, patiently studying Emily. She fiddled with the Book Scavenger logo pin she wore on her hoodie. She didn't know what to say. She was surprised by all this—Mr. Quisling pulling her aside to talk, someone contacting the school about *The Gold-Bug*, someone claiming the book was his. And this was the second time someone had claimed the book—Emily thought of the guest user who had messaged her through Book Scavenger the other day. "Do you remember the book I'm referring to?" Mr. Quisling asked.

"Yes," Emily said.

"And do you still have this book?"

"I . . . I don't." The lie came out of her mouth before she could change her mind about saying it. "I hid it again through Book Scavenger."

Mr. Quisling raised his eyebrows. "You did?"

Thinking of her conversation with the guest user on Book Scavenger and how he or she didn't know how many stories were in *The Gold-Bug*, she asked, "Why is this person so sure the book I found belonged to him? Maybe he's wrong."

He frowned. "Emily, if someone has gone to the trouble of looking up your profile and contacting your school, then I would give him the benefit of the doubt. Also, not that it should matter, but this person is a professional book collector. He's not another Book Scavenger player trying to trick you. This man believes that book belongs to one of his clients, and if it's the book he's looking for, he says it's very valuable. Not so much to you or someone else, but sentimentally it has significance for his client and, therefore, is valuable. It's also valuable in that this man says he will lose his job if he can't find and return the book."

"The man who called the school is a book collector?" Emily asked. Mr. Remora was a book collector. And he'd been looking for a book that belonged to Mr. Griswold when they walked in on him at Bayside Press. How many rare-book collectors could there be in San Francisco?

"Yes," Mr. Quisling said and continued on, not realizing that detail meant something to her. "Now, if you say you've already hidden the book, then I am trusting you at your word. But seeing as a man's job is on the line, why don't you try to retrieve it so he can take a look? If it's not the one he's looking for, you can return it to its hiding spot and the book can continue its Book Scavenger journey."

Did this mean Mr. Remora knew about Mr. Griswold's game? He didn't seem like the sort who would get excited about something like that. And Raven had said there were fifty copies total of *The Gold-Bug* hidden around the city, so if Mr. Remora was interested in it for the game, he could find his own copy. Maybe he didn't realize that Mr. Griswold had hidden the book and that it was missing on purpose.

"Earth to Emily." Mr. Quisling snapped his fingers. "You're not in trouble here. It's a simple task. You found a book that belongs to someone else. Retrieve it and give it back."

Emily nodded. "Yes, I'll try to do that."

And she *would* return the book to Mr. Remora. But she'd already made so much progress with Mr. Griswold's game. It couldn't hurt to finish it. That way, Mr. Remora would have the book back in his possession, and she'd have the satisfaction of solving an entire Griswold game. Everybody would win.

"So what did Mr. Quisling want?" James asked as they walked away from school.

Ahead of them a grocer sprayed down the sidewalk in front of his corner market. He released the nozzle as they walked by so the water stopped, then started blasting it again after they'd passed.

"You'll never guess in a million years."

"He selected you for a space mission? He's learning to play 'Heart and Soul' on the piano and needs you to play the harmony?"

Emily laughed. "Do you remember Mr. Remora? The book specialist who works for Mr. Griswold?"

"That guy we saw at Bayside Press and Hollister's? Of course."

"Well, apparently he's looking for *The Gold-Bug*. That might have been what he was looking for last week in Mr. Griswold's office. He saw my message in the Book Scavenger forums, saw Booker listed in my profile, and called our school. Our principal told the teachers, and because Mr. Quisling saw *The Gold-Bug* on my desk—"

"On the day that launched the Cipher Challenge, of which I will *triumph*!"

Emily grinned. "Right. And apparently the day that burned my *Gold-Bug* in Mr. Quisling's memory."

"*Your* Gold-Bug?" James smirked. "I thought it was Mr. Griswold's."

"You know what I mean."

"So why does Mr. Remora want *The Gold-Bug*? Does he know about the game?"

"I wondered that, too, but I don't think so. Raven said there are other copies to be found, after all, so why would he need this one? Mr. Quisling said the book is valuable for sentimental reasons, and Mr. Remora will lose his job if he doesn't get it back in Mr. Griswold's personal collection."

"So did you give it back?" James asked.

"Of course not!" Emily said. "How would we finish the game?"

James stopped walking.

"If Mr. Remora needs that book for his job, Em . . . maybe that's more important."

James's words stung, Emily couldn't deny it. "But we've already figured out some of the clues for the game! And he was so rude at Hollister's the other day."

"He was. But that doesn't mean he doesn't actually need the book."

"I *am* giving it back to him," Emily said, a touch defensively. "I just want to finish the game first."

"Sounds like a plan, then," James said, and they fell in step again.

CHAPTER

22

THE CHIME of jingle bells announced Emily's and James's entrance into Hollister's store. Even though Mr. Remora knew her only through her Book Scavenger profile as Surly Wombat and probably hadn't realized they'd crossed paths the other day, she still felt a stirring of butterflies when they stepped inside. Knowing that he was looking for her and the book would make it harder for her to act normal if he happened to be there again. But Hollister's store was empty, at least it looked that way from where they stood.

"Hollister?" James called.

They heard his whistle in return. They wound their way through the packed bookshelves, taking a detour by the crafts section so Emily could stoop down and check on the *Inkheart* book.

"Still there," she said. She regularly checked its

status on the Book Scavenger website, but you never knew if someone might have scavenged it but not logged the find.

They found Hollister in the middle of the store, sorting paperbacks out of a cardboard box. He held a book close to his eyes, then wagged it like a winning lottery ticket. "*One Flew Over the Cuckoo's Nest*! Nice used condition. That's a goodie!"

Hollister looked at them again as if he hadn't fully seen them the first time. "Well, hey there, you two! Come to pick through my fine literature selection?"

"Actually, I'm looking for books about ciphers or making up codes," James said.

Hollister tapped a finger to the tip of his nose, contemplating, then turned and with his swaying shuffle led them deeper into the book maze. Dusty lightbulbs dangled above and created dull pools of light to guide their way.

As they walked, Emily said, "We went to that restaurant you told us about, Hollister. Remember? The Black Cat?"

"You didn't go there," Hollister said. The floorboards creaked underfoot.

"Um, actually we did," James said.

Hollister stopped, leaned close to a bookshelf, and trailed an index finger across the spines as he scanned the titles. He pulled *Breaking the Maya Code* off the shelf and handed it to James, then gestured for them to follow him back up to the front of the store.

"The Black Cat's closed," Hollister said. "Been closed since the sixties."

James and Emily exchanged a look, uncertain if Hollister was teasing them or serious.

"Well, it must have reopened, Hollister, because we went there," Emily said.

"On Broadway," James added.

"There's your problem. The one I'm talking about was on Montgomery, not Broadway. By the Transamerica building—that old steel-and-concrete pyramid."

Emily stopped walking, and James bumped into her from behind.

"It closed?" Emily asked.

"In 1963. Same year President Kennedy was shot." Hollister pulled *Codebreaker* from a shelf and handed it to James.

James paid for his books. Once they were outside, Emily grabbed his arm and swung it like she was ringing a giant bell.

"We went to the wrong one! I told you it wasn't a dead end!"

"All right, all right." James laughed and pulled his arm free to hold his hands up in surrender. "I concede defeat! But there's only one way to find out for sure."

In the shadow of a pyramid-shaped skyscraper sat an old brick building painted white with green-paned windows. Gold letters spelled CANESSA PRINTING CO. at the top of the building, above four porthole-like windows, and again over an entrance on their right.

"A printing company?" James said. "That makes sense, with Mr. Griswold being a publisher and all."

"But the street address isn't right," Emily pointed out. "The Black Cat shared the building, but its address was 710. That one's 708."

James peered inside the street-level windows for 710. A group of four sat on the other side, looking at menus.

"Another restaurant?" he said, disappointed.

Emily tugged on the straps of her backpack and assessed the building and street. There was nothing Emily could see to identify this building as the former home of the Black Cat café, but the address matched what they'd found online, so it must be the right place. It was only a matter of deciphering what they needed to find.

Through her years of using Book Scavenger, she'd become accustomed to keeping an eye out for the odd detail. Clues and riddles could take you only so far, like how the clue for the book she and James first hunted took them to the pier at the Ferry Building. After that it was a matter of sleuthing—investigating crevices that would be a convenient place to hide a book-shaped object, observing a pile of freshly dug dirt, or noticing something out of place.

Emily scanned planters filled with flowers, two metal café tables, a sidewalk spotted with blackened remains of chewing gum, a flyer posted to the tree in front of the building, a parking meter decorated with orange and black. She was debating whether to pretend to have left something in the restaurant again or be direct and say they were on a scavenger hunt, when a breeze rustled the flyer tacked to the tree. A brand-new-looking flyer with a photo of . . . a cat? Emily went closer for a better look. A photo of a *black* cat.

"Check this out, James!"

Written in all caps in thick black marker under the photo was the following message:

LOOKING FOR A BLACK CAT? CALL SAMUEL

The bottom of the page was cut into fringe with a number printed on each tab:

(978) 067-9722 X649

"This has to be it!" Emily exclaimed. The flyer was crisp and all the numbered tags remained intact. Emily tore off a strip, and they headed back to their building as fast as they could go.

They raced up the stairs to James's apartment and kicked off their shoes. James grabbed the cordless phone from its stand on a side table.

"Read me the number."

The phone beeped with every number James

punched. Before she got halfway through, Emily heard a recorded voice speak.

"Who is it?" she asked.

James frowned. The recorded message repeated.

"It says we've typed too few digits. Try again," he said.

Emily repeated the numbers, but once again the recording came on halfway through the call.

"It must be because of the zero. I've never seen a phone number start with a zero," she said.

"Maybe it's not supposed to be a phone number. Maybe it means something else. A math equation? A cipher?"

Emily went to grab her notebook from her backpack when she saw the time on the Lees' grandfather clock. She groaned.

"I have to go. But we can work on this at lunch tomorrow."

"We were going to work on Mr. Quisling's challenge, remember?"

The sharpness of James's tone made Emily feel a twinge of guilt that, no, she hadn't remembered.

"Of course I remember," she fibbed. "We'll work on them both."

CHAPTER 23

EMILY CONTINUED to puzzle over the number
clue Friday and throughout the weekend. By
Sunday morning, her attempts to make sense of it had
amounted to nothing. And always floating around was
James's question about whether the game had actually
been finished before Mr. Griswold was attacked. The
Black Cat clue *had* led them somewhere after all, but
what if this number was now a dead end?

It didn't help that the last time she'd checked the
Book Scavenger forums, rumors were swirling that
Mr. Griswold wasn't doing well. One user, Captain-
Overpants, claimed to work in Mr. Griswold's hospital
and said that Mr. Griswold was still in a coma and
had been secretly moved to hospice care because he
was dying. But then someone asked CaptainOverpants
if he could verify his claim and he said no, and then a
bunch of people started jumping on him for fanning

the flames of rumors. The whole exchange was exhausting to follow. Emily clicked out of the forums and decided no news was just that—no news—and she wouldn't let any rumors get to her before she heard something real.

But that was easier said than done. She couldn't shake her worry that Mr. Griswold might not recover and that she could lose not only Mr. Griswold, but Book Scavenger, too.

That afternoon, her family was going to an outdoor concert at Golden Gate Park, which sounded like the perfect opportunity to get her mind off Mr. Griswold and his game. It also seemed an ideal time to hide a book for Book Scavenger. James's dad was in town that weekend, so Emily would be a solo scavenger. Funny how only two weeks ago she would have preferred it that way.

To get an idea of where she might hide a book, Emily did an online search for images of the music concourse and discovered there would be a fountain. She had once found a copy of *Escape from Mr. Lemoncello's Library* hidden in an aquarium at her previous doctor's office, and ever since she had wanted to hide one underwater. This looked like the perfect opportunity. All she needed to do was pick a book and seal it in a waterproof bag. She'd saved the Book Scavenger sack the aquarium hider had used. You could buy them through the website, and this one was printed to look like the interior of an aquarium with its teal color and pieces of coral. (Personally, Emily would have chosen the bag printed to make the book look like a treasure chest.) The aquarium camouflage in a fountain wasn't ideal, but it would work.

Now to decide which book to hide.

It was always difficult to choose which of her books to give away. Her most favorites were marked up with hearts and exclamation marks and other reading notes in the margins, so she would never part with those. But she collected copies of those favorite books to give away. Rummaging through her hideable book collection, she decided on *The Westing Game*.

When the Cranes left for the concert, a murky white washed the sky. There were no views of the bay on this overcast day. They walked past the street Emily's school was on and then walked farther, stopping at a small market/deli to pick up sandwiches, and then walked farther until they finally reached where her dad had last found street parking for Sal.

"We should have just walked to the park," Matthew said as he climbed into the back. "We're practically there."

"Only in San Francisco!" their dad replied.

Emily sat in the middle of the van and flipped open *The Westing Game*. She was in the middle of rereading the bit where Turtle sneaks into the mansion on Halloween when Matthew bellowed, "Look! Looklooklooklooklook." He pounded his index finger against the glass with every "look."

He'd startled Emily so much she'd almost dropped her book. She scanned the street trying to figure out what had gotten him so worked up. There was a bland brick building that looked more like a bank than anything else until she noticed the lit-up marquee that read THE FILLMORE.

"I'll see *you* in a week," Matthew said to the building as they drove by. Matthew had found a group of friends from his school who were going to the Flush concert, so their parents had agreed to let him buy a ticket. If it were anyone else who had already befriended an entire group to go to a concert with, it might surprise Emily, but this was Matthew.

"If we lived here, I'd work at the Fillmore," Matthew said.

"If we lived here, I'd ride a cable car every day," their mom chimed in. This was one of the games they often played. Imagining life, sometimes ridiculously, lived long-term in one place.

"If we lived here, my calves would become the size of small watermelons from walking so many hills," her dad said.

Emily watched gray buildings whiz by. The clinging white mist made all the wires that crisscrossed the city stand out like a cat's cradle.

"Your turn, Emily," their dad said.

"If we lived here, I'd live above a bookstore," she said, thinking of the apartments above Hollister's.

"Ooh, yes," her mom said. "If only."

And Emily wondered, why if only? "If only" implied "if only we could stay," and the idea of calling San Francisco home didn't sound so unreasonable to her.

When they got to the music concourse, the jazz was already in full swing. Her parents hadn't realized this was a Halloween-themed concert, and the front benches were filled with zombies, witches, and fairies. Even the stage looked dressed in costume as something out of Ancient Rome with an ornate dome carved with angels and columns flanking either side, but Emily knew from photos that that was how it always looked. Tables and pop-tents had been set up beyond the benches under frizzy trees, their leaves lit with orange lanterns. They passed the large fountain with a statue where Emily wanted to hide her book and continued to an expanse of lawn. An upbeat, bouncy number played as the Cranes wove in a single-file line around blankets and collapsible chairs and a dancing toddler dressed like a monkey. Emily's dad put his hands on her mother's hips and pretended to do an embarrassing conga that was mostly shrugging shoulders and the occasional kick. Emily was relieved when they found a clear space of grass to shake out their blanket.

"Anyone hungry?" Emily's mom sat down the bag of sandwiches.

"I'm going to hide my book," Emily said.

"Why don't you go with her, Matthew?"

Emily pretended to be very interested in adjusting the waterproof baggie around *The Westing Game*. It had been a while since she and Matthew had hidden a book together. He used to be really into it, maybe even more than Emily in the beginning. They fought about it back then because he always wanted to hide books in a way that made it super hard to find them, while Emily wanted her books found so she could read about their adventures as they traveled on to new places. Matthew dug into the paper bag and pulled out a pro- sciutto sandwich. Without so much as a glance or apol- ogetic smile her way, he said, "Nah. I'd rather go watch the guitarist."

Emily knew her cheeks reddened. She could feel them get hot. It was stupid of her to care. She had known he wouldn't want to join her. All she was going to do was walk the book over to the fountain and drop it in, anyway, so it's not like she needed a partner. But if it had been a few years ago, Matthew would have found a way to make something simple like that feel like a secret spy mission.

"Matthew, go with your sister," their mother said. "You can get up close to the music afterward."

"That's okay," Emily said quickly. "I'm not going far, and I'll be super quick. This one doesn't need two people anyway."

Before anyone could say anything more, Emily hurried to the fountain. She'd added a small stone to the baggie to help weigh down *The Westing Game* so it would stay underwater. When it seemed like nobody was paying attention to her, she dropped the book. With a *sploosh*, it went under. That night, when she got home, she would enter the clue onto Book Scavenger. She'd thought of a good one: *Where the wet things are between art and science*, encrypted in her and James's secret language to make it a little more difficult. *Art* and *science* referred to the de Young Museum and the Academy of Sciences, which were on either side of the concourse.

She sat on the edge of the fountain for a minute. A Dorothy and a Cowardly Lion played checkers on their blanket. Three small pirates held hands, shrieking in circles until they fell down. She could see her family's blanket from here. Her parents were dancing a clumsy, barefoot salsa on the grass. Matthew was nowhere to be seen, no doubt standing as close to the stage as he could manage. She looked down at *The Westing Game*, still submerged at the bottom of the fountain. She wished James could have come with her tonight. He would have liked the whole hiding-a-book-underwater thing. How odd that she could be a solo book hunter for years and enjoy it, but now it felt like something was missing to be on her own.

CHAPTER 24

MONDAY MARKED the third week of Mr. Quisling's cipher challenge. Nearly everyone had dropped out by now, having decided that doing homework would be easier than the work of creating and breaking the class ciphers. James and Maddie were both still into the challenge, but Emily figured it was more for the pride of winning their bet than for the homework passes at this point. The score was zero-zero, but at lunchtime James was confident that was about to change.

They sat at their table in the library, and James explained the mastermind code he'd come up with over the weekend, every so often looking over to where Maddie sat.

"I found this section about the Baconian Cipher," James said. Emily leaned in to hear his whispered words.

"Bacon, like bacon and eggs?"

"Exactly. A cipher that tastes delicious on any sandwich." James grinned. "No, Bacon was the guy who came up with it. With the Baconian Cipher, you use a combination of *A*s and *B*s to represent every letter of the alphabet. I was thinking about how computer programming is a type of cipher—it's called coding after all—and then I came across this Baconian stuff, and it gave me the idea to combine it with binary code."

"Binary what now?"

Instead of explaining, James pulled a sheet of paper from his binder and slid it over to Emily. A short paragraph typed at the top read: *Beware the ninja monkey. He likes banana bread and* drives a station wagon.

"This is a normal paragraph," she said.

"Emily." James tipped his head down. "You of all people should know normal-looking paragraphs can hide secret messages."

"Oh. Duh. Well, how does this work?"

James pulled another sheet from his binder—the answer key, Emily presumed. Every letter of the alphabet was assigned a combination of ones and zeros:

a = 00000
b = 00001
c = 00010
d = 00011

196

e=00100
f=00101
g=00110
h=00111
i/j=01000
k=01001
l=01010
m=01011
n=01100
o=01101
p=01110
q=01111
r=10000
s=10001
t=10010
u/v=10011
w=10100
x=10101
y=10110
z=10111

"These zeros and ones are called binary. For this cipher, a different group of ones and zeros represent each letter—*i*, *j*, *u*, and *v* double up because they're not used that much and it makes it more tricky," James explained. "So I take my secret message, which is *I like soup*, and convert it to binary. So *I* is 01000, *L* is 01010, and so on, until you have this."

James pointed to a paragraph on his answer key

made entirely of *0*s and *1*s: 01000 01010 01000 01001 00100 10001 01101 10011 01110.

"Then I made up sentences that used at least as many letters as there are digits in this ciphertext. *Beware* the *ninja* *monkey*. *He* likes *ba*nana *bread* an*d* dri*v*es a station wagon." All the letters that represent zeros are in italics, so if someone knows what I've done, they could decode this. I still think it'd be pretty hard though."

"This is so genius!" Emily said, a little too loudly. Maddie glared at them from across the room.

"Sorry," she whispered to James. But it was shout-worthy. She never in a million years would have figured out how to decode James's paragraph.

James dropped his pen on the cipher work and tipped his chair back. "No sorry needed. It will torture her to know she's doomed. So what about the black cat phone number? Any progress?"

"If you consider progress figuring out what it's *not*, then yeah, I made a ton of progress. It doesn't have the right amount of numbers to be a license plate number, and it doesn't work as an address for a location in San Francisco. Like: 97806797226 Forty-Ninth Street? You can turn it into a math equation, like add all the numbers to find a sum, but then what do you do with that? You just end up with another meaningless number."

"Do you have it with you? I can take a stab at it—"

A hand reached in between them and grasped James's copy of *The Book of Codes* from the table.

"I need to borrow this," Maddie said. "We're supposed to share. Library rules."

James hastily slid his binder over his cipher pages before clamping a hand on the book to tug it back.

"That's not a library book. It's mine," James said.

"Oh sure, like I'm falling for that."

As James and Maddie tugged the book back and forth in front of Emily, the bar code waved like a black-and-white flag until it finally got her attention.

Emily pushed up from the table and shouted, "Stop!"

James and Maddie froze. Heads all around the room turned in their direction. The school librarian popped out from behind a bookshelf. "Is there a problem?"

Maddie pinched her lips into a pout. She looked from Emily to James then said, "No problem," and flounced back to her table.

James warily watched the retreating mushroom head bob across the room. "Do you think she saw my cipher?"

But Emily was too focused on her discovery to pay attention to anything else. She tapped the bar code on James's book.

"Look! Look at this!"

Above the bar code were the letters *ISBN* and a string of numbers that began with 978, just like the phone number. Emily ran her finger along the numbers, counting in her head.

"*Thirteen* numbers, same as the phone number on the clue," she said.

James flipped over his other book. Its ISBN also began with 978 and had thirteen digits. Emily's collection of Poe works had another thirteen-digit ISBN number. Every book had a similar but unique number. *The Gold-Bug* had no bar code at all, but that made sense if Mr. Griswold had made it especially for his game.

"Mr. Griswold's clue leads to another book!" Emily said.

They ran to the computer bank to look up the ISBN number. In the search browser, there was an option for ISBN/ISSN Exact Match. Emily selected that and typed in the thirteen-digit number from the Black Cat flyer. Holding her breath, she clicked the red arrow and watched the computer do its thinking spiral, then slowly load a new page. *The Maltese Falcon* by Dashiell Hammett.

"No way," Emily said.

"That must be it!" James said. "But why did the flyer say to call Samuel? Are we supposed to do that, too, or do you think he just wrote that to make it look like a real lost-cat flyer?"

Emily clicked on the "About the Author" link for the book. "He used 'Samuel' because of that." She tapped the screen. "Dashiell Hammett's real first name was Samuel. Maybe he thought using Dashiell would be too much of a giveaway."

As exciting as it was to know she'd figured out another one of Mr. Griswold's puzzles, and must therefore be that much closer to the end, staring at the cover of *The Maltese Falcon* felt like starting from scratch again. Now what were they supposed to do with this clue? The satisfaction of accomplishing something could be very fleeting.

"I feel like this book is familiar for some reason. But I don't think I've heard of it until now," James said.

"It's set in San Francisco. Maybe you've heard of it because it has to do with the city," Emily said.

"How did you know that?"

"My parents gave it to me as a San Francisco–themed present before we moved here. Or maybe you saw it in my room."

"Yeah, maybe," James said. The bell rang, signaling the end of lunch. "Doesn't matter anyway. What matters *now* is that soon we deliver Her Royal Fungus with the cipher of doom. What an awesome day, huh?"

By the end of Mr. Quisling's class, Emily's mind had drifted away from the Roman Empire and back to *The Maltese Falcon* clue. She wrote *Dashiell Hammett* in her notebook and circled it. Around the author's name she wrote: *Born here? Wrote books here? School?* Because the Black Cat clue had led them to a San Francisco location, maybe this clue was meant to lead them to another spot in the city. She'd have to reread her copy of *The Maltese Falcon* to get more ideas.

"Mr. Quisling?" Next to Emily, James raised his hand. "Class is almost over. Are you going to collect ciphers for the week?"

Their teacher looked up at the clock and capped his dry-erase marker. "So it is. I assume you have one, Mr. Lee?"

"I do," James said, and flipped to the back of his binder. At the same moment, Maddie stood up.

"I have one, too." She walked her stack of papers to the front of the class and handed them to Mr. Quisling. She resumed her seat behind James, who was pulling pencils, crumpled papers, and textbooks from his backpack and piling them onto his desk.

"It was right here," he muttered.

"Excellent, Maddie." Mr. Quisling held the page forward for the class to see. The sheet of paper had a short paragraph at the top.

Something slithered in Emily's belly, as if a snake were winding its way around her stomach. All she could picture was their stuff, abandoned at the library table while they'd been at the computer bank discovering Mr. Griswold's next clue. Leaning across the aisle she whispered to James, "That isn't . . ."

"This looks interesting," Mr. Quisling said. "Your average paragraph about ninja monkeys—or is it?"

James looked up. "Hey, that's my cipher!"

"No, it's *not*." Maddie hit the perfect note of disbelief and outrage. "That's mine. I just turned it in."

James twisted in his seat to argue with her. "I spent all weekend working on that."

Maddie's eyebrows bunched together in a frustrated glare. "Funny, because *I* spent all weekend working on that, too."

If Emily hadn't just sat next to James at lunch and listened to him break down his new cipher and explain how it worked, she might be swayed by Maddie's performance.

Mr. Quisling turned the cipher around to study it. "Maddie's name is typed on this," he commented.

"Well, maybe she retyped it after she *stole* it from me."

"I didn't steal anything!"

"Enough!" Mr. Quisling said as the bell rang. The rest of the students shifted in their seats, packing up their backpacks.

"Mr. Quisling!" Emily raised her voice over the sliding desks and chatter that filled the hallway outside their room. "That's James's cipher. He showed it to me at lunch."

Maddie blinked her eyes rapidly, like she was fighting back tears. "Of course *she* is going to back him up."

"I said *enough*! It's clear something is amiss here, but there's no time to get to the bottom of this. You know how I feel about cheating." Mr. Quisling ripped the paper in two. He picked up the stack of copies Maddie had turned in and dumped them and the torn pieces into his recycling bin. "That cipher is invalid." He pointed a finger between James and Maddie. "For this week only, I will allow you to submit a different cipher. But if there is even the slightest suggestion that one of you has cheated, you'll be disqualified from the challenge completely."

Emily warily watched James shove his belongings back into his backpack. He didn't talk as they left Room 40. They walked silently past slamming lockers and laughing students.

"How did Maddie type her name on your paper, anyway?" Emily finally asked.

James shrugged. "It was a short paragraph. It wouldn't have taken her long to retype it and make copies."

"But why?" Emily said, incredulous.

"Maddie doesn't like to lose," James said glumly.

"But she had to know she couldn't win a home-work pass with your cipher."

"She didn't want to win a homework pass. She wanted to make sure I *didn't*, and she wanted to rub it in at the same time," James muttered.

"So she's threatened by you," Emily said, trying to shine a light on a bright side. "And she should be. You could still use your bacon-and-eggs cipher. Just submit a different encrypted message tomorrow."

She had hoped for a smile with the "bacon-and-eggs," but James didn't look up from the linoleum.

"Maddie stole the cipher key, too. Once you know how a cipher works, it's easy to break." He stopped abruptly in a hallway intersection. With his hands shoved in his hoodie pocket and eyes still on the floor, he muttered, "I forgot I have to do something," before turning away and getting swallowed by the crowd.

CHAPTER 25

"A WHOLE WEEK of sitting here and nothing," Barry said.

This was the second Monday afternoon in a row that he and Clyde sat in his beat-up El Camino parked across from Booker Middle School along with the cars of parents. He had thought it would be a simple thing to spot those kids again, but the more days they sat there staring, the more all these kids started to look the same. There were so many that poured out of the doors of this school, and there were different exits on all sides of the building, too.

"This is never going to work," Barry said.

"We'll find them," Clyde said.

Clyde dug his hands into his sweatshirt pocket, making Barry flinch. A shrieking chaotic mass of boys and girls ran down the sidewalk, jumped off the stairs, clustered in groups. Maybe if he could get them to line up and stand still for a minute, but they might as well be identical for as much as he could tell them apart.

"You're a high-strung kind of guy, aren't you?" Clyde said.

Barry bit at a cuticle. "Is this your idea of fun? 'Cause it's sure not mine—"

"Purple backpack," Clyde said and pointed.

Barry followed the direction of his finger without much enthusiasm. They'd seen purple backpacks before. And the longer they looked for these kids the more he wondered if maybe the backpack had been black or green.

The girl with the backpack was waiting for something, and that was when Barry spotted the boy crouched down, tying his shoe. That poky bit of hair standing up on his head—he'd watched that thing bob around when he'd been running behind it.

"What do you think?" Barry asked.

Clyde had the look of a cat narrowing in on his prey.

"Bingo," he said.

"Bingo," Barry agreed.

CHAPTER 26

JAMES WASN'T his usual chatty self on their walk home from school. Emily knew the cipher challenge would be a touchy subject after Maddie had ruined all his hard work, so she tried to distract him by talking about Mr. Griswold's latest clue.

"So, you don't know anything about Dashiell Hammett?" she asked. "You haven't heard of a park named after him, or anything like that?"

James was intent on watching a row of black birds huddled on a wire overhead and didn't answer.

Emily continued talking. "Every clue has led us to another book or story, so I'm thinking this one will too. Or here's another idea: Maybe there's an animal theme with the scavenger hunt—gold bug, black cat, Maltese falcon."

James gave a short huff and stopped walking.

"You know—" he started to say, but then something across the street distracted him. "Do you know them?"

"Know who?"

Emily scanned the people moving in and out of the stores and restaurants, the cars parked at the meters, the bus shuttling down the street.

"That car," James said. "Those men look like they're staring at us."

A long tan car idled up the block. The glare off the windshield made it difficult to see well, but the two torsos angled their way were clear enough.

"Maybe they're waiting for someone in the dry cleaners," Emily said, but she was glad the car was on the opposite side of the street.

The car rolled out of its spot.

"Never mind. They're leaving," James said.

They fell back in step, but Emily couldn't shake that feeling of being watched. When she looked behind once again, she saw the car arc in a U-turn at the intersection. Those men were turning around and headed in their direction.

"James," Emily said. "They're coming back."

"What the—" James looked baffled for only a moment before the expression dissolved into seriousness. "Okay, let's go this way."

James turned and headed toward Booker—and the approaching car.

"What are you doing? I don't think we should talk to them. I have a bad feeling about this."

"We're not going to talk to them," James said, marching forward. "They'll have to pass us and turn around again if they want to follow."

He was right; the street was lined on either side with cars parked at meters. The men couldn't even double-park their car without stopping traffic.

"Hey, we want to talk to you!" the man in the passenger seat called out the window as they rolled by.

Emily and James quickened their pace.

"We're not going to hurt you," the man added.

"Oh, well, now I really trust them," Emily muttered.

"Come on, I know how we can lose them."

People looked up from café tables as they raced by. A dog in the doorway of a clothing boutique yipped.

"This way!"

At the next corner, James ran across the street and up a hill inclined so steeply they couldn't see beyond the first block.

"Are you sure about this? I can't run very fast uphill."

"Trust me." James panted. "We have enough of a head start. Keep running, it won't take us long to get there."

Emily wondered where "there" was. Backpack straps gripped and head bowed, she bent forward and charged. She leaned over so far that her backpack was almost parallel to the ground. She felt like a turtle, and she was probably moving as fast as a turtle would run. The backs of her legs throbbed. Her bangs were matted with sweat. She kept her focus on the ground and tried not to think about how far she had to go, or who might be catching up behind her. Her breath came out in gasps. She was afraid she might collapse, but then she looked up and realized they'd reached the top of the hill. A few more steps and the ground was level again. She wanted to lean against the closest building, under the shade of a tree, and catch her breath, but when she looked down the hill, the tan car rounded the corner.

"C'mon." James wheezed. Thankfully he turned down the street they'd intersected, which was level. Their feet pounded the shadows of trees. Leaves crunched underfoot.

"We're almost there," James shouted.

Ahead, a line of cars slowly inched forward—a traffic jam. James reached the corner where the cars were all turning, and he stopped to wait for Emily to catch up.

"We can take the stairs."

"What sta—"

The road curved sharply downhill in a zigzag path, like the track of a sidewinder snake. At the bottom of the block it resumed a straight path that could be followed all the way across the city to the bay and Coit Tower on the other side.

"Welcome to Lombard, crookedest street in America." James panted. "Sorry we don't have time to take a picture."

They took small, fast steps down the hill until they reached the stairs, doing their best to dodge tourists and pedestrians.

A car honked behind them, followed by others like a cacophony of quarreling geese. Emily and James were more than halfway down the stairs when they stopped to look back. Over the hedge and hydrangeas that separated the road from the stairs, they could see the tan car had joined the parade inching down the street. The passenger-side door had been thrown open and one of the men was running toward the stairway. The driver was out of the car, too, slamming his hands on the hood and shouting.

And that was when Emily realized who the men were.

CHAPTER 27

E MILY CLUTCHED the railing. James yelled, "Go, go, go!" but she was transfixed. The charging man bumped into a camera set on a tripod. The camera owner—a burly man twice the size and height of the one chasing Emily and James—steadied his tripod with one hand and grabbed the pursuer with his other. The men argued.

James pounded back up the stairs and shook her arm. "Let's go!"

She spun around, feet moving as fast as possible. At the bottom they turned sharply, almost colliding with a woman painting at an easel, and kept running until they found themselves on a quiet residential street. Distant horns honked—reassuring bleats that the men were still being held back.

"What happened to you back there? Did you get zapped with a freeze ray?"

Emily's heart hammered in her chest. "Didn't you recognize them? Those men?"

"You did?"

"They're from the BART station. The security guards who chased us a few weeks ago."

"That's impossible. There's got to be more important stuff that happens in that BART station than tracking down kids who stick a bumper sticker on something. Finding Mr. Griswold's mugger, for starters."

James was right; it didn't make sense. But Emily was sure those were the BART station men. But how could they have found them? She replayed that Saturday afternoon: She found Mr. Griswold's book, her brother put the Flush bumper sticker on the ticket machine, the men shouted across the station for him to stop—

"Oh no," Emily said in a small voice.

"What?" James eyed her warily.

"They found my Book Scavenger card. With my username on it. I put it next to the trash can when I found Mr. Griswold's book. Remember? They probably went to the Book Scavenger website, looked up 'Surly Wombat,' and saw our school listed on my profile information. Do you think they followed us from Booker?"

"They found your card where you found Mr. Griswold's book?" James repeated.

A car sputtered through the intersection ahead,

causing them both to jump, but it was only a cab. James grabbed her arm and marched down a block to a screen of trees and overgrown bushes that concealed a small park squeezed between two buildings. Emily prickled with wonder at how well James knew his home turf. She would have walked right past and never guessed a swing set, toddler's slide, and teepee play structure were hiding behind the wall of foliage. James crouched in front of the teepee entrance and went inside on his hands and knees.

"Since when is plastering a bumper sticker on something that serious of a crime?" Emily said. Leaf shadows and sunlight dappled the backs of her hands as she crawled after James into the teepee. "Why would they go to so much trouble?"

"Hello?" James play-knocked her skull then shrugged his backpack to the ground. "Don't you get it? Why do you think they looked by the trash can?"

"Because they saw me put my card there."

"Because they saw you remove *the book* from there. They want *The Gold-Bug*, Emily." James worked the zipper of his backpack up and down until finally he said, "I think we should get rid of it." James looked serious and, actually, a little scared.

"We can't be *certain* those men were after the book," Emily said.

James spoke to his backpack instead of her. "I know you want to finish the game, but this feels too risky for a game we're not even sure was completed."

Emily sighed. Not this again. "It was completed, James. I'm positive. The Black Cat clue led some-where—don't you see? If Mr. Griswold hadn't finished his game that would have been a dead end."

James didn't look up from his backpack, so Emily tried a different tactic. "If those men used my Book Scavenger account to track us to Booker, then that's all they know about us. That we go to Booker. They don't have my real name or an address or anything. And I'll post to the forums that I don't have the book anymore. We'll walk home different ways, leave from a different school exit. They won't find us again." She was speaking faster and faster in her effort to persuade James not to give up.

"It's not just those men, Emily. There was that guest user on Book Scavenger who asked about the book. Then we found out Mr. Remora needs it. Now this. It's like the universe is telling us the book isn't ours."

"But it's not theirs!" Emily jabbed her thumb in the direction they'd come from. "If those men want the book that badly, then whatever Mr. Griswold's scav-enger hunt leads to must be valuable. He wouldn't want those men to have it."

"Why don't you give the book back to Mr. Remora?" James asked. "It belongs to him, and then we wouldn't have to worry about it."

James's suggestion was like a slap. "It doesn't belong to him."

"If he said he needed it for his job . . ."

"It's Mr. Griswold's book, and Mr. Griswold's game. He didn't create *The Gold-Bug* so it could sit on a shelf and be ignored. Mr. Griswold would want us to play his game."

"Would you stop saying that?" James's eyes pinched with hurt. "Just admit *you* want to play his game. That's all you've cared about since we found that stupid book. I've helped you with his puzzles, and you keep saying you're going to help me with Mr. Quisling's challenge, but you haven't."

Emily's anger at the suggestion of giving away *The Gold-Bug* melted into embarrassed horror when she realized that James was right. She hadn't helped him with the cipher challenge at all. The teepee filled with the twitters of a bird and distant traffic.

"But you didn't need my help." Her voice sounded so far away. "You broke Maddie's cipher last week, and what you came up with today was amazing—"

"And it got ruined in two seconds. Do you know how long it took me to come up with that Baconian idea? All that time wasted. Just because stupid Maddie stole it when we left our stuff to go to the computer."

The unspoken part of his sentence was "to look up the ISBN number." Mr. Griswold's game again.

James went on, "It might have been a cool cipher idea, but I still didn't win a homework pass, which means I still might lose my bet with Maddie. Anyway, it doesn't matter if I needed your help or not. I *wanted* your help. And you offered it."

"It's just a silly bet."

"Well, then I say *The Gold-Bug* is just a silly game. Does that make it matter any less to you?"

"I didn't mean—"

"It's not a game anymore, Emily."

It wasn't a game to her anymore, either. Those men were scary, but something valuable was at stake. Something that mattered to Mr. Griswold. And that made her determined to get to it first.

"It's important," Emily said.

"No. It's not." Each word pushed James's volume up and up. "I can't believe you care more about a stupid game than being a good friend."

James grabbed his backpack and crawled out of the teepee. His footsteps shushed on the dirt path as he walked away.

CHAPTER 28

EMILY SAT in the teepee for a good long while before she walked back to their building. James was right—she hadn't helped him with Mr. Quisling's challenge. But part of her was upset with him anyway. For her, playing Mr. Griswold's game was the equivalent of making it to the championships if you played a sport. It would be nice if he could see that and understand.

Emily stomped up the stairs to their apartment, dropped her backpack on her bedroom floor, and flopped onto her bed. The reindeer antlers James had given her on her first day of school rested on her windowsill. The photo of them with the antlers stretched over their heads was taped to the wall beside it, along with the newspaper clipping that she'd torn out about Mr. Griswold.

"He's going to be mad at me either way," Emily said to Mr. Griswold's photo across the room. She pushed herself up from her bed and found *The Maltese Falcon* filed in her suitcase of books. As she flipped through it, a memory nudged her. A memory of flipping through the pages of a different *Maltese Falcon* when she and James had visited Bayside Press. There had been a paperback in that pile of alleged games that Jack had showed them. Jack hadn't taken the idea seriously, but what if the person who'd sent it in to Bayside Press had been right? Jack said the person had found it playing Book Scavenger and thought it was Mr. Griswold's next game. Maybe it wasn't his *complete* game, but maybe they'd found one piece. The piece Emily was currently trying to figure out.

She ran down the hall to the front room, planning to do a search for *The Maltese Falcon* on Book Scavenger, but stopped short when she saw Matthew on the family computer. He was editing footage for another one of his stupid Flush fan videos.

"Matthew," Emily said. "I need the computer."

He had the hood up on his sweatshirt. When he didn't respond, she yanked it down, revealing his earbuds plugged in. Matthew turned, yanking out an earbud.

"What's your problem?"

"I need to use the computer."

"Sorry. I'm on it."

"Can't you use your phone?"

"Not for this."

"Matthew, come on. This will be quick."

"Wait your turn."

"Fine." Emily collapsed into the nearby couch. From her vantage point, she could see Matthew putting together another stop-motion video. This new video appeared to be made up of notebook paper drawings that got crumpled and uncrumpled, over and over. And it appeared to be taking him forever to finish. Emily jumped back up.

"I just want to check on one thing," she said. "It will be quick."

"Why don't you ask James? I'm sure he can spare one of his dozen computers for your games." He said *games* as if he'd said *pacifiers* or *tricycles*.

"He doesn't have a dozen computers," Emily snapped. "Anyway, this isn't your computer. It belongs to everyone."

"And I'm using it right now."

Emily was a shaken soda ready to pop. "Why are you always so mean?" she exploded. "You used to be fun. I used to think you were cool!"

Matthew looked at her sideways then back to the screen. "I can take a break." Matthew saved his work. "I'm hungry anyway." Matthew got up from the table and went back to the kitchen.

His low-key response to her outburst only made

her feel worse. Now he could add "dramatic" and "childish" to the list of reasons he didn't want to hang out with her anymore. Emily pushed thoughts of her brother aside and logged onto Book Scavenger. She selected "San Francisco" and then did a title search for *The Maltese Falcon.*

"Whoa." She straightened in her seat. Fifty-two copies hidden in San Francisco alone. She'd never seen anywhere close to that many copies of one book hidden in a city before. But it was a big city. She did a search for *Harry Potter and the Sorcerer's Stone* to compare against a typically popular book for hiding. Nine copies. There was definitely something going on with *The Maltese Falcon.*

She went back to those search results and looked under the User column. That showed the name of who had hidden the book, and again Emily was surprised. Three copies were hidden by different people, but the other forty-nine were all hidden by the same person. And not just any Book Scavenger player: Raven.

Emily clicked the message icon and typed "Raven" into the "To" field.

SURLY WOMBAT: Who are you?

RAVEN: I do not have the information you seek.

"Yeah, yeah," Emily said.

SURLY WOMBAT: Are you running Mr. Griswold's game?

RAVEN: I do not have the information you seek.

"Okay, fine. Be coy," Emily muttered. She looked at the list of hidden *Maltese Falcon*s. All of Raven's copies were hidden the week before Emily moved to San Francisco. She already knew from the one turned in to Bayside Press that there was a message of some sort inside—something that made the person who had turned it in think it was Mr. Griswold's game. Finding one of these copies had to be the next step. She looked at the San Francisco map on the Book Scavenger site and narrowed the choices to only show Raven's hidden books, since the forty-nine *Maltese Falcon*s were the only books Raven had hidden.

Every hidden book was marked with a star on the map, and the closest star to where they lived was in an area called Nob Hill. Out of habit, she almost declared the book so she could get double points, but—thinking of Babbage poaching her books—she pulled her finger back from the mouse right before she clicked. It wasn't like there weren't forty-eight more options to find if she declared this one and someone got to it before her, but Emily didn't want to run the risk of drawing someone's attention to it. Or alerting anyone that she was interested in it, she realized, thinking about those men who must know she's Surly Wombat.

She opened the clue without declaring the book, and it read: *Where he finished writing this.*

"Okay," Emily muttered to herself and opened a new web browser. She did an Internet search for "Dashiell Hammett" and "Maltese Falcon." There were almost two hundred thousand results. The top results were mostly about a movie that had been made of the book. She was about to search with different keywords when she saw a link to a map of sites referenced in *The Maltese Falcon* as well as places Dashiell Hammett had lived. She clicked on that. There were only two noted locations in the Nob Hill area. She hovered over one, and a bubble popped up that said, *Dashiell Hammett lived at 1155 Leavenworth Street when he completed the final draft of* The Maltese Falcon.

She'd figured it out! That was where she had to go. Emily did a victory spin in the computer chair.

She had to tell James. Sure, he was mad, but he'd be interested to know *The Maltese Falcon* clue led somewhere and to hear about Raven's role in the game. He'd probably even want to go with her.

Emily flipped to a clean sheet of notebook paper and, in their secret code, wrote, *Raven hid forty-nine copies of* Maltese Falcon *around San Francisco. One is at 1155 Leavenworth. Next clue!* She went to her room, slid open the window, dropped the paper in the sand pail, and raised the bucket. She stood on a chair and tapped their secret knock on the ceiling with the yardstick/tennis ball contraption. And then she waited. There were no footsteps above, no sliding of James's window. Emily tried the knock again.

Maybe he wasn't in his room. She lowered the pail back down, grabbed the note, ran down her stairs and out the front door to their building's landing, and pounded on the Lees' door. After a few seconds without any noise on the other side, she pounded again and then rang the doorbell. Two locks clicked, a dead bolt slid, and the older Ms. Lee opened the door. Even though James's grandmother was barely taller than Emily and swam in one of James's old Angry Birds shirts, she was still quite intimidating.

"Is your apartment on fire?" she asked.

"Um, no, I . . ."

"Don't knock so loud unless the apartment is on fire. I am not hard of hearing."

"Yes, ma'am," Emily said meekly.

James's grandmother gripped a wooden spoon in one hand and pursed her lips, waiting. For a moment, Emily couldn't remember why she was there.

"I was doing research for a . . . book report and found something I thought James would be interested in. Is he here?"

"One moment," Ms. Lee said. Up the staircase she called, "James! Emily is here."

Emily had expected James to appear, but instead she heard his voice reply in Chinese.

Ms. Lee turned back to Emily, her face softened

with an apologetic smile. "He's in the middle of a school project and can't be interrupted. Perhaps later? Or I could show him your research."

Ms. Lee held out her spoon-free hand.

"That's okay," Emily said, backing away. She knew James was mad, but he wouldn't even talk to her?

She had left her own front door wide open and walked back through, closing it softly behind her. When she reached the top of her stairs, she found her brother skulking about in the hallway and guessed he might have overheard her conversation with Ms. Lee. She ignored him and was about to enter her bedroom when Matthew said, "Phlegmily. I mean Emily."

"What?" She didn't bother turning around.

"I have some free time this week. If you want someone to go book scavenging with."

Emily waited a beat, expecting a punch line or her brother to start laughing and take his words back. When she didn't hear anything, she finally turned. Matthew scratched at the lines he'd shaved into his head and appeared to be studying the baseboards. He glanced up at her once, maybe to check if she was still there.

"Okay," Emily said. "Thanks."

CHAPTER 29

THE DAY AFTER her fight with James was the first time in the weeks since starting Booker that Emily felt lost in the big school. Not lost in the can't-find-my-classroom sense, but in the where-do-I-fit-in sense. With every school she'd attended in the past, she'd always started with an identity that pretty much saw her through to the end, whether it was "loner girl with her nose in a book" in New Mexico and Colorado, or "Matthew's little sister" before that. She wasn't always wild about the identity, but it was comfortable to have one and to feel like you knew the role you were supposed to play. At Booker she'd started from day one as James's friend. She didn't know what role to play anymore.

At lunch, it hadn't seemed right to hang out in the library without James, so she went to the cafeteria, which was about as loud as a marching band practicing in a bathroom. She saw Vivian, the girl from her English and social studies classes who'd first introduced herself as their class president. But Vivian was involved in a conversation with the other girls at her table and didn't look her way. Emily continued outside.

Booker had an enormous blacktop where they had recess and PE and lunch. Emily found a stretch along the school building that was empty (other than some pushy seagulls) and leaned against the wall, pulling out *The Maltese Falcon* and her bag lunch. *Hello, loner girl with her nose in a book. Haven't seen you in a while*, she thought.

In Mr. Quisling's class, James and Emily sat turned away from each other. Maddie took one look at them and said, "Uh-oh, things look tense for the clubhouse gang." She slid into the seat behind James. "Did somebody reveal the secret password to a nonmember?"

"Shut up, Maddie," James muttered. He was methodically solving another of his logic puzzles and didn't look up. Emily pretended to be too absorbed in doodling a maze onto the margin of her notebook to have paid any attention.

At the start of class, James bent over his backpack and pulled out a handful of long, skinny strips of paper. "I brought a makeup cipher for yesterday," he announced to Mr. Quisling.

Emily ducked her head to look at Maddie and was

pleased to see her gaping. She saw Emily looking at her and snapped her mouth shut. Her eyes were wide and blinking, and it occurred to Emily that Maddie might actually be nervous about losing her bet.

"Did you?" Mr. Quisling accepted the bouquet of strips, extending one to look at the letters written on it. "Interesting, Mr. Lee." Mr. Quisling gave an approving nod and distributed James's cipher to the class.

Emily looked hers over. It was unlike anything that had been turned in for the challenge so far, and unlike anything she and James had talked about cipher-wise. The strip read:

P
I

X
L

D
F

T
C

W
L

S

Emily wondered why the cipher was vertical instead of horizontal. And why were there five sets of two letters, evenly spaced, and then one letter at the bottom? Was the message five different two-letter words and then one one-letter word? Were there even five different two-letter words that could be used to make up a message? She didn't know how to start decoding this—not that she wanted to solve it or would turn in her solution if she figured it out. They might not be talking, but she still wanted James to win his bet with Maddie.

After school, just to be on the safe side with those men, Emily left through a different door from the main one they had walked out of yesterday. She took a different route, too, maybe to avoid running into James as much as to avoid those men if they were to come back. She didn't actually think they would come back, because she'd done something brilliant she was rather proud of. On Book Scavenger, she listed *The Gold-Bug* as hidden in the "Outer Sunset." She'd picked that neighborhood off a map because it looked about as far from their school as you could get without leaving the city. For the clue, she looked up that old language Maddie had used for the cipher challenge—Ogham—and used it to write out directions to an imaginary bench in a park. If the men were looking for *The Gold-Bug* as James suspected they were, and they were paying attention to what she did on Book Scavenger, then this would lead them on a bit of a wild-goose chase. She just wished James would talk to her so she could tell him they didn't have anything to worry about now.

When Emily walked in the front room of their apartment, she was kind of surprised to see Matthew sprawled on the couch, waiting for her. Even though he had said he'd go book hunting with her after school, she'd half-expected he would bail on her.

Matthew jumped up. "All right, let's go. I mapped out the address: 1155 Leavenworth, right?" He held up his phone for Emily to confirm.

"You remembered," Emily said.

Matthew tugged her ponytail as he passed by and headed down the stairs. "Of course, Phlegmily," he said.

"Lead the way, Barf-ew," she replied, but she was smiling as she followed her brother out their front door.

On the bus ride to Leavenworth Street, Emily wondered what James was doing. Probably studying in his room or hunched over his cipher books or logic puzzles with Steve defying gravity, like a diving board of hair sticking off his head. As if he'd been reading her mind, Matthew pulled out his earbuds and asked, "So what happened with James? Why didn't he do this with you?"

Emily shrugged. They passed a lady unloading grocery bags from the trunk of a car parked on the sidewalk.

Matthew was silent a moment longer then said, "He'll get over it, whatever it is. Don't worry."

"Easy for you to say," Emily said, still looking out the window. "You make a zillion friends every time we move. It's why you love moving so much."

Matthew snorted. "I don't love moving. If you asked me a few years ago, I would have rather bleached my hair and burned off my eyebrows again."

Giggles bubbled up at the memory, and Emily pressed her fingers to her lips to stifle them. She remembered her brother tearing out of a bathroom with a towel over his face shrieking, "It burns! It burns!" It wasn't funny at the time, but it was a *little* funny now that everything had worked out okay. Emily couldn't imagine there'd been a time he'd rather go through *that* again than move.

"Go ahead, laugh at my expense," Matthew said, but he was smirking, too. "This is how our life is. It can be cool in a lot of ways, you have to admit." Matthew waved a hand as if their bus, with the lone man gripping an oxygen tank and the Sharpie-scribbled seats, was what constituted his "cool." "But I used to hate moving."

"You really hated it?"

"Before we moved from Connecticut. Remember?"

Emily remembered Connecticut, but she didn't remember Matthew being upset about moving.

"I had just started a band with Ollie and his

232

brother. I didn't want to leave and start over somewhere new again. I even ran away, I was so mad."

"You ran away?"

"Not the real kind. But I went to Ollie's house and
told his mom I had permission to sleep over when I
didn't. Mom and Dad figured it out."

"Were they mad?"

"No. But you were."

"Me?" As hard as she tried, she had no memory of
any of this.

"You loved moving back then. Remember you
made us do the family map?"

Of course she remembered that. The family map
had hung in every kitchen since they'd made it. *The
Cranes Conquer America* was written at the top in
Emily's eight-year-old scrawl, back when she was into
putting smiley faces inside her *e*'s, *a*'s, and *o*'s. Metallic
stars dotted the cities where they'd lived.

"You got it in your head we could have an elk for a
pet when we moved to Colorado."

"I was going to name him Monty," Emily said.
She'd spent a lot of time drawing pictures of her and
Monty and the adventures they'd have in Colorado.

"I think I'd gotten Mom and Dad seriously recon-
sidering moving, and you thought I was ruining the
fun. That's when Mom and Dad let me get a phone to
keep in touch with my friends. And it turned out
Colorado was a cool place to live, although you never

got your pet elk, so you might not agree. What I finally figured out with all our moving is you miss out on stuff whether you stay or go. So I decided to just go with it. Embrace how we live."

There was a Jack Kerouac quote their dad loved to repeat when the family deliberated weekend plans. Emily said it out loud, "'What's in store for me in the direction I don't take?'"

"Exactly," Matthew said and inserted his earbuds.

If they'd stayed in New Mexico or Colorado or Connecticut or any of the other states, she never would have met James or ridden a cable car or found Mr. Griswold's book. Even though they'd only just moved to California and she and James weren't talking, she wouldn't trade these last few weeks away. Matthew was right—you missed out on stuff either way. Or you gained stuff, depending on your perspective.

CHAPTER 30

EMILY AND MATTHEW stood on the sheltered porch of 1155 Leavenworth. It was a corner building with a white-arched entry framed with black lanterns. The first story was beige brick, and the second and third stories were yellow, with the fire escapes painted to match.

"Do we go in?" Matthew asked.

"I'm not sure," Emily said. "All the clue said was, *where he finished writing this book.* His actual apartment belongs to someone else now, I'm sure, so I doubt we're supposed to knock on their door and ask if we can look around."

"Unless they're the ones who hid this book on Book Scavenger."

"Uh, yeah." Even though her brother had been making a nice effort since yesterday afternoon, she still hadn't confided in him about Mr. Griswold's game. Doing that would make it feel too much like she was replacing James, and she didn't want that. If she could have it her way, James would be here with them, too.

Matthew tried the front door, but it was locked. There was a call box to ring individual apartments to ask someone to unlock the door for you.

"He wouldn't have hidden it inside," Emily murmured, turning on the front stoop to survey the area. "Let's walk around the building."

Because the buildings were plunked right next to each other, they couldn't actually walk *around* the building. But they walked back and forth multiple times along the Leavenworth side and the Sacramento side, studying every nook and cranny for a spot where you could hide a book. There were windows just above the sidewalk at foot level, and more at head level, too. But Emily couldn't see any way they might conceal a book. There were no planter boxes or benches tucked next to the building, and the entry alcove was tidy and clear of anything booklike. Emily studied a fire escape ladder.

"Should I climb it?" Matthew asked.

"You can't reach up there." The bottom of the fire escape stopped at least a couple of feet above the front entry arch.

"Sure I can." Matthew proceeded to jump

repeatedly, not even coming close to reaching the fire escape, but he kept jumping nonetheless.

Emily turned and looked at the two trees in front of the building. Something caught her eye perched high amid the leaves. A large black bird peered down at them.

"Oh, spooky! Matthew, look—that bird is staring at us."

Matthew stopped hopping and looked up at the tree. They had a staring contest with the bird for a minute before Matthew said, "He sure is still. Do birds sleep with their eyes open? Hey, Bird!"

"Matthew!" Emily laughed, which only encouraged her brother.

"Yeah you, Bird! I'm talking to you!"

Still no reaction from the bird.

"That is really weird," Emily said.

"What kind of bird are you anyway, Bird?" Matthew hollered. "Are you a crow? Or maybe a—"

"Raven!" Emily realized. "That's it! That's the book I'm hunting!"

"You're a book, Bird?" Matthew hollered. "That's not confusing at all!"

"You wanted to climb something." Emily indicated the tree with a flourish. "May I interest you in this climbing tree?"

The trunk of the tree split in four directions, each branch thicker than both of Emily's legs put together. Her brother leaped into the palm of the branches and picked and pulled his way up to the fake raven. After he climbed back down and jumped to the sidewalk, he handed the bird to Emily. It was a wooden box designed to look like a raven. Emily popped off the front, revealing a compartment just big enough to hold a paperback book, which is where *The Maltese Falcon* sat.

"This is so cool!" Emily exclaimed. She put the lid back on the raven and turned the box around to inspect it.

"Now that's a scavenger who went all out. Must be Mr. Money Bags to be able to give away a box like that."

Emily gave the raven an affectionate pat. "Must be."

On the bus ride home, Emily flipped through *The Maltese Falcon*. It looked like an average paperback. Nothing written in it. Nothing hidden in it. It had all the publisher and ISBN and copyright info where it normally should be, so this was an actual published version, not a handcrafted one like Mr. Griswold's edition of *The Gold-Bug*.

Emily flipped back to the inside cover where a Book Scavenger tracking label had been placed. She had flipped past it the first time, assuming it had the registration number listed as was typical. But now she saw it did not. Instead of a tracking number there were six symbols:

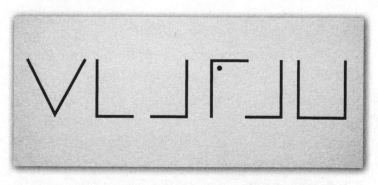

Emily pulled her notebook out of her backpack and the pencil from her ponytail and copied the symbols down. She began playing around with different possibilities for how to solve the puzzle—she rearranged their order; she drew them combined with one another like putting together a jigsaw puzzle. There were only six symbols, so was it a six-letter word? Or did each symbol represent a word, making it a six-word sentence? At one point she felt her brother studying her work. She looked over and he pulled out an earbud.

"Just so you know, I don't think your book scavenging is stupid."

Emily rolled her eyes.

"I don't!" Matthew insisted. "Not any more stupid than you think my Flush videos are. It was fun when we used to go book scavenging. Today was fun, too. I just like other stuff more now, so when I have a choice, I'm going to choose the other stuff."

"I don't expect you to choose Book Scavenger or doing anything with me," Emily said quietly. "But you don't have to be so mean about it."

James's words came back to Emily from their fight. She'd said Mr. Quisling's challenge was silly, and he'd shot back by calling Mr. Griswold's game the same and then asked her how that made her feel. Her brother talking about prioritizing his own interests over hers wasn't that different from her prioritizing Mr. Griswold's game over the cipher challenge. It made her feel sick to think she might have been dismissing James, a new friend she wanted to impress, the same way she'd felt her brother had been dismissing her.

"Matthew?" Her brother was about to put his earbuds back in, but he waited. "I don't think Flush is stupid, either."

"You better not." Matthew mock punched her arm. "They're not just great musicians, they're my buds."

"Oh, trust me. I know."

CHAPTER 31

AFTER EMILY and Matthew returned home, she spent over an hour trying to decode the odd little symbols on the flyer with no luck. The message was so short, using frequency analysis didn't amount to much help. Only the ⌐ symbol was repeated, but that could still be any letter. Even if she tried replacing it with a commonly used letter, she had no way of knowing if it was the right one, and it was incredibly difficult to fill in the other symbols in a way that made an actual word. Like if she used *E* for the duplicate symbol:

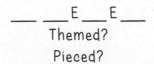
Themed?
Pieced?

Those were both words, but how would she know

which one was the *right* word, if either one was at all? Or if she used T:

$$\underline{\quad}\ \underline{\quad}\ T\ \underline{\quad}\ T\ \underline{\quad}$$

Rotate?

Entote?

Was that even a word?

Astute?

Or A:

$$\underline{\quad}\ \underline{\quad}\ A\ \underline{\quad}\ A\ \underline{\quad}$$

Cravat?

She had to look that one up to make sure it was an actual word.

Graval? Weasal?

Those were almost words, but they weren't spelled right.

She wadded up her paper and threw it across the room, where it bounced off the reindeer antlers that were now sitting next to the raven box.

"Yeah, I'd rather be working with him on this, too," she snapped at the antlers.

How had she ever enjoyed being a solo book hunter before? It was so... quiet and laughless working alone.

James's floorboards had creaked earlier, so she

knew he was home, but there was no way she'd ask for his help now. She had tried getting a hint from Raven on Book Scavenger, but there was no response. (Which was especially annoying because Raven's "online" light was green, so she was obviously ignoring her.) The only other cipher expert she could think of besides James was Mr. Quisling, and there was no way she would ask for his help, either. *Interesting form of note-taking, Ms. Crane.* He would probably dismiss her with some admonishment to study more and play less.

"Oh!" A bolt of inspiration struck. Emily dug through her backpack, gently laying her notebook and *The Gold-Bug* aside, then tossed out various scraps of paper until she found the bent calling card of that poacher who stole her book at the Ferry Building weeks ago.

Babbage. That was the name. She remembered Booker had been listed on the profile, too, so they were schoolmates. Not that that meant much, since it was such a big school. She probably had a stronger famil-iarity with the window cat she passed on her way there than she did with 99 percent of the kids at Booker. She would send Babbage a message and ask if he or she wanted to meet up at school to talk ciphers. Maybe she should even mention this new puzzle. Puzzle people usually couldn't resist at least looking at a new one, if not attempting to solve it. Fingers crossed Babbage would reply to her message.

On Wednesday at school she did her best to avoid James. She didn't need him anyway—she'd quickly formed a new clique with the seagulls who hovered near her at lunchtime. She flicked a piece of bread to a seagull she'd begun to call Bob, because of the way he moved his head up and down while he watched her eat.

"Tomorrow's Halloween, Bob," she said.

Bob twisted his head sideways and stabbed his beak at the piece of bread.

"Do the kids normally dress up here, Bob?"

Bob nodded.

"I don't know if you're trustworthy, Bob. I get the feeling you'd say anything for more food." She tossed another bit of crust his way.

There had been no word from Babbage the day before, so when she got home she went straight for the computer to check her messages again. Her mom was updating their *50 Homes in 50 States* blog with photos from the Golden Gate Park concert. Emily leaned over her shoulder.

"Can I check my messages real quick?" she asked.

"No, but you can check them quickly," her mom replied. "I love this one." The image she was resizing was shot through a crowd to focus on Emily perched on the fountain with her hands pressed flat next to her thighs. Her head was turned toward the de Young Museum, so all you saw was her long ponytail. Orange lights glowed in the trees. The crowd was blurry and colorful around her—someone's tutu and butterfly wings, a person with a unicorn head, Benjamin Franklin, and a group of people with neon-colored wigs. It was like looking down a bizarro rabbit hole to a hoodie-and-jeans-wearing Alice.

Her mom saved her work and stood up, patting Emily's cheek. "All yours," she said.

Emily logged into Book Scavenger, and a new-message notification greeted her. Babbage had replied! The message read: *I would be willing to meet with you tomorrow morning before school. I have first period in Room 40. We can talk there.*

Hearing back from Babbage gave her a lift, so she decided to try her luck again with Raven, who was, of course, online. She was beginning to suspect Raven must be an adult who worked at a computer all day, because she always seemed to be there.

SURLY WOMBAT: Hi, Raven. I found another clue.

RAVEN: I can't help you with that.

Emily sighed. Raven was such a stickler with the whole "ask in the form of a question" rule.

SURLY WOMBAT: Do you have a hint for solving the cipher in *The Maltese Falcon?*

RAVEN: Charlie, Sally, Lucy.

"What kind of hint is that?" Emily muttered. Beggars can't be choosers, though. She did individual searches for Book Scavenger players named Charlie, Sally, and Lucy, but there were hundreds of results. She'd have to think on this hint a bit more.

That night, in anticipation of meeting Babbage, she double-checked her bag for school, making sure she didn't forget *The Maltese Falcon*. She'd taken to always carrying *The Gold-Bug* and the Poe collection of stories with her, too, but because her backpack was so bulky she almost removed them. The two Poe books were the smallest ones and barely added to the bulk, so she left them in. Anyway, what if she and Babbage really hit it off talking about ciphers? She might want to tell him or her about Griswold's game, or at least show the original hidden message and how it worked. You just never knew, so it was better to be prepared.

Emily also squared away an idea for a Halloween costume, if you could call it a *costume*. She wanted something low-key so she could walk that line of not standing out in an embarrassing way if nobody actually dressed up, but also not looking like a stick in the mud if everyone did. She used plain white labels and cut out dots and dashes for Morse code and then stuck them on a black shirt like this:

—··· ——— ———

For the first time since she and James stopped talking, she was kind of excited for school tomorrow.

Thursday morning, Halloween, Emily got to school extra early. The hallways were nearly empty. Two teachers Emily didn't know stopped talking as she walked by. One dressed in a striped red shirt, matching knit hat, and round black glasses raised his hand in greeting, and the woman dressed as a mad scientist added, "Morning!"

Emily rounded a corner, passing the papier-mâché witch hats decorated by sixth graders that lined the windows of the library. She studied every student in the halls, wondering if one might be Babbage. A boy wearing a panda hat and a Giants jersey, two girls with cat-ear headbands and their faces painted with whiskers.

Room 40 was where she and James had social studies with Mr. Quisling, so she shouldn't have been surprised when she stepped inside to see him there, grading papers, but she was.

"Oh!" Emily stepped backward. "I'm supposed to meet a student here."

Mr. Quisling set down his pen. He hadn't dressed up for the holiday. "Surly Wombat?"

For a moment she thought he was asking if that

was the student she was meeting. Finally, she under-stood he was asking if *she* was Surly Wombat.

"You . . . *you're* Babbage?"

She knew adults played Book Scavenger, but she didn't think that meant teachers.

"At your service." His eyes flicked down to her T-shirt then back up. He cracked a smile. "Boo to you, too," he said.

Emily's face warmed. "I wasn't sure if kids dressed up for Halloween or not . . ."

Mr. Quisling nodded. "Clever. Subtle. I like it. So, you have a question about a cipher?" His eyes narrowed. "This isn't one of the submissions for class, is it?"

"No, no, no," Emily said. "It's not for school. It's just . . . something I was working on in my free time."

This seemed to satisfy Mr. Quisling. "Let's take a look."

Emily set her backpack on his desk and unzipped it to pull out her notebook. Before she laid a hand inside, Mr. Quisling cleared his throat.

"That isn't the book I think it is, I hope."

Oh *why* didn't she think before opening her back-pack? *The Gold-Bug* sat prominently on top of her note-book. She'd completely forgotten she'd told Mr. Quisling she'd hidden it through Book Scavenger and would try to retrieve it. As casually as possible, she shifted the book deeper into her backpack while she removed her notebook.

"I've already seen it. There's no use trying to hide it," Mr. Quisling said. "It will be much worse if you lie to me. You can trust me on that."

Reluctantly Emily said, "It . . . it is that Poe book. I *am* giving it back. Soon."

Mr. Quisling's mouth formed a thin, tight line. He wiggled his jaw as if he were grinding something between his teeth. His next words came out very slowly.

"You did hear me say someone's job was on the line for that book? A man could be fired if he doesn't have it."

"Yes," Emily said. She couldn't meet Mr. Quisling's gaze. From the moment she'd met Mr. Quisling, she'd been on his bad side. He must have a very different idea of the kind of person she actually was.

"Let me get this straight. You would rather a man lose his job so you can keep a book?"

With every word Mr. Quisling said, Emily shrank an inch.

"I wasn't going to keep—"

Mr. Quisling held up a hand to stop her and then turned it palm up.

"Give me the book."

She had to make him understand. "Mr. Quisling, it's not what you think." Before Mr. Quisling cut her off, she rushed on. "It's Mr. Griswold's next game. And I can prove it."

CHAPTER

32

MR. QUISLING dropped his hand to his desk and didn't say anything. Emily wasn't sure if that meant he was surprised or not. Mr. Quisling's expressions were like a closet of pressed gray suits. All pulled together, all professional, all respectable. But it was hard to tell from day to day if the gray suit he wore was the same or different from the one he wore before.

She flipped open *The Gold-Bug* to the Bayside Press symbol that had a raven in place of the seagull.

"That was my first clue," she said. "And then I found a secret message in the story. Mr. Griswold made this book with typos intentionally left inside. If you find the typos and list all the correct letters in one line, it spells the first sentence of another Edgar Allan Poe story."

Mr. Quisling picked the book up and flipped

through it as Emily recounted the rest of the scavenger hunt so far.

"And now I'm stumped with the clue I found in *The Maltese Falcon*. That's what I thought you could help me with." She reached for her backpack to grab the book, but Mr. Quisling held up a hand.

"I don't want to see it, Emily."

"But you could help me figure it out. We could work on the game together, and once we get to the end, *then* we could give the book back. I've been planning to give it back all along."

"If I look at your newly found puzzle, I am sure I *will* want to solve it. Which is why I don't want to see it." Mr. Quisling sighed. "I've met him, you know. Mr. Griswold." He patted *The Gold-Bug*.

"Then you should understand better than anyone," Emily pleaded. "People are saying he might . . ." Emily ducked her head, focusing on Mr. Quisling's desk. She couldn't say the words. She had stopped checking for updates on how Mr. Griswold was doing because she was afraid the news would be bad. "He would want his game to be played. He would want me to finish it."

Emily didn't look up, afraid Mr. Quisling wouldn't get it, just as James didn't.

"You're probably right, Emily," Mr. Quisling said. "And it's fascinating to learn about his game and everything you've figured out already. I'm glad you shared it with me, but that doesn't change the fact that we need to return this book."

Emily couldn't do anything but blink at Mr. Quisling. How could he want to return the book after everything she'd just told him? How could he resist not knowing what lay at the end of Mr. Griswold's game? She almost felt tricked.

"But why?" she finally managed to say. "I know who this book collector is—Mr. Remora. I've met him."

Mr. Quisling raised an eyebrow, which might be the closest he ever came to looking shocked.

"James and I took a tour of Bayside Press," Emily said by way of explanation. Now both of Mr. Quisling's eyebrows went up. "We ended up getting to go in Mr. Griswold's office. Mr. Remora was in there when he wasn't supposed to be. Later, we overheard him doing business at Hollister's bookstore, and he just wasn't very nice."

"You might have caught him on a bad day," Mr. Quisling said. "You walk into dangerous territory when you make judgments against a person based on limited interaction."

Emily couldn't believe Mr. Quisling was trusting the word of a man he didn't even know over hers. "Mr. Remora says he needs this book back for his job, but Mr. Griswold had already hidden it for his game. It wasn't supposed to be in Mr. Griswold's personal collection when I found it, so why would Mr. Remora be saying it should be?"

"Do you *know* it wasn't supposed to be in his personal collection when you found it? Do you have confirmation of that? Or are you making an assumption?"

"I don't have any proof, but—"

"Did this Mr. Remora lie about Mr. Griswold being his client?"

Emily tugged on her backpack zipper. "No."

"Did he lie about *The Gold-Bug* belonging to his client?"

"No."

"So you haven't actually caught him in a lie. What it sounds like you really want is a reason to keep the book for yourself, if only for a while. I'm sorry, Emily. I really am. I understand where you're coming from, but some things are more important than games. The possibility that a man genuinely needs this book for his own job security trumps any game, no matter how intriguing. Are we clear on this, or do I need to call your parents?"

Emily swallowed. "We're clear."

Mr. Quisling put *The Gold-Bug* in his top drawer and returned to his grading. Their meeting was over and on top of everything else, she hadn't even gotten help with the *Maltese Falcon* cipher. Emily left his room fighting back tears.

The hallway had filled with an assortment of costumed kids now that the first-period bell was about to ring. Emily bumped against a skeleton's backpack. "Sorry," she muttered. She turned corner after corner until she was in front of her locker. She spun the dial and tugged the door open, ducking her head inside under the pretext of sorting things into and out of her backpack. She wiped her nose and stared at the dark recess where *The Gold-Bug* had been.

Later that day, Emily averted her eyes from Mr. Quisling when she walked into social studies. He stood at the head of the classroom as usual, arms crossed and occasionally nodding at students.

"Good afternoon, Emily," he said as she walked past. She kept her head down but bent her mouth into a smile for politeness' sake.

She took her seat next to James, averting her eyes from him, too. She caught him looking at her when she pulled her binder from her backpack. Maybe it was her imagination, or maybe it was the Cookie Monster hooded sweatshirt he wore for Halloween, but she could have sworn he looked worried before he turned his attention back to his logic puzzles.

She had been using the back exit ever since those men chased her and James, but today that meant going through the crowds waiting for the haunted house/cafeteria. She wasn't in the mood for any of that, and it had been four days since they'd seen those men. She doubted they were even still looking for her, especially since she'd posted to Book Scavenger that she didn't have the book. Which, ironically, Emily realized was now true. So what did it even matter anyway?

She craved a familiar face and decided to brave

her regular route and stop by Hollister's. Before she pushed through her school's main entrance doors, Emily studied the idling vehicles in front. No sign of the old tan car.

The afternoon was hot and the sun intense as she walked up the street. Emily shielded her eyes, but still the glaring rays managed to bend their way around her hand, dulling her sight. A metallic pounding grew louder as Emily approached Hollister's. She stepped over a thick hose draped across the sidewalk that ran from a truck parked at the curb to the inside of the building next to Hollister's. The hose appeared to be connected to whatever was making the drilling noise inside.

Hollister's door was propped open.

"Emily-Who-Just-Moved-Here!" Hollister shouted over the drilling when she entered. He stood at his counter, wearing purple robes and a wizard hat topping off his dreads. He stepped out to close the shop door, which didn't totally silence the noise but did make it bearable. "Today's been a game of Pick Your Poison," Hollister said. "Suffer through that racket or work in an oven. That fan doesn't really cut it on a day like today." Hollister indicated a rotating fan that rattled in the corner. He returned to the book he'd been wrapping in brown paper. "No sidekick today?"

"James had other plans." Emily shifted words around the magnetic poetry tray on his counter. *Broken. Cloud.*

"Ah. So what's new with you? You still enjoying

Poe?" *Poe*. Mr. Quisling was probably talking to Mr. Remora on the phone at that very second to let him know Emily had returned *The Gold-Bug*.

To Hollister she said, "I carry the Poe book you gave me everywhere."

Hollister pulled a piece of twine from a spindle attached to his counter while Emily rearranged more magnetic words. *Hard. Fool. Magic*. He held the paper folded around his book with one hand and the twine in the other and looked from the pair of scissors lying near the book to the twine and then to Emily. "You mind?" he asked, nodding toward the twine.

"Oh. Sure." Emily picked up the scissors and leaned across the counter to clip the twine. She watched him wind it around the wrapped book and tie a neat knot.

"Presentation always makes a difference, don't you think?" He held the book up to Emily, twisting it to show all sides.

"You're really good at it," Emily said, thinking of the book-sculpture Bayside Press emblem he'd taken down about a week ago to make his window display Halloween-themed.

Hollister pulled out a notepad from the shelf under his counter and flipped through the pages until he found the one he was looking for. He held the notepad out. "Can't read my own writing."

Emily leaned forward. "It looks like 2634 Octopus to me," she read.

"Probably Octavia Street." Hollister jotted down the address on a sticky note and placed it on the wrapped book.

"Is that for Mr. Remora?" The question came with the memory of Hollister offering to deliver him a book the last time they were both in the bookstore. As soon as she asked the question, Emily realized she already knew the answer. Mr. Remora had complained to Hollister about living on Fillmore Street near the Fillmore, which stuck in Emily's brain thanks to her brother. She even almost remembered his address—it was something repetitive with sevens, like 1717 or 7171 or 7711.

Hollister studied her for a moment, his one tired eyelid dipping down as it always did. "How do you know Mr. Remora?"

Emily reminded him of that day. "You told us he's a rare-book specialist and Mr. Griswold is one of his clients."

"I remember now. Indeed, I did. And no, this isn't for him."

An idea occurred to Emily. It wasn't a well-thought-out idea, and it probably wasn't a *good* idea, but Emily asked anyway. "Do you need help delivering your books? I could take that one you just wrapped, and if you have Mr. Remora's book ready, I could deliver that, too. . . ." And then maybe when she delivered Mr. Remora's book, she could tell him she was the student who had found *The Gold-Bug* and ask if she could borrow it back for a short period of time.

Hollister adjusted his wizard hat. "Isn't that kind of you. Thank you, doll. But no, I cannot take you up on that offer, I'm afraid. Too young to be my employee for one. Even if that weren't the case, I wouldn't feel comfortable sending you around the city on your own to run my errands. Maybe if it was you and James together, but even then . . ." Hollister shook his head, dreadlocks swishing across his purple robes.

Hollister watched her push magnetic words. *Salt. Heart. Wake.*

"You know," he said. "I appreciate my customers. And many of them are fine, fine people. But not all book people are good people. Don't mistake shared interests with shared ethics." He tapped his pointy cap. "There's some wizardly wisdom for you today."

Hollister stepped away from the counter and fiddled with books on a nearby shelf, straightening some, pulling a title off one shelf and moving it to the row below. His words made Emily think about Hollister's former friendship with Mr. Griswold. Both were book people. Both seemed like good people. And despite not having been friends for the past thirty years, Hollister had cared enough to dedicate his window display to Mr. Griswold in a time of need.

"Hollister? Have you talked to Mr. Griswold since he's been in the hospital?"

If her question surprised him, Hollister didn't show it. "I don't believe he's in a conversational state," is all he said, but the lines of his face sagged.

"There are people on the Book Scavenger website gossiping about him," Emily said. "They don't think he's going to survive his attack." Emily wasn't sure if that was something she should have said, but she'd been carrying that worry in the back of her mind, and voicing it to someone who knew Garrison Griswold helped. "I don't like thinking about that," she said.

Hollister sighed. "Negativity has never been a friend to anyone."

"What was he like when you two were friends?" she asked.

He finished his fussing and surveyed his store, almost like he was scanning the room for what task he could do next. Emily thought maybe he hadn't heard her question or was just going to ignore it because he didn't want to talk about Mr. Griswold. But then he said, "Gary was young. Very creative. Ambitious. We idolized the Beats." He looked to her, some of his dreadlocks swinging over his shoulder. "You know the Beats?"

"My dad's a huge fan of Jack Kerouac."

"Good taste, good taste." Hollister nodded, and his wizard cap skewed to an angle. "The person Gary and I looked up to most was Lawrence Ferlinghetti. When we opened this bookshop, we fancied ourselves like

Lawrence Ferlinghetti and Peter Martin when they started City Lights."

"We? This bookstore used to be Mr. Griswold's, too?" She envisioned Mr. Griswold walking out from the back with a box of books to shelve, greeting customers as the chimes signaled their entrance. Was it possible to feel nostalgic for something you never experienced?

"This was before Bayside Press, of course. We were young. Too young to be a part of the Beat movement, but old enough to be influenced by it. But—also like Lawrence Ferlinghetti and Peter Martin—our partnership eventually severed. Ours less amicably, I'm afraid."

"Why?"

"Similar interests, different priorities. That may not make sense, how two people can be passionate about the same things and still find room for disagreement, but it happens."

"No, that actually makes a lot of sense," Emily said, thinking of her fight with James.

"Gary always had a grand plan, a way to make things bigger. My vision was to keep the bookstore small, a community place. Gary wanted to spread his energy and enthusiasm for the arts to as many people as he possibly could. Back then I thought his generous spirit had turned greedy, and we had a falling out. Over time I realized that, even though money and success came to him eventually, it was never his motive. Money changes your circumstances, but it can't change your core. A spiteful person becomes a spiteful person with money. A kind person, a kind person with money."

"James and I had a fight." Emily concentrated on lining the magnets into a row rather than see how Hollister reacted to her confession.

"That's bound to happen. Even with the best of friends."

"I don't think . . ." The drilling next door reverberated dully through the shared wall. Emily took a deep breath. "I don't know how to be a good friend."

Hollister blew a raspberry. "Nonsense. There's no 'how' about it. Just be. Just do. That's all a good friend is. That's what Gary did for me. He reached out for years, but I didn't appreciate it at first, and James might not, either. But if your intentions are good, and the friendship was true to begin with, he'll come around."

The mechanical pounding stopped suddenly, making the silence feel stark. The magnetic words scraped on the tray as Emily pushed them, absorbing what Hollister had to say. *Bird. Whisper. Shadow.*

CHAPTER 33

EMILY LEFT Hollister's. The drilling started up again and her footsteps fell in rhythm. Sweat trickled down her neck as she made her way up the shop-lined street and turned onto a residential one. She was looking up at a cat perched in a bay window when a voice she didn't recognize said from behind, "Hello, Surly Wombat."

Emily whirled around to see the two men from the BART station and Lombard Street. She stepped backward uphill, the steep slope forcing her step to be a small one.

"We're not here to hassle you," the tall man said, raising his hands.

The short man stepped toward her, and Emily instinctively took another uphill step back. "We want that book," he leered.

"Clyde!" the tall man snapped. The fake smile

disappeared. Beads of sweat dotted his upper lip like *he* was the nervous one.

Emily clenched fists around her backpack straps. All the buildings on this street had garages on the ground level and the houses stacked on top. Long flights of stairs led to front doors. Someone would have to be right at the window, looking down, to notice her. The roar of a vacuum drifted down, threading through the faded drilling.

"We don't want to hurt you," the tall man said.

Don't want to wasn't as reassuring as *aren't going to.*

A car door slammed up the hill, and Emily jerked to look behind her. Red rear lights of a car parked all the way at the top turned on, and the car eased away from the curb, driving away.

"The best thing to do is just give us the book. We know you have it."

The short guy—Clyde, the other had called him— stepped toward her again, but his friend swung an arm in front of him. "Just wait," he said.

"What—" Her voice croaked when she tried to speak. She started again. "What book are you talking about?"

"That one from the BART station," the tall guy said. "Let's not play games anymore, okay? That was clever what you did, posting the book like you hid it in Outer Sunset. We spent a good deal of time at that park, and we know it's not there."

Clyde flipped his hand in the air. "This is a waste of time! Let's just grab her bag and go!"

"No!" Barry snapped. "No," he repeated, more calmly. "We don't need to *steal*, okay?" To Emily he said, "Give the book to us, and we'll be on our way. You'll never see us again."

Emily had to think of something to do, and fast. These men could grab her without even taking a step—that was how close they were. And that Clyde looked like a dog who wanted to fight. The problem was, she really didn't have the book.

She could tell them that, but would they believe her after she'd already sent them clear across the city? And what would they do if they didn't believe her? She couldn't outrun them. Her only choice was to outsmart them. An idea came to her, but it was risky. It would only work if these guys knew as little about Mr. Griswold's book as she hoped they did.

"Is it Poe?" she asked.

"You know it is," the tall man said.

"A maroon cover?"

She swung her backpack to her front and tucked her chin to hide her nervous swallow as she unzipped her bag. She took another step backward and uphill. Any space she could create between them, the better.

"I was enjoying reading it, but if you need it that badly . . ."

Emily pulled out the collection of Poe stories from Hollister.

The tall man accepted the book, holding it at arm's length to study the cover before Clyde grabbed it and flipped it open. Emily swallowed again and stepped back, sure her bluff was about to be called.

Clyde turned to *The Gold-Bug*, which she'd marked up as she compared it against Griswold's to find all the typos. She did her best to look indifferent and bored.

"You wrote in it!" Clyde shook the book.

"I . . . I did," she said.

"You shouldn't write in books."

"It doesn't matter." His partner pulled him backward by the hood of his sweatshirt. "It's just a book."

The two men turned, and Emily watched until they rounded the corner and disappeared completely. She watched a few minutes more, and when the men didn't return, she drew in a long inhale and exhaled slowly.

Two books lost in one day. Not a good day for a book scavenger.

Emily stood on the landing of her building and stared at James's door. It had been three weeks since a strange boy made her laugh and then solved her cipher when she wasn't looking. Then—*poof!* A best friend where she'd never had one before. Easier than solving an Encyclopedia Brown–level clue in Book Scavenger. She wanted to tell James about those two men. And losing *The Gold-Bug*. And Mr. Griswold's past as co-owner of Hollister's bookstore. And that she'd discovered Babbage's secret identity. She missed James. Hollister's words—*just be, just do*—washed over her mind like a wave on sand. If Hollister were here, she imagined he would tell her to try knocking and see what happened. But she couldn't risk the possibility of Ms. Lee opening the door again instead of James. Of asking to see James and having him reject her.

She opened her own door instead and trudged up the stairs. She swung her backpack onto her bed, planning to do homework and to try to get her mind off losing what felt like everything important in the span of a few days. When she unzipped her overfull backpack, *The Maltese Falcon* tumbled out. After her meeting with Babbage/Mr. Quisling went downhill, she completely spaced on the fact that while she may have lost *The Gold-Bug*, she still had *The Maltese Falcon* and its clue. Maybe she hadn't lost out on everything, after all. If she could crack that clue, maybe she could still move forward with Mr. Griswold's game, *Gold-Bug* or no *Gold-Bug*, James or no James.

Bob the seagull had gotten a little too demanding about his bread, so on Friday, Emily went back to spending her lunch in the library. Being surrounded by books was comforting, even if she sat at a table by herself.

James was there, too, at a nearby table with those

twins, Kevin and Devin. Emily tried not to be obvious about it, but she glanced over at James every so often. Again she thought of Hollister and their conversation the day before. What she thought Hollister meant was that she shouldn't be afraid to take the wrong step with a friendship. Any step was a good one as long as you were trying to be a good friend. But sitting there in the library with the low, bouncy beats of reggae music spilling from the librarian's office and the hushed conversations broken up by the occasional rip of loud laughter, Emily felt too much potential for wrong steps, despite what Hollister thought.

One time when Emily glanced James's way, she caught him looking at her. He whipped his head back so fast to the card game the brothers were arguing over that Steve appeared to have momentarily laid down before bouncing back upright. Shortly after that, James put his cards down and pushed back from the table. Emily tried to look busy at work on the *Maltese Falcon* cipher. She was disappointed when James kept walking. He had been on his way to the bathroom.

After that, she tried to work in earnest, and, therefore, she didn't hear James come back.

"Pigpen," she heard his voice say from behind her.

She turned. "What?"

He'd been studying her paper over her shoulder. He pointed. "Pigpen. You'll see it."

And that was it. He walked away.

Emily studied her work again. The original cipher was written at the top of the page.

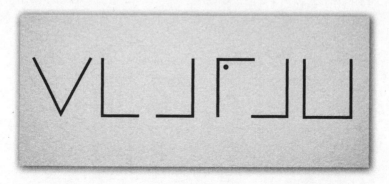

The paper was covered in her work trying to decode it, which looked like a bunch of unfinished hangman games minus the hanging men. She'd also written down Raven's hint: *Charlie, Sally, Lucy.*

"Pigpen," Emily whispered to herself, and she realized what James had seen. The names were all characters from the *Peanuts* comics: Charlie Brown, Sally, and Lucy. Pigpen was another character, but what did that have to do with the cipher itself? The solution was six letters long, and *Pigpen* was six letters. But that couldn't work, because the third and fifth letters were the same according to the cipher, and in *Pigpen* those letters were *g* and *e*. Not the same.

But *Pigpen* had to mean something. Emily went to the computer bank. All the results on the first page had to do with the cartoon character. She scrolled down and saw a heading for "Searches Related to

Pigpen," and in the list underneath that, the word *code* got her attention. Pigpen was the name of a cipher!

She printed out a Pigpen key:

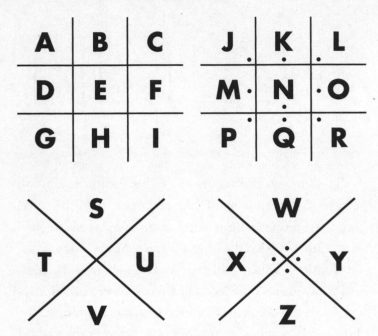

Once she had a key, it took her only seconds to figure out the solution to the *Maltese Falcon* clue.

SCARAB.

CHAPTER 34

S CARAB.

Scarab was the word Poe's narrator used in *The Gold-Bug*. It meant *beetle*, like the glittering gold one on the cover. Like the inky-black one on the inside page.

If *scarab* was the next clue, Emily had a sinking feeling she knew where Mr. Griswold was directing her. Back to *The Gold-Bug*. Back to the book that had been taken away.

Emily pressed her forehead into her hands, her elbows anchored to the library table. This was it. She'd reached the end of the line for Mr. Griswold's game. It was like working on a complicated jigsaw puzzle without knowing the final picture. Just as the pieces began to fall into place, and you could almost make out the image, someone came along and swiped it all onto the floor. And then vacuumed up the pieces for good measure. To choose to stop now would have been one thing. To have the power of choice taken from her made Emily feel insignificant and small.

She raised her head and caught James studying her. They both looked away as if their eye contact burned. The bell rang and Emily started to pack up. She zipped her bag closed when James appeared next to her.

"Did you get it? Pigpen?"

"Oh." Emily looked down for a second. "I did. Thanks for the hint."

Even if James could tell she was upset and asked her about it, she wasn't sure she wanted to explain why. James had wanted her to stop playing the game, and Emily couldn't bear the possibility of someone telling her that being forced to stop was for the best. All James said was, "I recognized the symbols from one of my cipher books. I was happy to help. Sometimes two eyes are better than one."

In a knee-jerk reply, Emily added, "No offense to the Cyclops." They exchanged small smiles before James walked away.

That afternoon in social studies, Mr. Quisling asked for any final attempts to break James's cipher. His long strip of letters was the only submission for the week. Emily held her breath, waiting to see if anyone raised his or her hand.

The room remained silent, and Mr. Quisling said,

"Mr. Lee, your cipher has survived the week. Congratulations on winning your first homework pass."

Emily couldn't resist peeking behind herself to look at Maddie, who scowled at her binder and scratched a doodle in the margins of her paper.

James punched his fists in the air and tilted his head back to shout at the ceiling, "STEVE SURVIVES!"

The class tittered, and even Mr. Quisling looked somewhat bemused.

"Would you—or Steve—please illuminate for the class how your cipher works?"

James stood in front of the class and held up his vertical strip of paper with letters on it:

"I used a type of cipher called the scytale. You take a vertical strip of paper like this, and you wrap it around a cylinder-shaped object." James held up a pencil. He wrapped the strip around it, and all the letters lined up horizontally. "To decode my message, you have to wrap the paper around an object with the same diameter as the one the original message sender used in order for the letters to align correctly. This pencil is what I used."

Vivian raised her hand and spoke at the same time. "Your message still doesn't make sense. You can't use nonsense words and expect us to figure them out—can he, Mr. Quisling?"

Before Mr. Quisling could reply, Emily spoke up. "Those aren't nonsense words," she said, realizing she could read James's message even though nobody else in the class could, and she smiled at what it said. "He used a substitution cipher to encrypt his message as a backup, in case you figured out the scytale. Right?" she asked James.

He nodded, smiling. James held up a piece of paper that showed their secret code. "This is the cipher key I used. Decoded, my message reads *Royal Fungus*."

When James sat back down, Mr. Quisling clapped. Emily joined in without even thinking about it. She lowered her hands quickly, embarrassed by her show of enthusiasm, but James gave her a half smile and Steve a "good job" pat on his tips. Small gestures, but they made Emily feel a million times lighter.

When the bell rang and everyone collected their things, James shuffled down the aisle and out the classroom without a glance her way. Emily didn't realize she must have been obviously watching him until Maddie stood beside her and said, "Looks like too little too late." She plumped up her mushroom-cap hair with one hand. Maddie was only trying to get under her skin, Emily knew that. And it worked, too, but not in the way Maddie might have been hoping for. Hearing her fear verbalized by Maddie, that her friendship with James was over for good, had the unexpected effect of making Emily realize how silly it sounded. It wasn't too late. And oddly enough, Maddie of all people had just given Emily a brilliant idea for how to make things right.

Back at her apartment that afternoon, Emily wrote a note for the bucket. All it said was:

B·N SXPPD
(I'm sorry)

She placed the note in the sand pail. She picked up the reindeer antlers and taped a paper towel to them, arranging the items to look like a white flag waving for a truce. She stuffed the antlers in the pail, making sure the flag would be visible in James's window once raised. When the bucket had been lifted, she secured the rope so the pail would remain there until James retrieved it.

A while later the ceiling creaked. James's window was opposite his door, so Emily knew he'd see the antlers and flag when he walked into his room. Whether or not he'd check it was another story.

The creaking stopped, then resumed again, and James's window slid open. His snorting laugh and the tinkle of a bell carried down through her open window.

He returned a response:

B'N SXPPD VXX
(I'm sorry too)

Emily sent a follow-up note:

ETF ZU VTWO?
(Can we talk?)

James came over, and they spent Friday evening catching up on the week.

"You had those men trekking all the way to the Sunset? And Babbage is Mr. Quisling?" He shook his head, disbelieving. "I stop talking to you for a few days and all sorts of stuff happens. The most exciting thing for me was dinner with my dad at Michelangelo's."

"Winning a homework pass for Quisling's challenge is nothing to yawn over. You're one up on Maddie now. You know she's stressing that she'll have to make her hair look like a toadstool. Which reminds me, I have a plan I think you'll like. I'm calling it: Operation Royal Fungus."

Monday marked three days since Emily had deciphered the scarab clue. It still stung to think about *The Gold-Bug* squeezed onto a shelf somewhere and Mr. Griswold's game going dormant. But it was the words of her brother, of all people, that comforted her. She'd rather have played some of Mr. Griswold's game than none of it at all. And things had been righted with James, so she hadn't lost everything.

On their walk to school, they rehashed the plan for Operation Royal Fungus. It hinged on them maintaining the appearance of their fight, so they parted ways before they reached Booker.

At lunchtime, James staked out a table next to Maddie's in the library, his latest code work spread in front of him. When Emily approached, James made a big show of scooping his papers together.

"Can I help you?" he asked. His anger and

annoyance was so palpable, Emily forgot for a second that they were pretending. "I . . ." she stammered.

Maddie nudged the girl next to her and jutted her chin in Emily's direction, which was exactly the motivation Emily needed to surge forward with the lines she and James had practiced.

"What are you working on?" she asked.

James didn't look at her.

Emily dropped into the seat beside him, their backs to Maddie. "James, come on. Are you still mad? You've won a homework pass now."

He gathered his papers and tapped them against the table. "No thanks to you. And Maddie could make a comeback, so I haven't won our bet yet. This new cipher makes my other one look like a preschooler's puzzle. There's no way I'm sharing it with you and risking it being stolen or copied."

"Your Baconian cipher would have been broken anyway," Emily said as James held the stack of papers behind him, hovering over his wide-open backpack. "I mean, binary code? Doesn't that seem kind of obvious? Especially coming from a computer geek like you."

"What?" James released the papers. The plan was for them to fall onto the floor instead of into the backpack, but for their scheme to be believable, neither one of them could look to make sure that was, in fact, what had happened.

"Besides, I saw that idea in a book," Emily continued with their script.

"Prove it."

James grabbed his backpack without looking at it and followed Emily as she marched across the library and disappeared between rows of bookshelves. When they were out of sight from the tables, Emily whispered, "Did she fall for it?"

James bent to a low shelf and slid aside books to create a tiny window. He crouched down and peered between the spines, watching for a moment before he held up a triumphant thumb.

"I practically dropped the papers at her feet," James said. "Of course she couldn't resist."

"Well, let's hope she uses them. And then the rest is up to Mr. Quisling. Hopefully he notices."

In social studies, James made a big show of looking for another missing item when Mr. Quisling collected the cipher challenge submissions. No surprise to Emily or James, Maddie turned in "her" submission for the challenge. Mr. Quisling accepted it and looked it over. Slowly he raised his head, his eyes locked onto Maddie like lasers.

"Is this a joke, Ms. Fernandez?"

What Maddie didn't realize was that the cipher wasn't James's. The cipher belonged to Babbage, copied word for word. It was a Sherlock Holmes–level cipher, and Emily and James didn't have a clue how to solve it. James had included a fake solution among the pages he pretended to drop in the library. They figured either Mr. Quisling would recognize his own work or later, when it went unsolved, Maddie would have to reveal her solution, which would prove to be a nonsensical answer key once she started walking the class through it.

Emily was so pleased that her trick had worked she almost missed Mr. Quisling's stare shift momentarily to herself. Almost. It was enough to remind Emily of an important detail she'd overlooked. Mr. Quisling knew *she* knew his Book Scavenger identity as Babbage. If he recognized his own cipher from the website, then it was a logical step to connect her to it. Emily studied the carved diamond on her desk. But Mr. Quisling addressed Maddie, not Emily.

"I know this cipher, Ms. Fernandez. And I know it's not yours."

"But I—"

"Cheating is not tolerated in this classroom, on any assignment. Furthermore, you were warned last week about the consequences of turning in a cipher other than your own creation. I'm disqualifying you from the contest."

James scribbled on his notebook and raised it for Emily to see *DUS!* or *YES!* in their cipher language. All they'd wanted was to give Maddie a taste of her own medicine. Having her disqualified was an added bonus.

"What?" Maddie cried. "That's not fair!"

"Disqualified. End of discussion," Mr. Quisling said. "You've wasted enough of our time."

In the hallway after class, Maddie stomped up to Emily and James.

"You set me up!" she cried so loudly students stopped to stare.

"Do you hear that?" James cupped a hand around his ear. "That's the sound of Steve celebrating my win. Don't worry—you'll look great as a redhead."

Maddie blushed. "Your win? I didn't lose. I was disqualified."

"I don't remember that being part of the bet. Do you remember that being part of the bet, Emily?"

"Nope."

"The agreement was whoever earned more homework passes or got to three first. Disqualification wasn't mentioned," James said. "I won one, and you have, let me count. . . . Oh, that's right—none!"

"Whatever. It's a stupid bet. I wouldn't have made you shave your head."

James snorted. "Right."

Maddie turned on her heel and marched away into the crowd.

"You'll start a toadstool trend!" James called after her. "Embrace your fate! Don't be afraid of your own destiny!"

"Do you think she'll do it?" Emily asked.

"Not a chance," he said. "It's okay, though. Watching her squirm was better than the toadstool hair. She probably *would* start a trend. Or she'd at least enjoy all the attention."

CHAPTER

35

SEA LION BRAYS carried from Pier 39 as Emily and James walked up to their building after school. The sound took Emily back to her first day in San Francisco, almost a month ago. Hearing wild barks in the middle of a city had been jarring, unexpected, but now they were soothing. It wasn't every day that she could hear them, so she knew the noise was a gift. She knew the city well enough now that she could track a route down their hill and through the grid of streets that stretched below to the general location of Pier 39.

They climbed the front steps of their building, which had once looked so starved and severe to Emily. Now it welcomed her like a familiar friend, the contrasting trim above the top windows like raised eyebrows surprised to see her again.

She invited James over to hang out, and as they walked up her stairwell, her apartment filled with skateboard thunder and Matthew chanting Flush lyrics.

"Sorry about that," Emily said. "Matthew's going to a concert tonight—" Emily was interrupted by whooping even louder than Matthew's singing.

Her parents burst from the kitchen, racing down the hallway toward them. Her dad held a carton of orange juice overhead, and her mom hollered behind him.

Emily and James pressed against the wall to let them run by.

"What's going on?" Emily shouted.

"It's a celebration!" her dad said. "All we had was orange juice. But I don't care! This is the most celebratory orange juice ever!"

Matthew rolled out of his room and dug his heel into the skateboard to flip it up to his hand. Freshly shaved swirls dotted his skull.

"Celebrating me going to the Flush concert? Aww, you shouldn't have."

"It sold!" Their mom clapped her hands. "*50 Homes in 50 States* sold! Our agent just called us with the news!"

"It sold?" Emily repeated.

Her parents passed out plastic cups of juice, but Emily was too shocked to accept one. Everyone but Emily hopped around, orange juice splattering the floor, and chanted with her parents, "We sold a book!

We sold a book!" Even Steve got in on the party with his bobbing back and forth. Her dad swung her ponytail like he was conducting an orchestra.

"C'mon, Em! This is a great day, great news!"

She remained in a firmly non-bouncy state. A feeling something like dread was overtaking her.

Emily yanked her ponytail from her dad's hand and marched to her room. The whooping and hopping dulled as her family and James watched her go. Why was she being such a Scrooge? She knew she was ruining the moment for her parents. How hard would it be to hop around, drink some orange juice, and pretend she was as excited as everyone else?

What an idiot she'd been. She sat on her bed, her backpack still on. She'd let down her guard and gotten herself attached to people and a place when she knew it would be inevitable that they'd move again. Her parents were publishing a book about living in fifty states, for Pete's sake.

James pushed open her door. "Are you okay?" he asked.

A horn honked repeatedly, and Emily heard her brother yell, "Showtime!" Of course he was totally unfazed. He leaned into the adventure and all that. No Jack Kerouac quote could help her now. There was something to be said for stopping to enjoy your surroundings, too, instead of always looking ahead to what came next. She didn't care what was waiting around the next bend. She knew it wouldn't be another puzzle-loving computer nut with a cowlick sidekick.

James shifted from foot to foot. "If now isn't a good time, I can go. . . ."

Emily grabbed her backpack and stood up.

"Now is the only time. Come on."

Her parents stood where she'd left them, leaned together in conversation.

"Emily," her mom said.

"We know you're not happy about our announcement," her dad said.

Emily thundered past them and down the stairs with James at her heels. She slammed the front door behind them. A station wagon full of Matthew's friends backed into the street, and Emily waved for them to stop.

She pulled open the back door. "Scoot over," she said to Matthew.

"What are you doing?" Matthew said. "You don't have tickets!"

"Just move," Emily said.

There must have been a don't-mess-with-me tone to her voice because Matthew nudged his friend and they slid over. Emily wedged herself on her brother's lap and James squeezed in next to the door.

"Where are we going?" James whispered.

"Mr. Remora's. I need to finish Mr. Griswold's game. Or at least try."

"You know where he lives?"

"He told Hollister he lives by the Fillmore." She nodded to her brother. "That's where they're going."

"But . . ." James plucked at Steve. "There are a lot of places to live around the Fillmore," he said carefully.

"I remember his address."

James raised his eyebrows.

"Well, I remember most of it. It's sevens and ones, like 1177 or 7171."

"Oh. Okay."

She could tell James was dubious about her impulsive plan, but she was determined to find Mr. Remora and ask him for *The Gold-Bug* back, even if she had to knock on every 1/7 combination address around the Fillmore.

They circled the neighborhood of the music venue looking for street parking. With every loop, Emily scanned street numbers. She knew Mr. Remora lived close enough to complain about the Fillmore, and 1717 was the closest possibility. That had to be it.

They finally found parking down a side street, and everyone piled out. Emily swung her backpack on and hurried ahead of Matthew's group. James was right beside her. When they got to the Fillmore intersection, Emily and James turned up the street, away from the music venue, running to cross in time before the light changed.

"Where are you guys going?" Matthew called.

Emily walked more quickly. She was determined

to do this, and stopping to explain herself to her brother would just slow her down.

Matthew left his friends and caught up to them, panting. "What's going on?"

"She's going to get a book," James said.

"You came all this way for a book? Can't it wait?"

Emily spun on her brother.

"No, it can't, Matthew. If you had Flush tickets and then someone took those precious tickets away, and this was your *one* chance to be a part of the Flush experience, what would you do? Would you be happy about it? Would you just say, 'That's cool. No biggie'? Or would you at least *try* to get your tickets back?"

Matthew stood with his arms crossed, eyes squinted in concentration like he was really imagining himself in this scenario.

"I'd get my tickets back, obviously."

"Well then, pretend my book is a pair of Flush tickets. That's how important this is to me."

Emily resumed walking, her backpack slapping against her with the forcefulness of every step. She assumed her brother would go back to his friends. Instead, she heard him yell, "Hey, guys, I'll catch up with you in a minute." Then he jogged past Emily and James, clapping his hands like a football coach.

"Let's move, people. We've got a book to rescue!"

CHAPTER 36

E MILY HAD her doubts, staring up at 1717 Fillmore. She'd expected something shabby and brown, like Mr. Remora's briefcase, but this was a tidy Victorian with a bright purple shop on the ground level and green stairs with prim white banisters leading up to the front door.

"So this is the home of the book thief?" Matthew said as the three stood at the base of the stairs. "What do you want me to do? Scale that tree? Break a window?"

"He's not a book thief, Matthew." Emily gripped her backpack straps and looked up to the front door. "He's a rare-book specialist."

She walked up the stairs.

"What are you doing? What is she doing?" Matthew said to James.

"It looks like she's ringing the doorbell."

"That's your plan?" Matthew said as he and James joined her on the front stoop. "You're going to ring his doorbell and just ask him to give you this book?"

Before she could second-guess herself, Mr. Remora opened the door.

"I don't eat cookies," he said, and was about to close the door on them when Matthew stuck his foot in the way and held the door open.

"Hold on. We're not selling cookies. My sister has something to ask you."

"Mr. Remora, I'm the student who posted about *The Gold-Bug* on Book Scavenger. I know Mr. Quisling gave it back to you, but I was wondering if I could look at it again."

"I don't know what you're talking about," Mr. Remora said.

"Don't you remember us?" James piped up. "We saw you in Mr. Griswold's office and Hollister's store."

Emily added, "We know you're a rare-book collector, and we know Mr. Griswold is one of your clients."

"Well. Good for you," Mr. Remora snapped. "I still don't know what you're talking about. Perhaps you should check again with your teacher."

"Didn't Mr. Quisling call you?"

"What part of 'I don't know what you're talking about' do you not understand?"

James and Matthew looked to Emily, waiting for

her direction, but she was stumped. Mr. Quisling had been adamant that Emily give up the book, that it was returned to Mr. Remora ASAP.

"Emily?" James asked. "Are you okay?"

A sickening feeling overtook her. She'd told Mr. Quisling about the game. He'd said he didn't want to look at the puzzle because he wouldn't be able to resist solving it.

"I need to sit down," she croaked.

Mr. Quisling never saw the *Maltese Falcon* cipher, but it would be easy enough for him to open *The Gold-Bug*, find the typos she'd marked, and put the pieces together himself.

Matthew swung an arm around her side, letting her lean on him, and pushed Mr. Remora's door with his free hand. Mr. Remora pushed back.

"What are you doing?" Mr. Remora sputtered.

"Can we come in for a second?" Matthew asked. "I don't think my sister feels well."

"No, you cannot—"

Matthew overpowered Mr. Remora, and he and Emily tumbled inside the house.

"I'm fine," Emily gasped, although her vision was spinning. There were books piled on every seating option, so she sat on the floor, not bothering to take off her backpack, and put her head between her knees.

"Emily?" That was James crouching next to her.

Raven had hidden forty-nine more copies of *The*

Maltese Falcon across the city. Plenty for Mr. Quisling to find, and surely he'd solve the Pigpen clue in no time. And then it was just a matter of time before he solved the entire game and uncovered the grand prize.

"How could I have been so dumb?" she moaned. Confiding in Mr. Quisling, of all people. Mr. Quisling. *Babbage.* Once a poacher, always a poacher.

She lifted her head trying to find something to focus on. The room they were in was half family room, half kitchen. Piles and stacks and towers of books were everywhere. Only a sliver of sunlight cracked through the closed drapes, making the room feel dreary. A dark hallway led to the back of the house.

"Can she have a glass of water?" James asked.

Mr. Remora had picked up his phone. "Get over here," he snapped into the receiver. "Right now."

Matthew crossed to the kitchen and opened cupboards by the sink until he found a glass. Mr. Remora threw his hands in the air. "Make yourselves at home, I guess."

"I'm sorry to have bothered you," Emily said. "I made a mistake."

From somewhere down the hallway, a door squeaked open. Mr. Remora closed the front door and flipped the dead bolt. The clomp of footsteps drew nearer until a tall, lanky man stepped out of the hallway.

"Uncle Leon, what's going on?"

The man speaking was one of the BART station men. Barry, Emily remembered from when she'd tricked him into taking Hollister's Poe collection. Barry looked from Matthew in the kitchen to Emily on the floor to James crouched next to her to Mr. Remora.

"What's he doing here?" Emily said at the same time Barry asked, "What are they doing here?"

Emily stood. Across the room on the kitchen island, under the glare of pendant lights, lay *The Gold-Bug.*

"You *do* have it!" she cried. Forgetting everything else, Emily ran and lifted the book from the island. The golden beetle greeted her, shining in the rose-hued light. So Mr. Quisling hadn't tricked her. But then . . .

"Why did you lie?" She faced Mr. Remora. James and Matthew flanked her on either side. Barry hovered across the room, looking as wary as she felt.

Mr. Remora remained by the front door, his arms crossed and scowling. "It's none of your business. Why does it interest you anyway? I didn't think Edgar Allan Poe was popular with children these days."

The doorbell rang. Mr. Remora twisted the dead bolt and tugged the door open.

"Took you long enough, Clyde," he snapped.

The short, burly man who'd been with Barry the other day stepped inside.

"What are they doing here?" Clyde crooked his

thumb in their direction. "Who's the new one with the spiderwebs shaved on his head?"

"They're swirls," Matthew said.

Barry stepped forward. "I thought you said we were done with the kids."

"Well, I was wrong," Mr. Remora said impatiently.

"It seems they've come to help us." Mr. Remora was small and wiry and balding, and at first glance he looked anything but intimidating. But the look in his eyes when he stepped toward them made Emily step back. "Let's drop the charade. We are both interested in that book for the same reason: Mr. Griswold's ridiculous game."

"You know about the game?"

"Of course I do. Not the specifics, per se. But he's been babbling about armchair treasure hunts for years, asking me to locate this or that book so he'd have a complete collection of the genre."

Barry cleared his throat. "Why don't you let these kids go? We can just chalk this up to a mix-up. You finish doing whatever you're doing with that book, and they can forget any of this happened."

"Why should I waste my time solving Garrison's game when I'm fairly certain this girl has already done so? Or is close to completing it, at the very least." To Emily he said, "That's why you're so desperate to have the book back, isn't it? So let's work together. I'll even let you have *The Gold-Bug* as a keepsake. You wouldn't be interested in the prize anyway. It's nothing a kid would like—no toys or candy."

"You know what the prize is?" Emily asked.

"Why else would I go to this trouble? Who'd want to do this for the fun of it?" Mr. Remora shuddered. "I hate games. What do you say? Care to share your secrets?"

If Emily could get the men away from the door they might be able to make a run for it. The kitchen was in the farthest corner of the room. That was where everybody needed to move to give them the best chance of breaking away.

"Well, you're right. We have practically solved it," she said. Her voice shook as she spoke. "But we're stuck on the last clue. It's a cipher."

James stared at her, mouth hanging open. He knew she was lying. They'd solved the last clue. Emily tightened her grip on *The Gold-Bug.*

"And what is this last clue you need to figure out?" Mr. Remora said "clue" with a little shiver, as if he were talking about snakes instead of a game.

"Do you have a pencil and paper?" She had her pencil tucked in her ponytail, of course, but she was hoping Mr. Remora would have to move somewhere else to retrieve one for her. And he did.

Just as she hoped, Mr. Remora walked into the kitchen. She noted that he hadn't relocked the door after he let in Clyde. Hopefully that would help, as long as they could cause a big enough distraction to get to the door first. Barry and Clyde shoved aside books and magazines on the couch and sat down. Clyde chewed at a hangnail; Barry watched Mr. Remora. They weren't as far from the front door as Emily had hoped, but it would have to do.

She turned to James. "You remember the last

cipher, don't you? I may need help remembering the whole thing."

James nodded slowly, trying to play along with Emily but unsure what she was planning.

As Mr. Remora rummaged through an overstuffed drawer, Emily mouthed to her brother *door*. He gave an almost imperceptible nod and took the slightest step away from her and toward the front door.

"Have you read all these books?" Emily asked Mr. Remora. Even the kitchen counters and top of the refrigerator were covered. Part of her was stalling and part was genuinely curious. Even if she didn't have to limit herself to one suitcase full, it would take her decades to collect this many books, let alone read them.

"No chitchat." Mr. Remora steered a notepad and pencil around a stack of American Revolution–themed novels.

Emily started to write and then faked a small coughing attack. "Could I have that glass of water?"

Mr. Remora sighed and picked up the full glass her brother had left by the sink. She took a small sip and smiled.

"Thanks."

Mr. Remora waved his hands in an impatient "get on with it" way.

Using her and James's secret code, she wrote out her plan, but made an effort to act like she was trying to recall the pretend cipher she was conjuring up. James caught on and chimed in, saying things like, "I think it was *T-A*, not *T-X*."

Her note read: "Make book chaos. Run."

It wasn't a genius plan, but it was the best thing she could come up with.

Barry's head dropped back on the sofa, eyes closed. Clyde flipped through a magazine so roughly it was amazing the pages didn't rip out. Matthew had inched about a foot closer to the door now.

"I thought you had the clue memorized," Mr. Remora said, sounding more disappointed than suspicious.

"You forgot this," James said. He glanced briefly at Matthew to make sure he was paying attention. Then in their cipher language James wrote *Now!* and many things happened at once: Emily threw her water at Mr. Remora, getting the American Revolution books wet in the process. Mr. Remora shrieked *"No!"* while James toppled tower after tower of books. Matthew leaped to the front door and swung it open, then turned back to kick a pile of books in Barry and Clyde's direction.

"What the—" Barry sputtered, startled from his nap. Inexplicably, Clyde started flinging magazines across the room like he was throwing boomerangs.

Mr. Remora's apartment was a flurry of flying books and crashing objects as Matthew, James, and Emily raced out the door, *The Gold-Bug* still in Emily's hand. Mr. Remora spun this way and that, uncertain where to go. He ducked from one of Clyde's hurled magazines and cried, "Stop it! Stop it! Stop it!"

The three darted into the inky night and across the trafficless street. Streetlamps illuminated their feet as they pounded down the sidewalk toward the Fillmore auditorium. Emily concentrated on the slap of their feet, the weight of her backpack bumping against her, urging her faster, faster, faster. She gripped *The Gold-Bug* tightly in her hand and tried to think of it as a baton in a relay she was desperately trying to win.

"Thief!" Mr. Remora's voice rang out.

Emily didn't think it was possible to go any faster, but his voice prompted an extra jolt of speed. Soon they reached the crowd lined up for the concert. They charged through, dodging people.

"Where's the fire, Crane?" one of Matthew's friends shouted.

"Stop the old dudes!" Matthew yelled back, throwing his thumb over his shoulder.

They passed the main doors of the Fillmore. Angry voices flared behind them. Emily dared a look back. A cluster of people clogged the sidewalk. She could hear Mr. Remora's nasally voice shouting, "Let me through! Let me through!" Barry's head was visible over the crowd, and Emily was sure he watched them round the corner. A gleaming black-and-gold bus was parked along the curb with the front sliding doors open. A man leaned against the bumper, taking a drag off a cigarette.

"Up here," James shouted, and the three raced up the stairs and onto the bus.

The inside was more like a giant motor home than a regular bus, with two diner-style booths on either side of the aisle and a mini kitchen. A velvet curtain concealed the back of the bus. Emily, James, and Matthew went straight to the tinted windows to see if anyone had followed them.

"What do you kids think you're doing?"

CHAPTER 37

IT WAS THE MAN who'd been leaning against the front of the bus. A toilet flushed from somewhere in the back, and a voice from behind them said, "Hey, Mikey. You had one responsibility—keep groupies off the bus. How hard is it?"

"Sorry, Trevor," Mikey sputtered. "They flew around the corner. It happened so fast I didn't even realize."

Matthew made a gerbil-like chirping sound. The color had drained from his face, and he was staring at Trevor with his mouth open.

"Trevor? As in . . . oh my gosh!" Emily clapped both hands over her mouth and completely forgot there had been a madman book collector on the hunt for them. This was Trevor, the drummer of Flush.

"Sorry we crashed your bus," James said. "We're not groupies or anything, er—" He looked at Emily and Matthew. "At least I'm not. I mean, no offense. I'm sure your music is great and all, my grandma is kind of strict about what I listen to and—"

James collapsed into the booth behind him. "Sorry," he said. "It's been a long night."

He let out a sigh and dropped his head back against the red pleather of the booth.

Trevor chewed on his lip piercing while he studied them. "Do these two talk?" he asked James.

Emily dropped her hands from her mouth. "Sorry," she said meekly. "I've never met anyone famous before."

Matthew let out another gerbilish chirp.

"My brother is seriously your number one fan. He's not normally like this."

Matthew sputtered, "Five...FiveSpade. I'm FiveSpade."

Trevor raised his eyebrows. "No way! *You're* FiveSpade? I thought you'd be older. No offense, man, but that LEGO Domination video was sick. I thought for sure you were in college at least."

Trevor dropped his guarded stance and shook Matthew's hand, pulling him in for a back pat, too.

"Man, this is a trip!" Trevor said. He went to the curtain and called behind it. "Zeke! Liam, Neil! Check out who's here."

A guy with a stubbly beard and tousled brown hair slid aside the velvet curtain and walked out, barefoot and in jeans and no shirt.

"Zeke!" Matthew said.

"'Sup."

Trevor gripped his arm. "Zeke—guess who this is."

Zeke looked Matthew up and down. "Liam's cousin?" he said.

"No, man. *FiveSpade*. Can you believe it?"

"LEGO Domination?" Zeke nodded. "Sweet."

Emily knew her brother was as shocked by this as she was, because he hadn't yet taken the opportunity to say "I told you so" and rub it in her face that the members of Flush really did know who he was. She dropped her backpack to the floor and sank into the booth next to James. Trevor's enthusiasm and cheer helped temper the stress from dealing with Mr. Remora.

James stared out the window. "See anything?" she asked.

He shook his head. "They haven't come down the street. We lost them."

They'd gotten away. Emily puffed her cheeks up and blew the air out slowly. They were safe now, on a tour bus with Flush, of all places.

All the members of Flush were in the front of the bus now, greeting her brother, aka FiveSpade. Neil opened the mini fridge and tossed around sodas. Liam hopped on the counter and started playing with a Zippo lighter, flipping it open and spinning it in his hand so it closed. Trevor was saying, "So 'Frisco's your home base, FiveSpade?"

Matthew nodded. "For now. But don't call it 'Frisco. Locals hate that."

Emily released her grip on *The Gold-Bug*, flexing her fingers. She'd been gripping it hard for so long the linen cover had left an impression on her palm.

Gently, she ran her fingers over the top. She tilted the book this way and that, watching the light play off the golden beetle. The last clue had been *scarab*, but so far she couldn't spot anything unusual about it.

"What do you see?" James whispered.

Emily shook her head. "Nothing." She opened the cover and scrutinized the inside scarab. A tinier version than the cover beetle, drawn in black ink. No numbers or letters or symbols printed around either one or hidden inside. Maybe she was wrong. Maybe the scarab clue had nothing to do with the book. Emily sagged at the thought of this. To have gone through all that drama for nothing . . . What if she'd gotten her brother or James hurt, and all for a book that didn't hold the answer she assumed it would. What would Mr. Remora have done if they hadn't escaped?

These thoughts spiraled in Emily's mind while she zoned out, watching Liam flick open his Zippo with a lit flame, then whip the top closed. The flame reminded her of the gold-bug story, where a message is revealed when parchment is heated up. Emily looked down at the black beetle and back to Liam.

"Could I borrow that?"

Liam looked scandalized. "You can't smoke!"

Emily blushed. "No, it's for an experiment."

Liam somewhat reluctantly held out the lighter. She tried rubbing her thumb against it like she'd just watched him do to make the flame appear, but she couldn't make it work. "Can you light it for me and wave it over this page?"

Matthew was still carrying on a conversation with the other Flush members. He'd relaxed into his normal self now and was describing the new stop-motion video he was in the middle of making.

Liam waved the lighter over the white page with the black scarab. "Like this?" he asked her.

"Maybe a little closer," she said when the page remained white.

"Too close!" Trevor yelled, noticing what Liam was doing. Liam jerked his hand back in surprise. The guys in the bus erupted in laughter.

"Sorry," Liam said with a grin.

"It's okay," Emily said. "It was probably a dumb idea any—"

"Look!" James pointed to the page. Lines, the color of weak tea, began to appear around the black beetle.

"I was right!" Emily waved Liam back to the book. "Do more! There must be invisible ink on this page. The heat makes it visible."

The group huddled around the book to watch as line after line slowly began to appear, revealing a map of San Francisco. The beetle marked a spot on the map labeled PORTSMOUTH SQUARE, RLS.

"That's it! We have to go there!" Emily said.

"Right now?" Matthew asked.

"I don't know, Em," James said.

In a low voice to James, she pleaded, "It's the end of the game. It must be. This is the treasure map that marks the spot. We lost Mr. Remora. He doesn't have *The Gold-Bug*, and he doesn't know about this map or have any idea where we'd be headed. If we do this tonight, we solve Mr. Griswold's game. We can call Jack at Bayside Press tomorrow, and we'll tell him about Mr. Remora, too."

James tugged thoughtfully at Steve, considering all this.

"Don't you want to see what Mr. Griswold's treasure will be?"

Finally he nodded.

She stood up from the booth. "We're leaving now," she said.

"Tonight?" Matthew asked. His face looked pained, like she was telling him he couldn't have a puppy.

"You don't have to go," Emily said. "I know you have your ticket."

Matthew gnawed on his lip, staring at the map. Finally, he shook his head. "Meeting you guys was cooler than anything I could have imagined," he said to the members of Flush. He turned to Emily. "But I'm not letting you two go off by yourselves. There'll be more concerts. I'm on your scavenging team whether you like it or not."

Trevor clapped Matthew on the back. "You're a good bro, bro. We're heading backstage in a minute here. You guys can borrow Mikey, and he'll drive you over, but you'll have to get your own ride home."

"And don't worry, FiveSpade," Trevor said. "We'll hook you up."

CHAPTER 38

EMILY, JAMES, and Matthew stood in the dark and deserted Portsmouth Square. The only light came from the dull orange glow of lampposts and the high-up windows of surrounding buildings. A fog had descended on this part of the city. It wrapped around trees and crept through bars of the playground.

"Do you know anything about this place?" Emily asked James.

"They call it the heart of Chinatown. A lot of elderly people hang out here during the day. My uncle comes here to play cards." He pointed toward the pagoda-style awning that sheltered picnic tables. A lump of sleeping bag was curled up on one of the benches, its dark form bold against the white fog. "I guess it's also a hot spot for homeless people." They'd stay away from that area if they could help it.

"So what are we looking for?" Matthew asked. He wore his new oversize Flush sweatshirt and hat, and he held a rolled-up poster signed by all the band members. They had also promised him VIP tickets to any future concert of his choice.

At the edge of the park, the silhouette of a miniature ship rose from the mist.

"Is that a pirate ship?" Emily asked.

Her feet squished in damp grass as she crossed to the statue, thoughts of treasure chests in her head. It was too dark to read the lettering on the face of the stone. Emily trailed her fingers over the engraving.

"Here." Matthew whipped out his cell phone. He cast the light of the screen over the words.

Emily read them aloud: "'To remember Robert Louis Stevenson'—" She gasped and clutched Matthew's arm.

"Watch the poster!" Matthew said, shaking her off.

"The map said *RLS*—Robert Louis Stevenson! He wrote *Treasure Island*. This has to be it. Whatever we're supposed to find must be somewhere near here."

Matthew continued reading the inscription aloud as Emily circled the monument, examining it more closely. James inspected the nearby benches.

"'To remember Robert Louis Stevenson: To be honest, to be kind—to earn a little, to spend a little less—to make upon the whole a family happier for his presence—to renounce when that shall be necessary and not be embittered—to keep a few friends but these without capitulation'—what does *capitulation* mean?" Matthew pondered.

"I think he's saying be a good friend without expecting something in return," James said as he poked a stick under a trash can.

Emily was crawling around the base of a tree, the knees of her jeans soaked and chilly, and felt a twinge of guilt remembering their fight.

Matthew finished reading the inscription: "'Above all on the same grim condition to keep friends with himself. Here is a task for all that a man has of fortitude and delicacy.'" Matthew turned off his screen light. "Huh. Sounds like a serious guy."

Emily's knee crunched against a hard object, and she yelped. She ran her fingers through the grass. Her fingertips brushed over something cold and smooth. She thought it was a pebble, but it wouldn't budge.

"Matthew, bring your light over here."

"My battery's running low." But he crossed to Emily anyway.

The stone was shaped like a beetle, flat enough to be concealed by the grass but bulky enough to catch a toe if you hit it the right way.

"It's like the story," Emily said. "In *The Gold-Bug* a beetle marks the spot where the treasure is hidden."

This had to be what Mr. Griswold wanted them to find. She'd been waiting for this moment since they'd first discovered Mr. Griswold's book. She thought she'd be jumping up and down with excitement, but instead she felt trepidation. Kind of like when you step on black ice and realize you're going to fall a second before you actually slip.

James tried to lift the beetle but couldn't. "Someone want to help me?"

Matthew held his phone aloft to light the ground, still protectively clutching his poster with his other hand. Emily and James tore at the grass and dug under the beetle until they could grasp it like a knob. It was attached to a stake in the ground. They see-sawed the stake back and forth to loosen the dirt until they could pull it free. The bottom of the stake widened into a mini shovel.

"Dig!" James said. "We're supposed to dig."

They used the shovel as well as cupped hands to scoop the dirt. They didn't have to dig long before they hit something solid, and soon a metal box was revealed. They pried the box from the ground. Emily undid the latch and opened the lid to reveal a yellowed stack of papers sealed in a clear bag. Taped to the front of the bag was a handwritten letter.

Greetings, Scavenger!

Congratulations! You have successfully completed my literary challenge and have proved yourself a master of riddles, puzzles, and navigating San Francisco and its rich literary history. You may be wondering about what you now hold in your hands. Allow me to indulge in a story:

In 1841, my great-great-great-grandfather Rufus Griswold made the acquaintance of a Mr. Edgar Allan Poe. Rufus Griswold was an accomplished editor, poet, and critic. In that day some may have argued that he was even more accomplished than Poe. Having similar aspirations and interests, you might assume that my great-great-great-grandfather and Poe would be fast friends. Sadly, you would be mistaken. Their relationship was professionally tolerant at best and a bitter rivalry at its worst.

Despite this, when Poe unexpectedly passed away in 1849, Rufus Griswold was named literary executor of his estate, to the surprise of many. Some claim he came about this by devious means and that Poe did not personally appoint him, but the fact remains that it was Rufus Griswold who was given access to the works of Poe and published a posthumous collection of his writings.

Several years ago, I was going through my family heirlooms when I came across a manuscript that was assumed to be a novel written by my great-great-great-grandfather. As I began reading it, the style reminded me of someone whose work I am quite familiar with. I kept my hunch a secret but had the manuscript authenticated by an expert. I am excited to tell you that the treasure you are holding in your hands is an undiscovered work by Edgar Allan Poe.

Bayside Press will publish this novel, and this letter certifies that you, dear Scavenger, will be awarded 10 percent of the royalties from the sale of this book on the condition that you agree to return the manuscript back into my care so it can be properly preserved and displayed in a public library collection.

I devised this scavenger hunt with the hope that anyone who made it to this point would appreciate *my gift as the treasure it truly is and treat it as such.*

Yours in pages and play,
Garrison Griswold

They stared at the letter in silence until the light from Matthew's phone snapped off. "There goes the battery," he said.

Emily lifted the sealed papers from the metal box and stood. She knew she was holding a one-of-a-kind literary treasure and should be feeling something along the lines of awe or amazement, but all she felt was disappointment. She was glad the phone had died so James and her brother couldn't see her face. After everything they'd been through to get here, why wasn't she happier to have reached the end of Griswold's game?

"Do you think it's worth a lot of money?" James asked.

"I have no idea," Emily said quietly.

"I do," a voice said behind them.

CHAPTER 39

Fog cloaked the three figures standing under the glow of a lamppost.

"Hand that over," Mr. Remora said, extending his hand. Barry and Clyde stood behind him.

Matthew groaned. "You guys again?"

Emily hugged the bagged manuscript.

"How did you find us?" James asked.

"You didn't think you fooled me, did you? Hiding on that tour bus? I knew you must be near the end of Griswold's game or you wouldn't have shown up at my house, so desperate to get your hands on *The Gold-Bug*. It was only a matter of time before you led me to this manuscript." He flexed his extended hand in a "gimme" motion.

"How did you know about it, anyway?" Emily asked. She scanned the park for an escape route. An iron fence enclosed the area. There was an opening to the street not too far away, but the question was whether they could outrun Mr. Remora and his goons for the second time that night. "Mr. Griswold's letter says nobody knew about it."

"Who do you think authenticated the manuscript?" Mr. Remora said. He shoved both hands deep into his pockets, pulling his jacket closed against the misty night. "I've worked for that man for a long time. I deduced his connection to Rufus Griswold within my first year of working for him. And *he* didn't find the lost Poe manuscript. *I* did. But there's no credit to me in that charming letter of his, is there? Of course not. We should have been partners. A fifty-fifty split. He never would have known what he had under his own nose if it hadn't been for me."

Mr. Remora paced in front of Barry and Clyde, his hands out of his pockets now, flinging in all directions as he talked.

"Then Garrison planned this cockamamie game without consulting me. You know what he said when I called him on it?" Mr. Remora jabbed a finger at Matthew like he expected him to respond. Matthew shook his head and stepped back. "He said, 'Oh, but you *will* be a partner, Leon. All you have to do is play the game—and win!' And he laughed."

Emily frowned. Mr. Griswold wouldn't have been that mean.

"When he told me his idiotic plan to give the manuscript away as a prize, like it was a honey-baked ham

316

or plastic trophy, I was horrified. That work deserves to be in a museum! Not buried in the ground like a bone, free to any dog that digs it up."

"Mr. Griswold agrees with you—he says so in his letter," Emily insisted.

"Ha!" Mr. Remora barked. "If he agreed with me, then it wouldn't be in your greasy hands right now. You're probably getting peanut butter all over it!"

"It's wrapped in plastic," Matthew said.

"And my hands are clean," Emily added nervously.

"You'll cut it up for paper dolls!" Mr. Remora waved his arms, the strands of his hair flopping erratically.

"Hey now, Uncle Leon," Barry said.

Mr. Remora whipped a finger toward him. "You don't get a say in this. I trusted you with entirely too much. This *child* has been more resourceful than you, Barry. You're worthless. You lose money that's not yours on horse races. I'm bailing you out with bookies left and right, and then I ask you to take care of one simple thing. And you screw that up, too." His shrill voice rang in the night.

Emily's eyes flicked from Mr. Remora to the fog-shrouded park in hopes of spotting someone coming to see what the noise was about. Barry shifted from side to side, eyeing Mr. Remora. Clyde yawned.

"Garrison Griswold was a fraud! He touted a deep love and respect for literature, but did you know he once used a first-edition Dashiell Hammett as a coaster? A coaster!"

Emily took a step back, tripping on the metal box, and stumbled in the hole they'd dug. She fell on her bottom, the manuscript clutched to her stomach. Her sudden movement alarmed Mr. Remora, and he shouted, "Don't move!" The next thing Emily knew, Clyde pulled a gun out of his pocket and pointed it at them.

"Dude," Matthew said.

"I thought you threw that away!" Barry cried.

"I told you that to get you off my back," Clyde sneered. "You think I want this to wash up and connect me with Griswold's shooting?"

From where she sat on the ground, Emily said, "*You* shot Mr. Griswold?" All this time she'd never questioned that it had been a random mugging in the BART station. She thought of how many times she'd refreshed the Book Scavenger forums for news on how Mr. Griswold was doing, how worried she'd been that he wouldn't recover. And she wasn't the only one who'd been affected by such a thoughtless, violent act—the mounds of flowers and books and stuffed animals left in tribute to him around the city were proof of that. The presence of Clyde's gun should have terrified her, but a wave of grief swelled for Mr. Griswold's current uncertain state, followed by a tsunami of anger.

"You shot him over *a book*? How could you do that? He did nothing but positive things! He might die now, and for what? How could you be that shallow and mean?"

The fury rising in Emily propelled her up from the ground and forward. With every step and every word the three men shrank back as a group, though Clyde didn't lower the gun.

"This isn't how it was supposed to be!" Emily shouted her words into the night sky, but it didn't make a difference. Mr. Griswold's game was over. He was still in critical condition. It didn't matter if the prize had been a valuable manuscript or a million dollars or a stuffed walrus. Mr. Griswold might die, and Book Scavenger might die with him. Nothing would change any of that. James and Matthew stood behind her, and Matthew placed a hand on her shoulder. Emily leveled her eyes at the three men. "You are pathetic."

"He shot him, not me." Mr. Remora pointed to Clyde. "But it had to be done. I certainly can't go publicizing that Poe manuscript if Griswold's still around. As it stands now, nobody knows it exists. It can be my discovery. Well..." Mr. Remora rumpled his hair, looking suddenly uncomfortable. "Nobody knows it exists other than you three."

Out of the darkness behind Clyde, a voice growled, "Make that four." There was a loud whack and Clyde dropped to his knees. The gun flew out of Clyde's hand and skidded across the concrete. Mr. Remora dropped to a crouch, covering his head, then peeked up scanning the ground.

"There!" Matthew pointed his Flush poster at the gun, and James ran to retrieve it. Unfortunately, Barry did, too, and got to the gun first.

Clyde's attacker stepped under a lamppost, bending over Clyde to make sure he was knocked out. The dreadlocks would have been recognizable anywhere.

"Hollister?" Emily asked.

"I hoped I'd see you kids here, but not under these circumstances," Hollister said.

Emily didn't have time to dwell on all the questions Hollister's presence raised. Barry swung the gun back and forth.

"Don't stand there, idiot. Do something," Mr. Remora hissed.

"What am I supposed to do?" Barry shouted.

"You're supposed to get me that manuscript, by any means possible," Mr. Remora said. Mr. Remora jabbed a finger in Emily's direction, punctuating every word. "Get. Me. That. Manuscript."

Hollister remained crouched next to the unconscious Clyde. He used one hand to clamp together Clyde's limp wrists while the other hand dug in his own pocket. "Leon, get a hold of yourself," Hollister said.

"You stay out of this!" Mr. Remora didn't even look Hollister's way. "Hand me the gun, Barry."

"They're just kids," Barry said.

"Don't let him talk to you like that," Matthew piped up. Barry swung the gun toward Matthew.

320

Emily pressed the manuscript even more tightly to her chest.

"He's using you, man," Matthew said. "He doesn't care about you. All he cares about is getting some stupid old manuscript."

"That *is* all you care about." Barry swung the gun back to Mr. Remora.

"Barry," Mr. Remora said in a calm, even voice. "That's not true. You're my flesh and blood. Give me the gun and I'll pay you double."

"How much is he paying you?" James asked.

"Five hundred dollars," Barry muttered.

"That's all?" Matthew said. "You know he's going to make bank on that musty old stack of papers my sister's holding, right? He wouldn't have gone to all this trouble if he was only going to make a couple thousand dollars."

"Don't listen to him," Mr. Remora said. "He's just a kid."

But what Matthew had said sunk in.

"You *don't* care about me," Barry said. "All you care about are books!"

Faintly, in the distance, Emily heard the wail of sirens.

"I called the police." Hollister removed his hand from his pocket to reveal a lit-up phone. "They'll be here any minute."

"Good," Barry muttered, his gun trained on Mr. Remora. "I'm sick of this gig."

CHAPTER 40

EMILY, JAMES, and Matthew sat under the pagoda awning with Hollister. They'd given their reports to the police, who were now finishing dealing with Barry, Clyde, and Mr. Remora.

At the moment, Mr. Remora knelt on the grass and wailed, "I had no choice! Griswold had no respect for literary treasures. He was a savage! He buried that manuscript in the ground! It's probably not even in an acid-free container!"

As they waited for an officer to escort them home, Emily finally had a chance to ask Hollister why he was there.

Hollister hunched on the bench, his dreadlocks draped forward over his shoulder. "It wasn't until the yelling got going that I woke up. . . ." He'd been in the sleeping bag that they'd spotted when they first arrived at Portsmouth Square. He seemed more shaken from everything that had happened than Emily, James, and Matthew were. "I'm so sorry I didn't get to you kids before. Things could have gone much worse than they did."

"It's okay, Hollister." James patted his back. "We're all fine now."

"Do you always sleep here?" Emily asked.

"Fairly often. Ever since you brought that book in my shop, actually."

"*The Gold-Bug?*" Emily asked incredulously. "Did you know about the game? You knew it ended here?"

"Yes and no," Hollister said. "You see, as I told you before, Gary and I go way back. Decades ago there was a treasure hunt revolving around a picture book called *Masquerade*. It became quite the phenomenon, and Gary was inspired. This was about forty years ago, but even that far back he planned on starting his game with *The Gold-Bug* and ending it right here with a nod to Robert Louis Stevenson. Those were the pieces of his plans that I knew. So when I saw your copy of *The Gold-Bug*, I recognized Gary's handiwork. I figured he'd decided the time had come to put the game in motion. I didn't know about the manuscript—and it doesn't sound like he knew about that himself until more recently. But it doesn't surprise me. I knew he wanted to give away something big, something that would get people talking. I decided to keep an eye on the place. Honestly, I'd been trying to figure out where he hid the treasure myself so it wouldn't end up in the wrong hands." Hollister nodded toward Mr. Remora, Barry, and Clyde to indicate the type of wrong hands he referred to.

"I have to apologize to you kids," Hollister said. "I thought this would be a harmless game. I didn't realize Mr. Remora or anyone else was involved. Not that I would have expected this from Leon—he's a prickly fellow, but I never would have guessed downright rotten. I wouldn't have sat by and watched you kids play if I thought you were walking into trouble. But Gary would be tickled to know you were the ones who solved his game. You get what he was all about. You understand the spirit of the game and have true love for books. That's Gary."

Before school the next morning, Emily walked into the kitchen to face her parents for the first time since seeing their pale, shocked faces when police officers had knocked on the door with her and Matthew in tow. She felt miserable for storming out the way she had. She knew her parents must have thought she'd overreacted to their news. She already knew what they'd say about that: "We have plenty of time left in San Francisco." But however long they had left could never feel like enough. Six months, nine months, a year. It never felt like enough time when you knew you'd be saying your good-byes soon. And how do you open yourself up to hellos when you're already preparing to say good-bye?

Her mom and dad sat at the kitchen table with family albums open in front of them. They were looking at a spread of pictures from a day spent in Estes Park in Colorado.

"Remember this, Em?" her dad asked.

A herd of elk had walked down the mountain road onto the main street in the village, meandering past stores as if they were souvenir shopping.

"So many good memories," her mom said.

"Only in Colorado," her dad said.

Emily knew where this was going. All the experiences and adventures they'd gained from the different states they'd lived in, and how lucky she was. How other kids memorized state capitals from a map while she visited them in person, or how she walked around Mount Rushmore instead of only reading about it, or how she recited the Gettysburg Address from Cemetery Hill, where President Lincoln gave the speech himself.

Her dad cleared his throat. "We didn't finish our conversation last night."

"I already apologized," she said.

Her mom flipped another page of the album. "Well, we feel like we owe you one, too."

"You do?"

"The lifestyle we've created for our family—your

mom and I know it's unconventional. That's part of what appeals to us about it. And we feel like you and your brother are getting a type of education that can't be bought or found by attending the same school year after year."

"I know," Emily said. So far she was missing the apology part of her parents' apology.

"We realize we've been a bit selfish," her mom said. "And you and Matthew are getting older. You're developing your own independent dreams and aspirations, and they may not sync with ours. Last night made us realize that we want the whole family on board for our next move. You know we love our surprises, but it never occurred to us what kind of stress that might cause for you, not knowing when and where we might move to next. So we'll stay in San Francisco indefinitely and make the decision to move on as a family when we're all ready, whether that's a year from now or five."

"Seriously? But what about your book deal?"

"What about it?" her mom asked.

"Your book is about us living in all fifty states. We have a lot more to go before we're done. If we stop now, you won't be able to write your book."

"Our book is about our *quest* to live in all fifty states. We have plenty of material to work with."

"You mean we're not moving again?"

Her dad stood from the table and swung an arm around her shoulders. "We'll keep it open for family discussion, but for now we'll call San Francisco our home for as long as you and Matthew want it to be. Once you guys go to college, your mom and I can resume our nomadic ways."

Emily put one arm around her dad's waist and the other around her mom, still seated at the table, and brought them together in a group hug. "You guys are the best!"

CHAPTER 41

ONE WEEK LATER Emily and James returned to the Bayside Press building, this time with Matthew in tow, to meet with Mr. Griswold's assistant, Jack, and discuss their prize for winning Mr. Griswold's scavenger hunt. The Poe manuscript had been turned over to the police at Portsmouth Square, and Emily had no idea what to expect from the meeting. She knew she should be excited—she'd dreamed of playing a Griswold game, let alone winning one—but she'd felt deflated about the whole thing ever since the run-in with Mr. Remora. The elevator doors opened to the wine-and-silver-blue lobby.

"Did a giant barf cotton candy in here or what?" Matthew said.

Jack leaned against the receptionist's desk, waiting for them. Just like the first time they met him, he was wearing an argyle sweater-vest. Jack greeted

Emily and James with hugs and a handshake for Matthew.

"Follow me," Jack said, ushering them down the hall. "He's eager to talk with you."

"He who?" Emily asked.

Jack stopped in front of a set of double doors. It had only just registered that this was Mr. Griswold's office when Jack pushed the doors open and there was Mr. Griswold himself. He sat in a wheelchair, striped in Bayside Press colors, and admired the golden hare medallion still on display around the bust of Poe. Was she hallucinating?

"No way," James said.

"Old book dude!" Matthew called out.

Emily slugged her brother and then fiddled with the pencil in her ponytail. Her palms felt sweaty, and she wiped them on her jeans.

Mr. Griswold wheeled himself closer and smiled, his bushy mustache lifting up at the edges. He looked exactly like his photo in the newspaper clipping, but less gray.

"You must be Emily, James, and Matthew. A pleasure to meet you three! Emily, I understand you have been a loyal Book Scavenger user over the years."

"You're not in a coma," Emily blurted, then mentally slugged herself. She'd daydreamed about this moment forever, and that was how she greeted her idol?

Mr. Griswold chuckled. "Come in, come in." He

wheeled back and gestured to the couch nestled between bookcases. "We have a lot of catching up to do, don't we?"

As Emily, James, and Matthew seated themselves in Mr. Griswold's office, Jack perched on the arm of the couch and launched into an explanation.

"The police suspected from the beginning that the BART station attack was premeditated," he said. "Largely because none of Mr. Griswold's personal belongings were stolen."

"Except one important one," Mr. Griswold added with a wink.

While Mr. Griswold had been in a coma, there had been a security breach at the hospital, and people feared his life was still at risk, so he had been secretly relocated. Hospital staff noticed that he was missing, and a rumor spread that he had died, which his team decided not to address until his health stabilized. Hearing this, Emily realized that the Book Scavenger user CaptainOverpants, the one who'd claimed to work in Mr. Griswold's hospital, hadn't been making up the rumor he'd gossiped about.

"I remember encountering those two men in the BART station, and then the next thing I know, I'm waking up a month later in a strange place with an incredible headache and no recollection of how I got there, or any awareness of how much time had passed. Jack has been filling me in on all that transpired. And, boy, has a lot transpired."

Mr. Griswold's eyes crinkled with kindness as his gaze settled on Emily. "I'm setting the record straight about my, er, vitality this afternoon, but after all you've been through I wanted you to hear the news directly from me first."

Emily's mouth hung open. She wasn't sure if she'd closed it once or even taken a breath the entire time Mr. Griswold and Jack had been talking. A mixture of relief and awe swirled inside as she processed that Mr. Griswold was sitting right in front of her. It all seemed a bit dreamlike.

"I hope you enjoyed my literary treasure hunt, despite Mr. Remora's antics," he said.

"We did," Emily said, her voice a near whisper. She swallowed and repeated herself more loudly.

Mr. Griswold clasped his hands in his lap, studying the Poe bust as he talked. "Ever since I learned about my relation to Rufus Griswold and the role he played in Poe's life, I have felt remorse for how my ancestor treated Poe after he died. You see, Rufus took advantage of his position as Poe's literary executor. He altered some of Poe's letters and writings and compiled them into a posthumous biography in an attempt to paint Poe in a very negative light."

"Why would he do that?" James asked.

Mr. Griswold shook his head. "I'm not sure anyone knows. Rufus's lies and fabrications weren't fully revealed until long after his own death, so he never had to explain himself. He and Poe had a contentious relationship, to be sure. Toward the end of Poe's life, there was a woman they were both friends with, and so some speculate there was a love triangle in play." Mr. Griswold shook his head once again. "I don't know the why, but to go out of your way to spread lies about someone after he has passed away, well, I can only imagine what a sad and bitter man my great-great-great-grandfather must have been."

Mr. Griswold dragged a finger across the charms that dangled from the golden hare medallion.

"When I discovered the Poe manuscript, an idea clicked for me. I had long been a fan of Poe's short story 'The Gold-Bug' and thought it would be fun to emulate the treasure hunt. Once I'd found the manuscript, I realized I not only had the perfect prize in hand, but I could make amends to the ghost of Poe at the same time."

Something that had been bothering Emily for the last week was nudged free as she listened to Mr. Griswold speak.

"What about . . . what about Mr. Remora?"

Mr. Griswold sighed sadly. "Yes, Mr. Remora. I am so sorry about Leon. I had no idea he could be capable of . . . so much awfulness." He grimaced, his mustache folding into the deep lines of his face. "He knows books and literary history incredibly well—I always forget that not all book people are good people."

Emily tilted her head, surprised to hear that.

Hollister had said nearly the same thing a couple of weeks ago.

Mr. Griswold continued. "I feel like I should have known or seen red flags, but when I have a game in the works, I can get . . ."

"Obsessed?" Jack offered.

Mr. Griswold smiled. "I was going to say hyperfocused. I get so intent on orchestrating my plans and keeping them a secret that I suppose I have a tendency to stop observing what's really going on around me."

"Like losing yourself in a good jam," Matthew said.

"Exactly." Mr. Griswold punctuated the word with a tap of his finger against the wheelchair arm.

Emily still wasn't completely satisfied. "Mr. Remora said that *he* found the Poe manuscript. He said that he deserved to be partners with you, fifty-fifty."

Mr. Griswold scoffed. "Technically, he *did* find the manuscript—I suppose that part is true. I hired him to sort through and archive my family's papers and heirlooms, in addition to helping me with my book collection. I never expected to uncover a Poe manuscript, of course, but I knew there were some potentially valuable or historically interesting items. I even had Mr. Remora sign a nondisclosure statement to assert that he would not divulge information he learned or claim ownership of anything in my possession.

"Not to mention, I compensated him for his work.

Compensated him very well, in fact. But I don't think it was the money that ultimately mattered to him. I think it was the glory of discovering a lost Poe. And you and I would understand a bit of that, wouldn't we, Emily? The thrill and satisfaction of a treasure hunt? It's what Book Scavenger's all about."

"Not *all* about," she said. "It's about a community of book lovers, too. And sharing books and adventures with friends." Her eyes flicked to James, and she felt shy all of a sudden, but he was smiling.

Matthew elbowed her. "And brothers."

"I think Mr. Remora knew that with me involved," Mr. Griswold continued, "he'd only be a footnote in the story. Without me, he could orchestrate a different scenario for him to 'discover' the work, thereby ensuring the spotlight would shine fully on himself."

Emily had told herself she didn't believe Mr. Remora's claims about Mr. Griswold, but it wasn't until right now, hearing Mr. Griswold explain his side in person, that the weight of those negative words truly evaporated.

"There's something I still haven't figured out," James said. "If you were really unconscious that whole time, then who was Raven? Was it Jack?"

Jack pointed to himself. "Me? I've never even heard of Raven!"

Mr. Griswold chuckled. "Raven is right here." He wheeled himself toward a bookcase that opened to reveal a small room filled with computer equipment.

"This is Raven. My virtual assistant. She's a computer program designed to assist players in the scavenger hunt."

"I knew it!" James made a triumphant fist. "I knew there was something weird about her. But why did you activate Raven if you weren't planning to start the game right away?"

"The simple answer is, I wanted to cross it off my to-do list. Sounds silly, doesn't it?" Mr. Griswold adjusted his glasses. "Raven was programmed to reply to user queries only if they used the trigger phrase 'The Gold-Bug.' Once you made that initial contact with Raven, she could respond to other questions, but she wouldn't interact with you without the first *Gold-Bug* prompt. And so, because of that, and because nobody has ever posted about *The Gold-Bug* in the history of Book Scavenger, I activated Raven. I didn't anticipate it being a possibility that Raven would be put to work, because I wasn't planning to hide any copies of *The Gold-Bug* until right before the game began."

"And so everything Raven told us was preprogrammed?"

"Yes," Mr. Griswold said. "She was set up to give specific clues or bits of information if someone used the right prompts."

"That's why she kept saying the same thing over and over whenever we wrote 'The Gold-Bug,'" James mused.

"So why didn't she always reply?" Emily said, thinking about the times she'd seen Raven's green online light but didn't receive a response to her messages.

"I programmed Raven to answer eight inquiries from a user at a time. If you used up all eight, then Raven wouldn't respond to you for another forty-eight hours. Just my attempt to be a little tricky."

Mr. Griswold cleared his throat. "Now it's time for us to get to the fun stuff. Your prizes."

Mr. Griswold explained that while the original Poe manuscript would be lent to a university collection where it would be displayed in an exhibit and studied by scholars, Bayside Press would be publishing a copy of Poe's posthumous novel. Emily, James, and Matthew would split 10 percent of the royalties earned from the sale of the book, to be deposited into a scholarship fund for each of them. In addition, they were each gifted a laptop and invited to be founding members of a teen advisory board for the Book Scavenger website.

"I have one more token of appreciation in mind, but for now I'd like to keep that a secret," Mr. Griswold said.

"You know, there was someone else who helped us, too," Emily spoke up, a little shyly. She wasn't sure how Mr. Griswold would react to this, but she felt compelled to bring it up anyway. "I think he's an old friend of yours—Hollister?"

The corner of Mr. Griswold's mouth twitched as an unreadable emotion briefly waved across his face.

"Ah. Hollister," Mr. Griswold said softly. "We haven't spoken in ages, I'm afraid."

"Well, it's never too late to reach out to someone. That's what he told me, actually."

Mr. Griswold smiled. "Did he now? That's sound advice. Very sound advice indeed."

CHAPTER 42

EMILY LAY on her bed, finishing a book James had lent her called *Rhyme Schemer*. They planned to hide it at Pier 39 that evening when they went with her family to the Lighted Boat Parade.

There was a knock on her door, and her dad opened it, letting in the sounds of the Flush holiday album Matthew had been making the family listen to on repeat since Thanksgiving.

"A package for you," her dad said, raising a medium-sized cardboard box he balanced on one hand.

Emily jumped up and grabbed it. The Bayside Press logo was stamped on top.

"They're here!" she squealed. Mr. Griswold had said he was sending her advance copies of the new Poe novel. His final prize to her, James, and Matthew would be inside the book.

"I have to tell James!" She put the box down and raced to her window. A colorful strand of holiday bulbs dangled around her window, reflecting off the rain-flecked glass. She moved the antlers, *The Gold-Bug*, and the raven box from the windowsill to the floor before sliding the window up and reaching for the pulley rope, now slick with rain.

Her dad chuckled and left, letting the door close behind him. Once the bucket was at her level, she grabbed her notebook and scratched out a message:

HXXOS TPU KUPU! EXNU XAUP!
(Books are here! Come over!)

The next fifteen minutes seemed like the longest minutes ever as she waited for James to come down. She finished *Rhyme Schemer* and then paced her room until he poked his head in.

"Finally!" Emily clapped her hands.

James held up a thin paper bag with a logo on it for sourdough bread. "I thought of a good bookstume," he said. "The clue can be something about lost bread, or a book that wants to be edible." He snapped his fingers, an idea occurring to him. "We'll make up the clue using altered poetry, like the character does in *Rhyme Schemer*!"

Emily grinned. "Yes, yes, yes. Brilliant. But first—*Look!*"

She dragged a ballpoint pen across the tape sealing the Bayside Press box. The flaps popped open to reveal paperback books of *The Cathedral Murders: A Posthumous Novel* by Edgar Allan Poe. They weren't the final, final books, but Jack had said these advance copies would be like a dress rehearsal before the official performance.

Emily removed a copy and squeezed it between her hands, breathing in the paper smell. She flipped through the pages, wondering if the last prize would be another hidden puzzle. But it wasn't. It was a special mention in the introduction of the book:

> *One fall day Emily Crane and James Lee, two San Francisco middle school students, found what they thought was an innocuous copy of an Edgar Allan Poe book abandoned in a BART station. Little did they know that this book, a reprinting of Poe's short story "The Gold-Bug," would lead them on a wild scavenger hunt across San Francisco, culminating in the discovery of the manuscript for the very novel you now hold in your hands.*

The introduction went on to tell the story of Mr. Griswold's plans for his game and how Emily and James unraveled all the clues.

"I can't believe it. We're in a book!" Emily exclaimed.

"We're famous book hunters!" James said.

They spent a few quiet minutes looking through their copies of the new Poe book until Matthew poked his head in. His lopsided Mohawk had been shaved away, leaving short and stubbly hair everywhere except for his long bangs. "Dad said the books are here?"

Emily held one out to him. "Page five," she said.

After skimming the introduction, Matthew said, "There's nothing in here about my awesome kung fu moves to stop Mr. Remora!"

"That's because that only happened in your dreams," Emily said.

"Oh, right." Matthew flicked his bangs out of his eye and smiled.

"But you get a mention for the *Maltese Falcon* clue and, of course, Portsmouth Square."

Matthew pointed to the bread bag on the floor.

"What's the bread for?" he asked.

James slid *Rhyme Schemer* inside the bag. "It's a bookstume."

Matthew made a face and shook his head. "No, no, no. If you're going to dress a book up like a sourdough loaf, you need to make it look more convincing than that. Hold on."

Matthew left the room, and James turned the wrapped book this way and that. "I guess it does just look like a book in a paper bag."

When Matthew came back, he carried a roll of toilet paper and sheets of newspaper. He crumpled a sheet of newspaper with one hand and gestured for the book. "You put the paper on top to add bulk, like a real sourdough loaf. Now"—he nodded to the roll of toilet paper—"mummify them together so they stay in place."

James wound toilet paper around the book as

Matthew held it and the balled-up paper in place. Emily opened the sourdough bag to check for size.

"Squash it down more so it will fit," she said.

Emily smiled at the heads of her brother and James, bent together in concentration. When they finished stuffing the bread bag, Emily held up the concealed book, twisting it to view from all angles.

"Now, that's a bookstume," Matthew said.

From the hallway, Emily's mom called, "Time to head out, everybody!"

"Let's go hide it," James said. "You ready, Em?"

"I'm ready."

And she was. She was ready to lean into their next adventure.

AUTHOR'S NOTE

Although this story is entirely fictional, there are many factual bits woven throughout. Here is some background.

RUFUS GRISWOLD

Rufus Wilmot Griswold is indeed a historical figure and contemporary of Edgar Allan Poe. Outside of his relationship with Poe, Griswold is best known for publishing the anthology *The Poets and Poetry of America* in 1842. The animosity between Poe and Griswold might have begun in earnest when Poe wrote a review of this anthology in which he criticized the selection of poets (even though Poe's own poems appeared in it). To further complicate the situation, it was actually Griswold himself who'd paid Poe to write this review, presumably expecting Poe to say only favorable things. Things went downhill from there between the two men until Poe died unexpectedly (and mysteriously) in

1849. Griswold published the infamous obituary Emily and James quoted from: "Edgar Allan Poe is dead. He died in Baltimore the day before yesterday. This announcement will startle many, but few will be grieved by it." Griswold signed "Ludwig" to the obituary instead of his own name, perhaps afraid of public reaction, but his identity was soon revealed.

It seems unbelievable that someone who would write an obituary with this much malice toward Poe could also be named the literary executor for Poe's works, but that is in fact what happened. Some sources say Poe named him as his literary executor before he died, but others suggest Griswold manipulated himself into the position after Poe's death through arrangements made with Poe's mother-in-law. Griswold went on to publish a posthumous collection that included a slanderous and partially fabricated biography of Poe. Griswold embellished Poe's letters and writing to portray him as an egotistical, mentally unstable alcoholic and drug addict prone to bitter jealousy. Although the biography was contested by Poe's friends and supporters, it remained the primary resource about Poe for twenty-five years. Today, Griswold's characterization of Poe often endures, even though biographers—such as Arthur Hobson Quinn in his 1941 *Edgar Allan Poe: A Critical Biography*—have documented the fabrications that Griswold made.

At the time of his death, Poe left behind an unfinished story about a lighthouse keeper, but as far as I know, there is no unpublished novel-length manuscript. Finding an unpublished novel would be especially rare, as Poe is known primarily for his short stories and poems and published only one novel. If such an item were discovered today, it would be worth a considerable amount of money. A first edition of Poe's first published work, "Tamerlane and Other Poems"—widely considered as the rarest book in American literature, with only twelve known copies—recently sold for over $600,000.

"THE GOLD-BUG"

What Raven says about "The Gold-Bug" is true: It's a short story published in 1843 that was popular in its day and brought attention to cryptograms and secret writing. It's not one of Poe's better known works today, perhaps because it doesn't fit the Gothic, horror style people often associate him with. In "The Gold-Bug," the protagonist discovers and attempts to solve a cryptogram, which he hopes will lead him to buried treasure.

Poe is credited with originating the detective-mystery genre with his character Le Chevalier C. Auguste Dupin, who appeared in three short stories: "The Murders in the Rue Morgue," "The Mystery of Marie Roget," and "The Purloined Letter." Some classify "The Gold-Bug" as one of Poe's detective stories because the narrator and protagonist work like detectives to unravel the mystery of the gold-bug and decipher the encrypted message. But a true detective story is supposed to present all the clues for the readers so they can attempt to solve the mystery alongside the detective, and "The Gold-Bug" withholds information until the end.

CIPHER CHALLENGE

Poe was a fan of ciphers and cryptography. He not only incorporated a cipher into "The Gold-Bug," but he also wrote essays about the subject. While writing for *Alexander's Weekly Messenger*, he issued a challenge to readers to submit cryptograms for him to crack. He received numerous submissions, which he claimed to have solved himself. It was this that inspired Mr. Quisling's cipher challenge in *Book Scavenger*.

MASQUERADE

Masquerade is a picture book written and illustrated by Kit Williams, an English artist, who collaborated with his publisher to launch a treasure hunt in which the clues were hidden within the book's illustrations, ultimately leading to buried treasure. *Masquerade* was published in 1979 and launched a phenomenon that had millions of people searching for the treasure—a golden hare medallion on a chain that Williams had crafted himself—until it was found in 1982. *Masquerade* initiated a literary genre called "armchair treasure hunts." *Quest for the Golden Hare* by Bamber Gascoigne is an excellent recounting of what happened both before and after *Masquerade* was published.

BOOK SCAVENGER THE GAME

The book-hunting game is a product of my imagination, but the idea came about as many do: by merging several sources of inspiration. The first is a website called Book Crossing (bookcrossing.com). Book Crossing offers a wonderful way for readers to share their used books by "releasing" them into the wild. The books can be labeled and tracked online, so you can follow the journey of where your book goes. I love the idea of setting a beloved book free to have new adventures and connect with new readers. I first learned about Book Crossing in 2003, around the same time I heard about two other popular pastimes: geocaching and letterboxing. Geocaching is an outdoor world-wide treasure-hunting activity in which people use a GPS device to find small containers. Each container typically holds a logbook and small trinkets. Letterboxing is similar to geocaching, but the hidden boxes each contain a unique rubber stamp. Participants carry a sketchbook, an ink pad, and their own rubber stamp. When a letterbox is found, the participant swaps stamps, marking his or her sketchbook with the one from the letterbox and marking the letterbox logbook with his or her individual stamp.

Book Scavenger began with a vision of kids finding a book in a BART station, leading them into a mystery. What book do they find? What is the mystery? I imagined a story in the spirit of some of my favorite movies and books when I was young: *Goonies*; *It's a Mad, Mad, Mad, Mad World*; *The Westing Game* by Ellen Raskin; *From the Mixed-Up Files of Mrs. Basil E. Frankweiler* by E. L. Konigsburg; and *The Egypt Game* by Zilpha Keatley Snyder.

I love puzzles and ciphers, so I decided there must be one hidden in this mysterious, found book. To help me brainstorm what the secret message might be or mean, I turned to books, most notably *Mysterious Messages* by Gary Blackwood, *Codebreaker* by Stephen Pincock, and *The Book of Codes: Understanding the World of Hidden Messages*, edited by Paul Lunde. (You may recognize these titles from James's research for the cipher challenge.) Through reading more about the history of ciphers, I learned that Edgar Allan Poe was an avid fan. Those were the beginning seeds for this story.

In addition to the historical references, the majority of the San Francisco locations and figures and their historical significance are not made up. The Ferry Building, Pier 39, City Lights bookstore, the original Black Cat, Lombard Street, the music concourse at Golden Gate Park, Dashiell Hammett's residence, the Fillmore, Portsmouth Square—those are all places that exist. The first Black Cat that Emily and James go to was based on an actual restaurant, but that restaurant closed over the course of my writing this book. Even the secret park that Emily and James go to is based on a real place I used to walk past on my way to and from work, although I have since tried to find this park after moving away from San Francisco with no luck. Maybe that's the magic of the city in play: It will only reveal its secrets to you when you're an insider.

There are more small details that are allusions to something outside the story. I had fun peppering these in, and you might enjoy spotting them and deducing their significance.

ACKNOWLEDGMENTS

Book Scavenger is the realization of a dream I've held onto since childhood, and I'm filled with gratitude to so many people. In particular, this book would not exist without the following people.

My agent, Ammi-Joan Paquette: Thank you for your insight, your unflagging enthusiasm, and your friendship.

Christy Ottaviano, I am overjoyed to call you my editor. Thank you for believing in me and taking a chance on my work. You are brilliant at what you do.

Everyone at Henry Holt, thank you for ushering my book into the world with such care and enthusiasm. A special thank-you to the production editor, Christine Ma, and to Sarah Watts for her fabulous illustrations.

To the following writers who read and critiqued *Book Scavenger* through the good, the bad, and all the stages in between, I am so appreciative for your feedback: Vanessa Appleby, Michelle Begley, Ann Braden, Maryanne Fantalis,

Mike Hassell, Megan Kelly, Audrey Laferlita, Shari Maser, Jeannie Mobley, Laura Perdew, Rachel Rodriguez, Katherine Rothschild, Jennifer Simms, Kiersten Stevenson, and Elaine Vickers.

Thank you to Cheryl Klein: Without your early encouragement, I would have given up on this story a long time ago.

My gratitude goes to the following teachers and administrators who shared their time and expertise with me: David Green-Leibovitz, April Holland, and Emily Peek. Thank you, also, to Gabrielle Dean, curator of literary rare books and manuscripts at Johns Hopkins Sheridan Libraries, who kindly answered my questions about Poe and rare manuscripts. And to Kimberly Ng, Rachel Rodriguez, Katherine Rothschild, and Laura Young-Cennamo, thank you for letting me pick your brain about San Francisco living when I couldn't be there in person.

I am also grateful to the following friends and family who were readers of early drafts: Justin Bertman, Cade Chambliss, Dianne Chambliss, Jeff Chambliss, Kayla Chambliss, Laura Chambliss, and Sammie Peng. Your encouragement and enthusiasm for the story helped keep me pushing on.

I would be remiss not to mention the following teachers whose words and actions absolutely shaped the person and writer I have become: Mrs. Peterson, Mrs. Buckley, and Mrs. Adams—my first-, second-, and third-/fourth-grade teachers—who helped foster my love of reading and writing; Andrew Althschul, who taught my first creative writing class at UC Irvine: Through taking your class I was reminded of how much I enjoy writing and creating stories; Michelle Latiolais, from whom I could have taken every class at UC Irvine if it were possible: You helped me believe I wasn't ridiculous for imagining my name on the cover of a book, or a byline of a story; Lou Berney and John Fleming, my mentors at Saint Mary's: Thank you for looking past my shy exterior in the kindest ways possible and helping me uncork the quirky writer inside.

My writing has also benefited greatly from the conferences, classes, and resources offered by the following organizations: Book Passage Children's Writers and Illustrators Conference, SCBWI, Better Books Marin Workshop, and the Lighthouse Writers Workshop in Denver.

Writing is a solitary, sometimes lonely act, and writing and rewriting a novel over a decade would have made me mad without forging a connection to the children's literature community. Thank you to SCBWI, Verla Kay and the members of the Blueboards, Erin Murphy and the community she has nurtured through her agency, the Fearless Fifteeners, and EMU's Debuts for providing outlets for writers to come together and support and encourage and commiserate and heal and grow.

Also falling in the "thank you for keeping me sane" category are my friends who have been there for me through the highs and lows, especially Michelle Comstock, Lisa Evans, Valerie Kovacovich, Michelle Mason, Sammie Peng, Jennifer Quong, Katherine Rothschild, and Laura Young-Cennamo.

Finally, and infinitely, I am so grateful for my family. My parents, Tom and Dianne Chambliss, who are my friends, my role models, my cheerleaders: Thank you for all the ways you've supported and encouraged me over the years. Jeff and Laura, you are the best brother and sister-in-law a person could hope for. Your support and encouragement have always come across loud and clear. Cade and Kayla, it's an honor and joy to be your aunt. You are part of the inspiration behind these characters, and I hope this book makes you proud. To my father-in-law and mother-in-law, Roger and Julie Bertman, your generosity and thoughtfulness are greatly appreciated. To my son, Nils, you are a daily inspiration to do better and be better. The world is a happier place because of you. And, finally, to my husband and best friend, Justin. You have supported my dreams in countless ways. This wouldn't be as meaningful without you by my side. I love you all.